The New Frontier

Other Books by Wayne L. Wilson

Soul Eyes
Kate, the Ghost Dog: Coping With the Death of a Pet
A Whole New League
(Swinging For The Fences: Life In The Negro Leagues)
Famous Fighters
(Footsteps To Freedom: The Underground Railroad)
Sam Cooke (Righteous Rockers)
Stagecoach Mary (Wonder Women: Heroines Of History)
Little Richard (Righteous Rockers)
Chuck Berry (Righteous Rockers)
Renaissance Italy (That's Me In History)
Allen Iverson (Blue Banner Biographies)
Tony Blair: Real-Life Reader Biography
Careers in Publishing and Communications (Latinos at Work)
Careers in Entertainment (Latinos at Work)
Shakira (Real-Life Reader Biography)
Bruce Lee (Real-Life Reader Biography)
Freddie Prinze, Jr. (Real-Life Reader Biography)
Julia Roberts (Real-Life Reader Biography)
Voices For Civil Rights (I Protest)
Voices For Peace (I Protest)
The Blackfeet (We Were Here First: The Native Americans)
The Seminole (We Were Here First: The Native Americans)
The Pueblo (We Were Here First: The Native Americans)
The Shoshone (We Were Here First: The Native Americans)

As Contributing Writer
The Hoop Kid From Elmdale Park
Elite Squad: A Sci-Fi Intergalactic Basketball Adventure
African American National Biography
Encuentros: Hombre a Hombre

THE
NEW
FRONTIER

A Novel

by

Wayne L. Wilson

ISBN: 9781951122874 (paperback) / 9781951122881 (ebook)
LCCN: 2024933275

Kinkajou Press
9 Mockingbird Hill Rd
Tijeras, New Mexico 87059
info@kinkajoupress.com
www.kinkajoupress.com

Content Warning: This book contains descriptions of corporal punishment of minors (spanking and verbal abuse), attempted kidnapping, and racism that may be disturbing to some readers.

Publisher's Note

Content Warning: *Racial Slurs*

This novel takes place in 1961 and involves a Black family moving to an all-White neighborhood in Los Angeles. As such, the characters experience racism and bigotry, much of it involving racial slurs against the Black characters. Scenes also exist that involve Black characters using racial slurs with other Black characters in other context and settings. We have chosen to keep these words within the context of the story as the author wrote them because they are integral to the narrative as well as to the history and time when this story is set. The real impact that these words have on the characters is important to how the story is told and to remove the words, or to sanitize them, would lessen the impact that the author intended. However, that does not mean that either the publisher or the author condones the use of racial slurs, stereotypes, or bigotry either historically or today. While we have chosen to keep these words in the context of the story this does not make it appropriate for these words to be used or spoken outside of this setting and story. Such insensitive language was not appropriate to use at the time this book is set and is not appropriate to use during our present time.

We encourage you to talk with your parents, family members, teachers, clergy, a trusted adult, or your friends about how racial slurs and language were used in the past, how they are used today, and how we can stop using them while acknowledging how their use in the past has shaped the world we live in today.

Dedication

In loving memory of my parents, Charles and Shirley Wilson. They would have loved this book. Although, I'm pretty sure they were leaning on my shoulders and whispering ideas for the story while I was writing it.

To my daughter, India, you continually bring me so much joy, love, and inspiration.

To Brenda, thank you for being such a wonderful and loving partner. You've been by my side during some of my most life-altering times. I'd say you are my "muse", but I think you prefer it when I call you my "moose" instead.

To all the urban pioneers who have been ostracized and battled discrimination due to living in a place where you are not accepted because you look different and/or may have dissimilar religious beliefs.

The Bogeyman: A monstrous imaginary figure used in threatening children; a terrifying or dreaded person or thing.

Webster's Dictionary

Prologue

I became a pioneer at the age of 12. But instead of a covered wagon we traveled to the "New Frontier" in a blue Buick.

Kids posted on the walls and even on rooftops like pigeons, gawking as if we had stepped out of a spaceship instead of an automobile. White faces peered through cracked open front doors, parted curtains, over back fences, and even from behind newly posted "For Sale" signs. A few curious people trod onto their porches. The bolder ones stood on their lawns, arms crossed like they were cemented, and whispered from the corner of their mouths.

For the very first time my dark skin felt uncomfortable on my body.

Hadn't they ever seen Negroes before?

I already hated living there. I wanted to go back home, hang out on our old street, and play tag with my friends. But that was not to be. I had a new home now.

Maybe, if just one person had smiled, I may have been all right...

But instead, I got sucker punched.

I had no idea I'd left the warmth of my old neighborhood for one that was wrapped around me like an icy blanket.

On a hot and sweaty summer day in 1961, my life dramatically changed. I never imagined that moving to another neighborhood would make me struggle to prove to others and to myself that I was just a normal kid like anybody else.

Chapter 1

The first move took place in the spring of 1949. My father and very pregnant mother packed their belongings and popped a bus wheelie out of the small town of Langston, Oklahoma to reap the golden harvest of opportunities Los Angeles, California proclaimed.

I was born months later on June 5, nothing special, except on that same day, six years later, the place of my birth, James Monroe Hospital, burned to the ground in a spectacular fire!

My mother saw it as a sign from God that I was destined for greatness. My father said he read in the newspaper the hospital fire was the result of arson. Daddy joked I was more of a "gift than gifted." He hadn't finished paying the last of my hospital bills, and the fire destroyed all the records. Mommy argued that the cause of the event had absolutely nothing to do with its significance.

Daddy remarked, "I don't know, Jolene... Seems to me as much trouble as this boy gets into, he might be more of a devil than a saint!"

He laughed hard.

Not my mother.

"Grant, that's not funny."

"What?" he asked, his laughter dying quickly.

"After all we've been through?" she huffed.

"Oh now, honey, c'mon, it was just a joke. Calm down."

"Don't you tell me to calm down, Grant Cole! Don't you

3

realize how blessed we are to even have a child?"

Her eyes, filling with tears, shifted to mine. She got quiet and abruptly left the living room. Seconds later the bedroom door slammed.

"Aw c'mon, Jo, you know I'm only kidding," Daddy muttered to the vibrating walls.

"Kidding about what, Daddy?"

He playfully cuffed me upside the head and cushioned me in his arms.

"Champ, if you're such a genius, why do you ask so many questions?"

I really don't think he expected an answer. He held me so tightly to his chest I could barely breathe, let alone talk.

Yeah, it's true... I drove my parents nuts with questions. Couldn't help it. To me the world was one gigantic playground bustling with enchantment, mystery, adventure, and monsters... but I'll talk more about that later.

I just graduated from Perry Avenue Elementary School and will be in sixth grade in the fall. I was excited about it, but I wondered if I'd have as much fun as I did in elementary. Those were the days of the great lunch pail wars—boys against girls, Barbie and Minnie Mouse versus Gumby and Mighty Mouse.

We'd square off during lunch, the girls on one side and the boys on the other, armed and ready for combat with our trusty metal lunch pails. Someone would blow a whistle and you'd hear: "Charge!" Next thing, we're bonking our opponents with lunch pails. Sometimes it got downright medieval as we fenced and thrust pails at each other. I witnessed some hardcore injuries from those fights—scraped knees, knots, and bruises to the head. I don't really like to admit it, but to be honest, the girls won most of those battles.

We lived in a cottage on 43rd and Perry Avenue, just below Leona Blvd in South Central Los Angeles. The cottage hid behind a two-story house where our landlords, Mr. and Mrs. Evans lived. Besides collecting money, they never seemed like landlords. They treated us like family. Mr. Evans worked as a porter at Union Station for over 20 years. He was rarely home, but when he was, he and Daddy would sit on the Evans' front porch, watching people and cars, playing checkers, talking politics and business, and drinking beers. My father still claims no one taught him more about being tight with a buck than Lavay Evans.

To find us you had to cut around the front house and hike down a narrow pathway to the back. We shared a tiny, squared area of grass in the rear with the Evans. Our front yard was the Evans' backyard.

I slept in my parents' bedroom in a little bed until I was five. Then they switched me to a space called a foyer which was near the front door. I don't think it exactly thrilled them for me to sleep in their bedroom, but it suited me just fine. Especially since there was a strange and deadly creature running around loose in the city known as the bogeyman. I heard this beast snatched children during the night and whisked them away to some haunt where they were never heard from again.

The rumor was this monster could slip through a window and be found in your closet or lurking underneath your bed. The best way to prevent it from attacking was to keep a light on in the bedroom. The bogeyman hates light as much as a vampire hates the dawn. I'm a little better now, but when I was younger, I reminded my parents of that fact every time they tucked me in. But, they'd forget, until I'd wake up in the middle of the night, in darkness, and screaming like a banshee.

My father tried his best to convince me that the bogeyman was just a myth, but he was wrong. Every kid knows the bogeyman does not kidnap adults. My suspicion was the creature didn't find them very appetizing.

I knew all this because my best friends in grade school, Jamelle and Terelle Johnson told me so. They were identical twins and experts on monsters. Jamelle was the oldest by two minutes. He had a tiny scar on his forehead and bragged it came from fighting pirates. Terelle told me different. He said Jamelle got it from tripping over a phone cord and banging into the dining room table.

The twins say they saw the bogeyman one night hunched on a tree branch glowering down at them. Jamelle thought at first it was a cat, but Terelle swore the bogeyman changed from a hideous monstrosity into one.

Who could argue with that? Especially when a man could turn into a werewolf at the mere sight of a full moon.

That's why I constantly checked under the bed with my flashlight. Usually I waited until my father joined me. You see, Daddy wasn't afraid of anything. And, he was big enough to lift the whole house if he wanted to.

My greater concern was for my mother's safety; although, I found out she could swing a pretty mean broom.

One day while lying on my bed and flipping through a comic book, I heard crunching sounds under the bed where I stored my stash of potato chips, cookies, and candy.

Was it the bogeyman?

The noise stopped as soon as I climbed off the bed. I hesitantly lifted the covers and peeped under the bed. Pairs of beady red eyes stared back at me!

"Mooooommmmmm!!!"

She swooped into the room faster than a hawk.

"What in the world is wrong, Samuel? I was outside hanging up the laundry until I heard you scream."

My finger shaking, I pointed to the bed.

My mother got down on her hands and knees and warily peered under the bed. Startled, she fell backwards, but in a single motion amazingly bounced back to her feet and raced into the kitchen. Instead of calling the police, or better yet, the army, she swiftly returned with a broom.

A broom? Are you serious?

The bogeyman picks his teeth with a broom! I figured she was in shock as she poked under the bed with it. I prayed that the bogeyman wouldn't pull the broom and my mother under the bed with him.

One blink later, mice scurried out from underneath the bed, fleeing in all directions. Screaming louder than Tarzan, my mother whomped the floor with the broom like she was beating a tom-tom. The rodents scampered back and forth seeking refuge. I tried to scoop several of them into a shoebox, until my mother shot me a warning glance, meaning cool it or you'll be the next victim of the killer broom. I wisely grabbed my bat and joined the fray.

We chased the pack outside the open backdoor. Panting victoriously, I combed the house for mice escapees with my upraised bat. That was fun!

Unfortunately, my exhausted mother didn't share my excitement. She immediately examined my arms and legs for bites. Satisfied I was okay, she warned me not to mess with mice or rats because the vermin were dirty and could give me rabies. Later, she went into the kitchen to finish washing dishes.

I surveyed the room once more to see if I could locate any more critters. Disappointed, I went into the kitchen to grab a snack. My mother didn't hear me come in. She sat on the kitchen chair with her back to me gazing sadly out the window. I eased back out the door, hoping my growling stomach wouldn't give me away. The peanut butter and jelly sandwich would have to wait.

That evening my mother and father had one of those muffled arguments behind the closed bedroom door. I couldn't hear everything they said, but it was the first time I overheard a conversation about moving.

I'd turned 11 the month before one event in particular made me realize we'd be moving soon: Senator John F. Kennedy accepting the Democratic nomination for President on July 15, 1960, at the Los Angeles Memorial Coliseum:

"For I stand tonight facing west on what was once the last frontier. From the lands that stretch three thousand miles behind me, the pioneers of old gave up their safety, their comfort and sometimes their lives to build a new world here in the West... Their motto was not 'every man for himself'—but 'all for the common cause.' ...

We stand today on the edge of a New Frontier—the frontier of the 1960's—a frontier of unknown opportunities and perils—a frontier of unfulfilled hopes and threats...

Beyond that frontier are the uncharted areas of science and space, unsolved problems of peace and war, unconquered pockets of ignorance and prejudice, unanswered questions of poverty and surplus. It would be easier to shrink back from that frontier, to look to the safe mediocrity of the past...

But I believe the times demand new invention, innovation, imagination, decision. I am asking each of you to be pioneers on that New Frontier."

My mother sat cross-legged in the middle of the living room floor, me on my knees, as we worked on a puzzle. The box cover design was a brontosaurus emerging from the water and chewing on palm leaves. My father sat stoically in his armchair, a newspaper spread across his lap, and one hand grasping a transistor radio he listened to through an earplug. His eyes were fixed on the television screen. Sometimes a hint of a smile crossed his lips.

I badly wanted to ask him who'd win a fight between a triceratops and a woolly mammoth but figured this might not be a good time.

Kennedy ended his speech, the crowd went ballistic, and my father catapulted from the chair like it was a trampoline. His deep bass rumbled: "Jolene, did you hear him? THIS is what I'm talking about!"

He stripped the plug from his ear and laid the radio on the table.

"We are a part of that New Frontier! It's a new day for Negroes and ain't NOBODY gonna hold us back! You're always talking about fate and destiny... Well, our destiny is to be right here in California. Wasn't no American dream for us back in Langston, that's for sure!"

He paced back and forth waving his newspaper, eyes dancing wildly. "Soon as escrow goes through, we're getting out of this rat trap!"

"What crow, Daddy?"

He burst into laughter. "Escrow is not a bird, Champ." He spelled the word for me. "It means we're waiting on the final approval for our new house. But it will go through. You just worry about what color you want your new bedroom to be painted!"

"I get my own bedroom?"

"That's right, sport! And, we're gonna have our own backyard, too!"

Okay, now I was into it.

"See his face, Jo? Tell me that boy isn't excited!"

He squatted and grabbed me in a headlock with those pork chop arms.

My mother continued searching through puzzle pieces for the missing tail.

"What about you, Jo? Aren't you excited, too?" The excitement in his voice dropped. He let me go. I socked him in the shoulder, cracking my knuckles.

"Uh, yes, Grant, I am," she remarked softly, with a weak smile.

Daddy frowned.

"Oh no, here we go. Thought we already did this dance."

"We did, Grant... it's just..."

"It's just what, Jo? Baby, I know you're not gonna start crying the blues again about leaving this stinking out-house!"

"Call it what you want, but we've had some good times here, Grant. It has been our home... you know... ever since Samuel was born."

"Uh, huh... it's our home, but it ain't our house. We don't own it! That's why you work at the damn grocery store part-time and I work two, sometimes three jobs, so we can save up our pennies!"

"Grant, you don't need to curse in front of our son."

I didn't mind. I'd finally found a puzzle piece for the tail.

"You think I joined the army cuz I loved hanging out with Uncle Sam?!"

"We have an Uncle Sam? Was I named after him, Daddy?"

"No, son," my father sighed, "it's slang for the U.S. Government."

I didn't know what slang meant, but decided to ask another time.

"What I'm saying, Jo, is fortunately, I gained a few skills and saved up a little of that G.I. money. I don't know about you, but I don't plan on living in nobody's shack for the rest of my life like I'm some poor-ass tenant farmer!"

We're poor? I thought you had to be unhappy to be poor?

"Grant, I'm tired of living this way, too. I just wonder sometimes if we made the right decision... you know? Things are moving so fast."

"Not fast enough if you ask me. Jolene, I'm 30 years

old and sick and tired of paying my dues—it's time!"

My mother quietly sifted through the puzzle pieces.

"Mom, what are you doing?"

"What do you mean?"

"You just put one of the tail pieces back in the pile."

"Oh, sorry."

"It's okay, Mom. I'll get it."

"Jolene, we may live in a toilet, but I'll be damned if I let us get flushed. That's why I gambled when we really didn't have the money and bought that new Buick. For me, that car represents our hopes and dreams for a brighter future!"

"Mommy, I found one of the pieces for the tail!" I declared.

My father rolled his eyes.

"Good, Samuel. Hush now, your father's talking."

"Yes, ma'am." I clicked the piece onto the growing puzzle.

"Jolene, you know a couple of schools gave me scholarships to play college basketball..."

My mother nodded and self-consciously pulled on her forefinger.

"But being the oldest, I had to drop out and get a job to help Mama with the bills and my brothers and sister. She couldn't do it alone. So I enlisted in the service for four years right after graduation to make more money. They offered Negroes some pretty good benefits. I don't want Samuel to go through the same crap I went through."

"I know, Grant, I know," she whispered, her voice quivering. She folded her arms protectively. "It's just... I get real nervous and scared sometimes. I know what to expect here. I don't know what's waiting for us over there."

The flames in his dark brown eyes went down as he scooted over to her.

"Honey, trust me. It may start out rough, but it's all

gonna work out for us as a family. You, me, and Sam are going to enjoy living there. I promise."

He kissed Mommy on the cheek and affectionately squeezed her. Finally, she worked up a smile, even though her eyes glistened.

"Honey, I'm as sentimental as you are about this matchbox. We've had good times here... especially after this water-headed boy came into our lives."

He reached across and thumped me on the head.

"Uh, uh, Daddy, you're the one with the water-head!"

I punched his rock-hard leg with my fist and tried to pretend it didn't hurt.

"Yeah, this place was cool for a hot minute... but I'm ready to live in a *real* home. Listen, those Negroes ain't sittin' at lunch counters all over the South cuz the eating's good! And the Congress of Racial Equality organized Freedom Rides integrated with Blacks and Whites to battle desegregation. When those buses arrived in the Deep South, the riders were beaten savagely by White mobs. All these folks are making sacrifices so we can be free to equally live our own lives. Like Senator Kennedy said, we got to be pioneers, too! It's a new frontier. You with me?"

She nodded before burying her head in his shoulder and holding his arm.

"Mom, I need help finding the rest of the pieces for the tail!" I shouted.

Chapter 2

It took a year before we finally moved. Apparently, something went wrong and the escrow didn't go through on the first house. My father was very upset. I heard him say angrily to my mother that even though he qualified and filled out all the paperwork correctly, it was something he had no control over. But those escrow people learned nothing stops my father from getting what he wants. Finally, the escrow went through on another house. Daddy was over the moon about it and said we were very lucky to get the house. So, we were scheduled to move in sometime in early June 1961, the same month I would turn 12. And once again he talked about us being pioneers.

I really didn't get all this pioneer talk. I mean, I'm sure being a pioneer might be kinda fun... especially if they let us trade in our Buick for a covered wagon like the one at Knott's Berry Farm. And then gave us a picnic basket loaded with their fried chicken, biscuits, and Boysenberry jam! Except Terelle and Jamelle said the stagecoach was better. It was cool when the bandits showed up to rob you.

I got tired of hearing about Senator John F. Kennedy running for president. My father was crazy about him. All he ever talked about was Kennedy this, Kennedy that, and how he's gonna change the country. Daddy cut out every article in a paper or magazine that showed Kennedy's name.

Even in Ike's Barbershop, Kennedy's name was constantly mentioned with my father leading the pack. Another presidential candidate named Richard Nixon sometimes popped up, but that was usually due to Ike. If you liked Kennedy, Ike LOVED Nixon. If you liked water, Ike LOVED air. Basically, Ike LOVED a good argument. You could talk about anything in his three-chair shop. It was a hangout where everyone could talk about whatever they wanted to. I didn't like getting a haircut, but I always enjoyed being in Ike's Barbershop. I loved hearing all the chatter, loud talking, laughter, and debates, even though I didn't always understand the conversation.

Ike had a sign up outside the door that read: "Ike's Place. The barbershop where we're always cuttin' it up! Come on in!" What I especially liked to stare at was the barber's pole outside the shop. The emblem reminded me of a giant ice cream cone with its red, white, and blue colors spinning underneath a huge white ball.

Inside, the shop was already filling up. As soon as we walked in you immediately got a strong whiff of hair tonics and talcum powder. Five men sitting on padded folding chairs lined up against the wall opposite the barber chairs. We found a spot to sit on a beat-up, faded red couch next to a woman who shook her head disgustedly while combing her son's hair. He restlessly squiggled in her lap.

Above her head was a large sepia-toned print containing photographs of men and boys' haircuts and hairstyles ranging from short cropped, to longer hair, to cuts with parted hair, to hair straightened with lye relaxer or "conked" (Daddy jokingly called conked hair "fried, dyed, and laid to the side"), to a pompadour style featured in a photograph of the wild musician Little Richard. Along the wall, Ike had photographs of celebrities and entertainers you could get your hair styled or cut like, such as Sidney Poitier, Harry Belafonte, Sammy Davis, Jr., Ray Charles, Chuck Berry, and Nat King Cole.

"Junior, stop all that kicking and settle down so I can get these naps out your head. Then Ike won't have to spend all his time combing through it."

"Bessie, he messed up your boy's hair that bad?" Ike questioned.

"Sure did, Ike," the woman answered. "Next time, I'm waiting till you get back from vacation. He did a horrible job!"

"Sorry about that, Bessie. I'll talk to Pharris when he comes in later... Probably came in that day all sleepy-eyed from staying up all night with that gal he's been seeing lately. How about I give you half off today to make up for it?"

"Appreciate that, Ike."

Ike pulled the chair cloth, which looked like a giant apron, off his customer and shook the hair off it. He quickly swept the hair off the floor as the customer got up and paid him. He then slapped the arm of the metal and leather barber chair with a towel and gestured for the next customer before saying to my father, "Okay... now, Mr. Grant Cole, I sho nuff am glad you're here today, cuz I got a ton full of questions to ask you."

"Whatcha wanna know, Ike?"

"All right... can you please tell me why any self-respecting Negro man, such as yourself, would ever want to move south of Century Boulevard?"

Ike's domed head rose above his crown of salt and pepper hair. He wore thick squared glasses and a white barber's shirt. He stood with his scissors and comb hovering over a man's head, eyebrows raised, waiting for Daddy's answer.

"Aw, Negro, get off the man's back. He can live any damn place he wants too as long as he's got the money! Count it, BB—that's 20!"

Over in the corner near the entrance to the bathroom,

Chester slammed the domino on the wiggly card table as BB jerked upright. There was a piece of paper underneath one of the table legs to keep it balanced. Overhead, there was a poster of the new movie: *A Raisin in the Sun* staring Sidney Poitier and Ruby Dee. BB quickly covered his flipped dominoes with his hand.

"Now ain't that some stuff!" Ike replied, smacking his gum louder. "Chester, you best keep focusing on those dominoes cuz you don't know what the hell you talkin' about. Lynwood is just a hop, skip, and jump away from where Grant's moving. Not too long ago, my cousin almost got lynched there!"

"Lynched?" Chester peeked over the cupped dominoes in his hand.

"You heard me—lynched!" Ike snapped. "You think it's any different here than Mississippi? The California sun and the Hollywood stars just hide the glare better! We got our own Klan—y'all remember them spook hunters?"

Chester slid a domino across the table into the zigzag shape of the dominoes. "Yeah, I remember them bastards... On the back of their club jackets they had this cartoon darky with a noose around his neck. They all lived out there in South Gate, Bell, and Huntington Park. Used to attack any brotha crossing east of Alameda, like a crocodile waiting for somebody to step into the water."

"Nigga, please... like they waited..." BB grumbled. He straightened out the dominoes. "Sometimes you didn't have to be anywhere near their neighborhood. They'd hop in the car and drive west looking to beat some colored man's ass! But that was back in the forties and fifties... They ain't around no more."

"Tell it to my cousin!" Ike barked, chewing his gum more rapidly. "They may have new names and faces, but the hate ain't changed one bit."

"Yes Lawd!" Chester agreed, intently studying the

dominoes in his hand. His feet tapped to Howling Wolf singing "Back Door Man." Wolf's gravelly voice and bluesy guitar blasted from a radio that sat on a table loaded with magazines and newspapers such as the *L.A. Times*, *Los Angeles Sentinel*, *Time*, *Ebony*, *Jet*, *Life*, *Sports Illustrated*, *Popular Mechanics*, and *Boy's Life* and *Highlights* for the kids.

"My cousin stopped at a red light and rednecks threw rocks at his car like it was a bullpen. He stepped on the gas and flew outta there like a bat outta hell!"

Ike popped his gum as he clipped the man's hair. He turned around to the wide cabinet behind him. Three mirrors affixed against the wall sat behind each of his three chairs. Ike sorted through an array of clippers and razors till he found the best one to line the man's hair on the front, sides, and back.

"I ain't done yet... Then a PO-liceman pulls him over and gives him a ticket for running a red light!!"

"Say what?"

"Yeah, buddy... that's when he found out the cop was deaf and blind."

"C'mon now, be right."

"If I'm lying, I'm dying. My cousin says he told the PO-lice he ran the light because they was throwing rocks at him. The cop says he was camped out inside his car at that same corner and didn't see no people throwing rocks. So my cousin says, 'I guess you don't hear them hollerin' nigger, either, Officer?' Man, do you know, he say that policeman grinned and said, 'You're right, I don't hear a thing,' and wrote him a dang speeding ticket on the spot."

"What kind of stuff..."

"Yes, sir! My cousin said he ain't been back that way since. So don't tell me you can move anywhere you want just cuz you can afford it!"

"I don't know, seems to me... BB, you put my score down? Okay, seems to me a man pays his money, he's got the right to live where he wants."

"What the hell you know about that, fool?" Ike asked, gum popping like gunshots. "You ain't paid me for the last two haircuts!"

"Now why you wanna bring that up in front of everybody? You know when I gets paid you is covered... Why you write 15, when you only got 10, BB?"

"So, Cole, I'm still waiting on an answer. Why do you want to move to... where'd you say, Fisher Place? Yeah, that's it. I mean, look, you a grown man... you can do whatever you want to... but I'm just curious, man... I..."

"Uh, am I going to get a chance to speak, Ike?"

"Don't start with me, Cole," Ike said sternly, pointing his scissors at my father and sneaking a wink at me.

My father chuckled, then got serious.

"Look, we got brothas and sistas down South demanding their rights and getting beat up and sometimes killed for it."

"Amen," shouted one of the patrons.

"You know, that ain't right," another one chimed in.

"No, sir, it ain't," shouted BB as he snatched another domino from the pile while Chester smugly grinned.

"All because we want to be treated as equals," someone said.

"I'm a man like anybody else!" yelled another patron.

"Well, King and all those folks ain't knocking on the backdoor no more. They're kicking them open and this time the rope is around Jim Crow's neck!"

"You ain't said a wrong word, yet, Cole!"

"Uh, huh, go'n and tell it, son!"

"So, I guess they inspired me. In my own way, I'm trying to do my part. The opportunity presented itself, and like everybody I'm just trying to get mine."

"Damn... sho can't argue with that," Ike replied, scissors clicking. "What you think about what my man, Cole, is saying, Mr. Sullivan?"

Sitting in a rocking chair, Mr. Sullivan tugged on his scruffy salt and pepper beard. Piled high on the coffee table in front of him lay *Jet* magazines. He rarely read them. He usually flipped through the pages of each one until he reached the center photo featuring the weekly swimsuit model. He held it close to his face and turned it at all angles.

"Lawd have mercy... this child is blessed with a body that won't quit! Looka here, looka here... I swear she could turn back the hands of time for this old man... yes indeedy... hmmm."

His eyes strained to lift from the photo. "Uh, what y'all asking me? Oh, yeah... the way I sees it... man got to do what a man got to do. Cole can't be worrying about what us folks is saying. He's got a pretty wife at home and that fine lookin' youngsta over there to think about. Shoot, I'd get the hell away from you Negroes myself if I could afford to. Y'all ain't about nuthin' anyway."

His wheezy laughter drifted through the shop as he slapped his thigh.

"Oh, now ain't that cold," Ike said, laughing as well.

"Y'all know I'm teasing... but seriously, back in Alabama, I couldn't even drink out the same water faucet as them crackers. So if Brother Cole can get himself a nice house on the same block as them Caucasians, then all power to him. But ain't no good-byes... I guarantee he'll be back here to see us."

"He better be!" Ike worked Royal Crown pomade into his customer's hair.

"Oh, don't worry, we'll be back at least once a month for a haircut."

"Cole you ain't got a choice," replied Mr. Sullivan. "If you try to get a haircut in one of their barbershops, you might get your head cut off instead of your hair!"

Everyone hooted and hollered, including my father.

Mr. Sullivan returned to the *Jet* center photo. "What-you-say, girl!"

Chapter 3

My father still chuckled about that "head cut off" comment as we drove home. He repeated it to my mother later and she laughed, too.

A barber chopping somebody's head off?

That's funny?

While they laughed, I sat in terror. Plus, the escrow on the house had gone through. Now my parents' sole focus was on moving to a place where bloodthirsty barbers roamed.

What could I do?

I needed advice from a higher authority. I figured out whom to ask.

Mattie White.

Mattie White knew God personally. She told me she had conversations with God and his son, Jesus, all the time.

Wish I could talk to Him.

I got down on bended knees every night and prayed at my bedside, but God never uttered a word to me, not even a whisper. My mother claimed He heard everything I said... but I don't know... I'm still waiting to hear *His* voice.

Mattie swore I'd hear it someday, but only if I read my Bible regularly and kept an open heart. She grumbled that my chances would improve if my parents got me baptized. I asked why she doesn't tell them.

"Not my place," she'd grunt.

My mother always chuckled when I used to mispronounce "foster" and called Mattie my "frosty" mother. Mattie White babysat most of the kids in the neighborhood. She'd let all us kids call her Mattie. Never met Mr. White. He died years before I was born. Mattie couldn't have kids, so after Mr. White died she quit her job cleaning houses and become a foster mother. She loved children and claimed their presence enriched her life and helped her to move forward. This was one of those things she said God talked to her about before she made a decision. "God's will," she called it.

I got my chance to discuss more about God with her the following Sunday. My mother was asked to work the store due to someone on the night shift calling in sick. My father worked as a janitor in the evenings, so he couldn't watch me.

"Honey, can't we find anyone else?" he grumbled as he hurriedly threw on his coveralls.

"What's wrong with Mattie?"

"Ain't nothing *wrong* with Mattie. What's wrong is that damn Holy Roller church she wants to take him to."

"Who else are we going to call on a Sunday at the last minute? Mattie said she'd be fine watching Samuel as long as she could take him to church with her. You know she never misses a Sunday night service. Besides, Samuel likes spending time with her."

"Yeah, well, I don't know if he wants to spend time watching all those crazy folks acting up and jumping around like they got ants in their pants!"

"Not ants... the Holy Ghost."

"Uh, huh, well, maybe he ought to go with me. He can help me empty the wastebaskets and vacuum."

I loved vacuuming!

"Grant, you remember the last time? You came home complaining about how much Samuel slowed you down. Especially after he knocked over the ink blotter and spilled black ink all over the carpet. It took you forever to clean it up! Let Mattie take care of him."

"All right, fine… but don't blame me when he comes back with his eyes bugging and tongue hanging out like the *Creature from the Black Lagoon* movie.

"Oh stop!" she laughed. "A little church won't hurt Samuel."

"That's no church—that's a carnival!"

***

"Mattie, you want me to help you dry the dishes?"

"No thanks, Sam, I'm almost finished! Lord it's so hot tonight!" Mattie exclaimed from the kitchen. Water gushed from the faucet and plates clattered on the counter. She went back to singing:

"Jesus loves the little children, all the children in the world, whether Yellow, Black, or White, they are precious in his sight, Jesus loves the little children of the world."

I spun around and raced to the far side of the living room. As I leaned forward, Jesus kept his eyes on me the whole time from his position on the mantle. I ducked behind a bookcase and peered through the slats, but Jesus' blue eyes locked on mine. No matter which angle, I couldn't evade Jesus' gaze. I tiptoed up to the picture and stared at it. Jesus stared back, his eyes serene, and his light brown, shoulder length hair highlighted by a halo. The longer I stared at the portrait the more it seemed he was looking at me like, "Boy, don't you know who you messin' with?"

Mattie came around the corner, wiping her hands with a dishtowel. She eyed me suspiciously as one of her thick eyebrows arched.

"Boy, what you doin'?"

"Trying to see if Jesus can still see me."

"Jesus is always watching you no matter where you are." She grinned, amused by my antics.

"Oh."

"If you're not too busy..." Mattie chuckled, "do me a favor and get me my hat in the closet—the one with the pretty roses on it! It's time to go to church. She slapped the dishtowel over her shoulder as she returned to the kitchen once again singing, "*Jesus loves the little children.*"

The temperature had cooled a bit, but the night air remained humid. Sometimes Mattie grabbed my arm with her free hand when she started feeling tired as we walked to church. Most of the time she used her free hand to wipe away the perspiration settling onto her face. Her other hand grasped a Bible that she cocked purposefully in her arm, like a halfback carrying a football.

Mattie was a portly woman with hips spread out like a catcher's mitt. She waddled when she walked, constantly bumping me with her hips... but I liked it... It felt comforting in a way. It let you know she was there.

The walk was slow due to Mattie stopping now and then to catch her breath. At one point she sat down on the steps of a vacant building, breathing hard and grimacing. She must have been in a lot of pain. She lifted the tail end of her dress to just above her knees and massaged them. It stunned me to see how tremendously scarred and flat her knees were... like they had been leveled with sandpaper. They were swollen on both sides. I guess my expression betrayed my thoughts.

"Years of scrubbing too many people's floors, honey."

"Oh," I said, unable to tear my eyes away.

We continued our walk, and then I remembered what I needed to ask her.

"Mattie, can we talk?"

She answered by whacking me on the head with her Bible.

"Boy, you know better than to insult your Mattie like that. Of course you can talk to me. What's on your mind?"

"What does Jesus' daddy look like?" I asked, rubbing my head.

"You talking about God?"

"Uh, huh."

"I don't know... but I'll betcha God has the kindest and warmest face you've ever seen."

"What about his hair?"

"Probably whiter than mine."

"You think he has a beard?"

"Yeah... I see a long, thick, and bushy one, like Santa Claus." She smiled, her eyes twinkling above the huge raccoon-like black circles underneath. The dark folds clashed against her fair skin and seemed to give birth to all the freckles littering her face.

Suddenly the sounds of an organ and banging tambourines filled the overheated night air. Mattie clutched my arm and we hurried our pace. I bumped alongside her like a balloon on a string.

The Jordan Family Christian Center used to be a small movie theater before it changed into a storefront church. Most of the cinema seats had been ripped out and replaced by wooden pews. The theater billboard above the building's entrance—that once announced each week's feature films—now read:

FROM HERE TO ETERNITY!

Starring: Jesus Christ
Directed by: The Holy Ghost
Produced by: God Almighty
Written by: Pastor G.K. Veasey

Welcome! Limited Run! Last chance!

Once inside, Mattie rushed to find a seat. I begged to

sit in one of the movie chairs on the side of the aisle, but Mattie said she was too big to sit in one of those. We sat a couple of pews from the front. I noticed the walls were lined with canes and crutches. There were even some smoking pipes lying on the floor. I tapped Mattie's shoulder and pointed to them.

"Them the folks that got healed."

Healed? Was that what she said? I could barely hear over the raucous music.

"What are those pipes for?"

She leaned into my ear close enough that her lips tickled.

"Mr. White got cured of smoking here… but it was too late… he still died of lung cancer. But it's all right… Now he's praising the good Lord in heaven!"

Eyes closed, she clapped her hands in time with the music. I slipped my arm through hers and clapped, too. But I wasn't about to close my eyes.

There were only about a hundred people inside the church, but the music was loud enough to rock the Los Angeles Coliseum. A small church band made up of an organ, guitar, violin, and drums played on stage like they believed they were an orchestra. The congregation joyfully sang the church anthem. I could tell some people didn't know the words, but they sang with just as much emotion as those that did. So I joined in, pretending I knew the words too, until Mattie gave me a look. Then I just hummed.

Those who didn't sing bobbed their heads while their lips moved speedily in prayer. Others cried, tearfully laughed, or waved one hand heavenward. A bright-eyed girl, who'd turned around earlier in the front row and smiled at me with her crooked teeth, now had her hands fluttering above her head. Soon her glazed eyes fixed on a slight and bespectacled preacher with glistening, jet-black processed hair who strutted onto the stage.

He grabbed the microphone with a confident air that didn't fit his appearance. He shook his head, deeply moved, as he studied the congregation. He joined them in song, and I was surprised to hear a beautiful deep voice rise above the music. After the song ended, he spoke. He was not an eloquent speaker, but his rough street voice had enormous power.

"God is great!"

"Yes he is, Pastor Veasey!"

"I get goose bumps when I think about how much He loves us!"

"You should look at my arms, Pastor!" someone shouted.

I was already looking at mine.

"I'm going to say it again—God is great! Somebody say Amen!"

A chorus of Amens greeted him.

"His greatness blessed us with the music of the spirit... music that can lift your heart from the depths of despair and make it soar above the clouds!"

"Praise Jesus," Mattie replied softly, rapidly fanning herself with two church programs. There were so many people in the congregation fanning themselves it looked like a sea of butterflies.

"Music is not the only thing that will move our hearts this evening!"

"What you say, preacher!" shouted an elder, wiping his sweaty forehead with a handkerchief.

"There is a powerful and divine force that can change the hearts of men!"

"Tell 'em about it!"

"The Holy Ghost!"

"Say it again!"

"I said the Holy Ghost!"

"Yes, Lawd!"

"The same Holy Ghost that can turn a mouthful of silver into gold!"

"Did mine last week!" somebody testified.

I quickly looked around. I wanted to see that person.

"It's time to celebrate! Tonight we are going to have us a party!"

"Now you sayin' something!"

"A Holy Ghost party!" the Pastor shouted as he grabbed the microphone and sashayed back and forth across the stage. "And we all know, ain't no celebration like a Holy Ghost celebration!"

"Hallelujah!" the faithful yelled.

"Then let's get this party started!" he yelled back as he removed his glasses and passed them off like a baton to one of the elders behind him at the altar. That's when I noticed something wrong with his right eye. It seemed like there was a marble stuck in it. I yanked on Mattie's arm.

"Mattie, look! He's got a glass eye!"

"Hush! You just now seeing that? Maybe you need *your* eyes checked."

"But..."

"He got into a prison fight, and somebody stabbed him in the eye."

"He was in prison?"

"Yes, and that's when Jesus came into his life."

"Jesus was in prison with Pastor Veasey?"

Mattie sighed. "Samuel... just listen to the sermon. We'll talk later."

"Who needs a miracle this evening?" Pastor Veasey bellowed.

His gaze was piercing, even with the deadened glass eye. The answer was immediate as people rose to their feet, arms raised and palms outward. The band cranked up a soulful spiritual. Pastor Veasey strolled down the aisle.

"Don't be shy. The Lord ain't gonna be shy when he comes back to earth in all his splendid glory as judge and jury. He's not gonna be shy when he casts sinners into the Devil's arms. Don't be shy. God's not gonna be shy when he rewards the faithful with a life of everlasting happiness.

"All He wants is your love, your devotion, and for you to CONFESS your sins and REPENT! That's how ETERNITY will come to you. I can guarantee it! Sears can't guarantee their products will last forever. And Ford's not giving you a lifetime guarantee on a new car. But if you believe in the cross of Jesus Christ, I can promise you eternal life. That's God's guarantee in exchange for your souls.

"And like this church, God don't care what color you are. When Jesus comes there's no time for any of that foolishness! All the races will come together, and all believers will be filled with the power and the glory of God! So don't be shy, step forward and be proud to receive the Holy Ghost because YOU are the CHOSEN!"

And that's when things got real blurry for me. My father's words galloped into my head: *That's no church... that's a carnival.*

Lots of people stepped forward. The band's music got even louder along with thunderous foot stomping, wailing, hands clapping, and cries of hallelujah. I was fascinated and afraid as images swirled around me like a cyclone.

The preacher laid his hands on a frail, silver-haired woman who had a slight hump in her back. Earlier she had stood wobbling, barely able to hold on to the pew. After he touched her, she lifted her head and howled like a coyote, then spun in circles. She finally tumbled to the floor, jerking and kicking as she rolled all over it. She pushed away the hands of anyone trying to help her. She gradually rose up under her own strength.

People kept surging towards the preacher. He'd kiss them off the forehead with the palm of his hand, and they'd collapse to the floor or jump and scream. Some writhed across the ground like snakes. Others just passed out. Mattie cradled me in her arms.

"Don't be afraid, child. It's only the Holy Ghost doing His work."

Only? Yeah... knowing a ghost floated around waiting for his chance to leap inside somebody's skin wasn't exactly what I'd call comforting.

My greatest fear was that the Holy Ghost might decide to hop inside of me. I listened closely when Pastor Veasey said, "You have to be ready for the Holy Spirit... you gotta open up and allow him to come inside."

Well, I wasn't ready yet. So I decided to close all my bodily openings, starting with pinching my nostrils with my fingers so he couldn't slip through the air holes. Next I worked on being as tight as I could be, keeping my body stiff, and making my breaths short.

But I soon gave up the struggle... too tiring... plus, I was starting to get dizzy. If the Holy Ghost was going to jump inside me then so be it. Besides, it may not be all that bad... Some folks burst into giddy laughter, and they hadn't even been drinking. I never saw adults act this way, except when they got drunk at my parents' parties. But they were also good to each other.

A team of women huddled around a hysterical woman who'd lost her husband weeks ago. They laid their hands on her and prayed. Soon her screams became faint sobs.

Pastor Veasey strode over to a huge, burly man with a jagged scar across his cheek. The man rocked back and forth in the pew. At times, he'd clap his hands rapidly and angrily. His large hands were shaped like beefy cymbals, and he'd smack them together like he was swatting a mosquito.

Pastor Veasey gestured for the man to stand up. The man faced him with his head bowed. Resting both hands on the man's shoulders, the preacher said, "How long you been out of jail?"

"I just got out two days ago, preacher," the man replied, fidgeting.

Veasey knowingly nodded. "Then you've chosen the right place, my brother. Welcome to the House of the Lord. This is where God plans to set His sinners free. Through the gospel of Jesus Christ, let the Holy Ghost enter this man so he can praise God for all eternity!"

Veasey held the back of the man's head with his right hand and shoved his other hand against the man's forehead, grasping him in a headlock. He did so without fear of a man that looked like he could have broken the pastor into a million pieces. The man dropped helplessly to his knees, dazed. If Mattie hadn't held my arms, I'd have broken an Olympic sprint record out of the church. Snot bubbled out the man's nose, and he foamed at the corners of his mouth like a rabid dog. He jabbered in an unknown language like he was under a spell.

I clutched Mattie's arm. "What's wrong with him, Mattie?"

"He's speaking in tongues, boy."

Tongues? I stared at him to see if he had more than one tongue in his mouth. The talking tongues sounded more like gibberish to me, but then other people started babbling in their own strange tongue language.

The band triumphantly struck up a rousing gospel number, and the aisles got crammed with dancing parishioners. An old lady with an ostrich feather hat hypnotically bounded from her pew with outspread arms. She kicked off her shoes and pranced on the seat of the pew.

I wondered what Mattie thought about this madness, but she was eyeing another woman around the same age sitting quietly in her pew with a faint smirk.

"Whatcha lookin' at, Mattie?"

"Child, I'm waiting to see how long it's gonna take Sista Vita to get sanctified. She ain't one to let Sista Rosa upstage her for too long."

Sure enough, Sista Vita dramatically snatched off her shoes, flung her hat toward the altar, and launched into a chicken wing-flapping dance down the aisle. She wildly swung her hands as she passed each pew. Pretty soon the other woman danced alongside her, and it looked like a tribal dance fest.

"Look at 'em! Praise God!" Mattie clapped and laughed.

I don't know how I looked about this time, but Mattie stopped applauding and stroked my head.

"Honey, you look tired. You wanna lie down? We can leave in a minute."

"I'm not tired. I want to stay up."

"That's not what your eyes say."

I fought to open them wider to prove it to her, but it was a losing battle.

"Are you afraid if you fall asleep the Holy Spirit might grab ahold of old Mattie and cause her to act a fool?"

I said no, but my face shouted YES.

"I've been there... but I promise, you don't have to worry about that, Samuel. I carry the Holy Ghost in a permanent place inside my heart, so I don't need to get out there and do a stomp and buck dance tonight. You go on and go to sleep if you want. It'll be all right."

That's all I needed to hear. I was too tired and overwhelmed to worry about the Holy Ghost anymore. Before I closed my eyes and laid my head on Mattie's shoulder, I saw Pastor Veasey leap into the air like a Masai warrior, his processed hair no longer smoothed down. It was upraised, spiky, and wild, looking like a deranged rooster. The Holy Ghost had seized him, too.

***

Shuffling noises startled me during the middle of the night. Had the Holy Ghost found out where I lived? I got scared all over again until the potent scent of ammonia drifted into the room. Daddy was home. He wearily leaned against the bedroom door, his figure silhouetted by the overhead hall light. He found me sitting up in a chair next to their bed, reading a comic book by flashlight.

"Hi, Daddy," I whispered so I wouldn't wake my mother.

"Hi. How come you're not in your own bed in the front room? Can't sleep?"

"No."

He smiled.

"I understand. Go ahead and keep reading, you'll fall asleep soon."

A moment later he went into the bathroom, and I heard screechy knobs being turned followed by sputtering metallic coughs as water streamed out of the shower. I did fall asleep in the chair until Daddy walked in smelling like Ivory soap. He eased into their bed. He leaned over and smugly whispered to my loudly snoring mother, "Told you he wouldn't be able to sleep."

He knew she heard him. She's a light sleeper... and never snores.

Chapter 4

All the talk about moving made me kind of angry. I don't think my parents had any idea how much this would affect my life; especially since I had become a schoolyard legend...

On our walk to school one morning, Terelle, Jamelle, and I were having our usual conversation about bogeymen, werewolves, vampires, and other creatures of the night. While we argued about whether Frankenstein's monster could beat up the Wolfman, I didn't see an uncovered manhole. I dropped straight down, just like Alice in Wonderland, into a pit of darkness. I landed in the arms of a man wearing a construction hat, goggles, and hefty orange coveralls caked with dust. He stood on a ladder and was just as shocked to see me as I him.

"Son, uh, are you all right?"

I nodded my head; but I felt kinda wobbly. I'd skinned my arms and knees against the narrow walls. Sharp pains zinged from the scrape marks.

Farther below, another voice rose up: "Larry, what the hell's going on up there?"

"It's all right, Ed. This little colored kid fell down the hole, but I caught him. He's fine! Isn't that right, kid?" he asked nervously.

"Oh for Christ-sakes, that's all we need... some kid's parents suing the city. I told you we shoulda posted more signs and blocked the area off better!"

"Hey, kid, you sure you're okay?" He dusted me off.

"Yeah, I think so."

I stared straight into his goggles, hypnotized.

"He *thinks* so? Great, we're fired!" groaned the voice down below.

The goggled man grinned as he kept brushing me off. "Don't listen to him. He doesn't know what a tough kid you are. Right?"

"Uh, huh."

"Okay, then grab a hold of the ladder, son. Got a tight grip? Good. Now, let's climb up. It's only a few feet to the top. There you go."

His thickly gloved hands gently held me by the hips as I climbed each step carefully. At the last couple of feet the ladder ended, so he hoisted me up into the bright shining sun where I grabbed the ledge and spilled forward. He held onto my legs until he was certain I was safely on top.

"Watch yourself, okay, son?" he said. "Bye!" His head and goggles disappeared. I heard laughter below, mixed with a curse word or two.

As I squinted into the harsh sunlight, I made out Terelle and Jamelle standing there, mouths ajar, staring at me like I was a ghost. They weren't alone. News travels fast in a schoolyard. A mob of kids gathered around the manhole. They had heard about it from our on-the-spot reporters.

The story going around school later was that the mole men captured me and I miraculously escaped. I looked the part, too—clothes tattered and dirty. I tried to tell everyone that a workman caught me but a jury of my peers refused to hear of it. I was in shock or just being modest. Terelle and Jamelle claimed the mole man yanked me down by the head, kicking and screaming. If I hadn't bravely fought to free myself from his grasp, his huge claws would have ripped my arms off. The goggles hid the ugly snout sticking out of his face.

Soon, the twins even had me convinced. They said the mole men hypnotized me into thinking they were just workmen. Why else did all the caution signs go up a day later along with plastic blocks and ribbon to cordon off the area? I'd uncovered their secret hiding place, and they didn't want any adults to get wind of their evil plans for world domination.

I warned Mrs. Carlson, our blonde, fifth grade teacher, about the hole and who lived there. She covered her face with her hands and made a snorkeling noise. I chalked it up to hysteria. A glimpse of a smile showed between her fingers. She patted me on the head and told me not to worry. I don't think teachers understand these kinds of things, even though I thought they knew everything. I vowed to protect Mrs. Carlson with my life if the mole men invaded the classroom—mainly because she was very pretty, and I had fallen in love with her.

The word about my adventure with the mole men spread quicker than the measles. Even Sheri, with the curly hair and shiny caramel skin, was impressed. I once paid her a nickel to kiss me on the cheek. After hearing about my tangle with the mole men she kissed me on my cheek for free. Oh yeah, it gets even better. She secretly held my hand on the bus during a field trip to the museum. She made me promise not to tell anyone at school—but not at home!

Once I got home I rushed to my mother who was in the bathroom putting on makeup and gave her a big loving hug.

"Oh my, what's going on?"

"Guess who kissed me today and held my hand on the field trip?"

"Somebody kissed you?" She grabbed a brush and started working her hair.

"Yeah."

"You mean, yes?"

"Yes... Sheri, the prettiest girl in school kissed me on the cheek!"

"Oh?"

"She's the prettiest girl in the school!"

"I heard," my mother said, carefully putting on her lipstick. She smacked her lips. "So, how do I look?"

"Good."

"Prettier than Sheri?" she teased.

"No, Sheri is *really* beautiful, Mommy!"

Judging by the look on her face—wrong answer. Probably not a good time to mention I was in love with Mrs. Carlson.

"You think she's more beautiful than your mother?"

Uh, oh... I'd stepped into quicksand and, unlike Tarzan, had no vine in sight to grab onto and pull myself out. I forgot how sensitive my mother could sometimes be. The teasing tone in her voice disappeared.

"Hmmm... I remember a time when you used to say no one was more beautiful than your mother... Guess that's changed," she sighed, gazing into the mirror and brushing her hair again.

"No, no, you're the most beautiful woman in the world, Mommy, and she's the prettiest girl in school."

I was relieved to see her smile.

"Samuel, I think you're learning the art of diplomacy."

I didn't know what diplomacy meant, but she didn't look as hurt as before, so it must be good.

I really did believe my mother was the most beautiful woman on earth. People said she looked like an actress named Dorothy Dandridge. Every time she got a compliment like that it would launch a yard-size smile on her face, and she'd act like no one ever told her this before. "Really? You think so? Thank you!"

Chapter 5

I was extra nice to my mother for the rest of the day and the hurt faded. I may have fumbled the ball at home, but I still scored a touchdown at school. My meeting with the mole men made me famous.

Unfortunately, there was a downside to fame. It began with two words:

Edgar Bradshaw.

While my PR agents, Terelle and Jamelle, nurtured my image, one of another kind already existed. Edgar Bradshaw was *the* consummate school bully. He was the baddest dude to walk a schoolyard since Shaka Zulu. And easy to spot with his stocky toad-like body, thick bruiser arms, and tiny little beads of hair balancing on his head like muddy black marbles. Jamelle was convinced he came from an ancient tribe of ape-men. No one knew where he came from and nobody asked. He knew everyone was afraid of him and it thrilled him.

The word *tough* didn't exist before his birth.

The drums say he may have murdered his parents. How else would you explain his appearance? He walked out the house with holey jeans and uncombed hair. My parents would have used me for fish bait if I had done that!

They say Edgar once fought four kids and held them in a headlock that lasted for weeks. It took more than a dozen policemen to pry those kids from his monstrous arms, and when he finally let them go they had Gumby shaped heads as they tumbled to the ground, gasping for air.

Our paths had to cross someday. One morning he startled me by jumping in front of me out of nowhere with his behemoth body. I suspected he hid behind a tree. The twins swore he slept in the highest branches of that tree and lived on birds and fried chipmunks.

I'll never forget those immortal words: "You got a quarter?"

Being confronted by that humongous frame was like being injected with a truth serum. When he talked his speech was croaky and slurred and his droopy mouth looked like someone had stuck a fishhook in it.

"Y-Y-Yess!"

After a nerve-wracking amount of fumbling through my pockets, I fished out a quarter that melted into the palm of his hand.

Ignored were my pleas that I now had no money to buy milk for lunch or that I'd get in trouble with my parents. Made no never mind to him. Instead, his eyes widened, his hands balled up into fists, and he threatened to knock my head off. Edgar never used lotion so his ashy skin looked as if he had been standing in the middle of a campfire. His scarred and meaty hands looked like he pounded them daily against rocks for exercise. If he could do that to himself, then beating me up would be a joy. That's why I'd almost ripped a hole in my pocket trying to pry the coin out.

Drinking water wasn't all that bad.

He snagged my money, snarled, and began to lumber away. But then he abruptly swung around. I had this horrible feeling that he had a change of heart (what heart?) and decided to beat me up anyway. I braced myself and envisioned my head rolling down the sidewalk.

He planted his fist against my nose.

"You tell anybody about this and I'll beat you stupid!

Got it?!"

It hurt to even nod my head against Edgar's granite fist. My only comfort was that none of the other kids laughed or teased me, since they were all scared of him.

I figured I wasn't the only one he made a profit from. Pretty soon I expected to see him open the "Bradshaw Elementary School Bank."

For the next few days, "my money or my life" became my newest slogan. I didn't see Edgar every day, but whenever I did my hand was already sewn inside my pants pocket as I frantically searched for another quarter. I dropped money into his outstretched hand like it was a tollbooth crossing.

The only wisdom I gained from this experience was that I was a milk addict. I suffered bouts of severe milk withdrawals during lunch.

But I also discovered that, in the face of danger, sometimes the greatest strategies can emerge. How could Edgar take my money if he never saw me? So, I took a different route to school.

Except, I didn't account for the extra blocks and time my detour took. I got to school 30 minutes late and without a written excuse! That afternoon, Mrs. Carlson sent me home with a note tagged to my lapel asking my parents to call her. Depressed, I trudged home, knowing my fate.

The electric chair?

No.

A hanging?

No.

A lethal injection?

No... All just wishful thinking.

Those methods were humane compared to my mother's great narrow belt. The belt didn't kill you; it just hurt, plain and simple. You've seen people on television hung or electrocuted, but when have you seen a whipping on TV?

Never. Much too frightening and graphic... especially when the victim was a kid.

Oh, and one last thing... Mrs. Carlson must have been psychic. She called my home and told my mother that she had a feeling I might misplace the note and forget to tell her to call... which, funny enough, I had.

I sat trembling in the corner of the bedroom in my little wooden red chair. The palms of my hand sweated nonstop while I awaited sentencing. I prayed for a natural disaster—an earthquake, tsunami, hurricane, alien invasion—anything that would disrupt the oncoming tragedy about to occur. The phone conversation between Mrs. Carlson and my mother felt like it lasted forever. All my mother said was, "Uh huh, uh huh... I see... Uh, huh... Well, Mrs. Carlson... thanks for letting me know. Don't worry, it won't happen again. You have my word. Samuel will be on time from now on!"

Then I got the look.

My mother eased the phone onto its cradle. It didn't click, it went "uh, oh." Tears bobbled down my face as I watched her unfasten the belt she wore with her fancy new red dress. My mother talked just as fast as she spanked me.

"Samuel Scott Cole, don't-you-ever-let-me-catch-you-being-late-for-school-ever-again! Do-you-hear-me?"

The rapid-fire belt made me scream loud enough to awaken the dead at the Forest Lawn Cemetery. Thankfully, the spanking was short. A fountain of tears streamed from my eyes as I stood there rubbing my behind.

Seriously, were whippings legal?

"Samuel, why were you late for school?"

Like a fish out of water my mouth moved but made no sound.

"Boy, don't let me ask you again!"

She reached for her belt again, and speech erupted

from out of nowhere!

"Edgar B-B-Bradshaw, h-he keeps t-t-taking m-m-money f-from me, and h-he is real b-big, and s-s-scary... so I h-h-had to f-f-find a n-new w-way to s-s-school. I-I-I d-don't ever w-want to go b-back to school again..."

I never finished due to collapsing into a heap on the floor.

My mother sat me down on the bed with her. Her eyes softened. I sensed the momentum swinging to my side. I laid my head on her shoulder.

"Oh, Samuel... why didn't you tell me this was going on?"

I shrugged, sniffling like crazy. "I hate him, Mommy!"

She rubbed my back. "Samuel, what do you think your father is going to do when I tell him some ignorant bully is taking your money every day?"

"I don't know... come down to school and beat him up for me?"

She smiled. "You know better than that. Here's the deal... if that boy tries to take your money again—you're not going to let him! We work too hard to let some undeserving soul just take our money. Understand?"

What I understood was, they didn't care about losing their son to a fist fatality.

Her high cheekbones jutted out more than usual. "Tomorrow you WILL go to school and you WILL stand up to Mr. Edgar! If he threatens to beat you up you WILL NOT back down! You WILL make sure he knows he's been in a fight, win or lose. Afterwards, I promise he won't ever bother you again. You hear me?"

"Yes, Mother."

Unbelievable... she actually told me I might lose. Isn't it written down somewhere that parents are supposed to protect their young? This was no ordinary boy. He was a beast that lived in the highest treetops!

"If it helps, Samuel, I'll tell you about the time I had a fight."

"You?"

I was genuinely surprised. I couldn't imagine my beautiful mother in a brawl, unless, of course, she carried the magical attack belt with her.

She laughed. "Yes, me, silly. I was around your age and there was this big old fat girl who used to pick on me. My girlfriends said she was jealous of me. She used to snatch my food all the time. Samuel, I've never lied to you and I won't start now. I was scared to death of her. Finally, one day I had enough. I was sick and tired of being hungry at school. She made her usual demand for my food and I refused to give it to her."

"You did? What happened?"

"Well, I had very long hair then, and she grabbed my ponytail and yanked it hard. I hated having my hair pulled about as much as I hated not eating. I grit my teeth, closed my eyes, and swung as hard as I could, fearing this girl was going to kill me... but when I opened my eyes, she lay on the ground in tears and holding her stomach. All the kids laughed at her, happy to see her finally get her due."

Wow! Forget my father... maybe I could get my mother to beat Edgar up.

"And you know what? She never bothered me again. So you have to fight him, no matter how much it scares you. Edgar needs to know you'll stand up to him. If you don't, I'll find out about it sooner or later. And if you're late for school again, next time I'll let your father deal with it!"

And then there are things far worse than death.

That night I played with my toy soldiers for the very last time.

Mommy must have told Daddy anyway. The next morning I watched cartoons on our black and white television set until my father shut it off and insisted that I stand up so he could teach me how to box.

The lesson went fairly well. I learned how to beat up his hands. The problem was, Edgar couldn't care less about fighting—his specialty was maiming.

As it turned out, the next school morning turned out to be one of the best ones in my life. Edgar never showed up.

I was so happy I became teacher's pet the whole day.

But on my way home, my real-life nightmare appeared out of nowhere.

"Got some money?"

I closed my eyes and clenched my teeth.

"E-E-Edgar? I d-d-didn't know you were at s-school today."

"I wasn't, boy. I go to school when I feel like it!"

"Oh."

"Why? You don't like it?" He bumped my chest.

"No... I mean, you can do what you want."

"That's right, punk. And I want my money!"

A circle of kids gathered around us, the majority standing respectfully to Edgar's side.

I hung my head and stared at my feet.

"N-No."

Edgar gasped.

The crowd gasped.

Terelle and Jamelle gave me an it-was-nice-knowing-you look.

"Say what?" Edgar bumped my chest again.

"No... I m-mean, I d-don't have no more money."

He shoved me. "You better have it tomorrow, stupid, or you-know-what!"

I hated my parents at this moment.

"No. I c-can't g-give you any more money—ever."

Everyone gasped again.

Edgar was stunned. "You can't what?!" He pushed me.

That alone hurt.

"My mother said I can't give you my money."

Kids giggled.

"Your mother? Why you little sissy, I'm gonna kick your...!"

I didn't hear the finish because I took off like a wild rabbit, cutting through alleys, zigzagging, doing everything I could to lose Edgar; but he was hot on my tail followed by about 30 screaming kids with clanging and banging lunch pails.

I tried to ditch him in every way I could, including running through an old hotel. I ran straight through the front entrance, past the lounge, and out the exit, but only managed to remain steps away from Edgar's outstretched arms. We skirted through street traffic, honking horns, screeching cars, alleys, and backyards. Kids foaming at the mouth shadowed us, excited to see the massacre.

Huffing and puffing, I ran around the Evans' house right up to my front door and banged loudly on it. My mother opened the door and I stumbled inside.

"Lord, what in the world..."

Edgar braked to a stop and froze. Every kid behind him froze, too. A few kids recognized my mother and turned to tiptoe away until she said:

"Hey! Are you the boy that's been picking on my son?"

Edgar's mouth fell open. He didn't know what to say.

And shockingly, she shoved me back out the door.

We stood there goofily staring at each other. Edgar was just as confused as me until my mother said, "Well, my son is not afraid of you, so if you want to fight him so bad, go ahead, hit him!"

I gaped at my mother in horror.

This can't be my real mother! An alien must have inhabited her body!

Edgar eyed me like I was the last ice cream cone in the

desert. He cocked his fist and reached back to Mississippi. His fist made an atomic smack on my cheek. The pain jolted me and though I teetered, I stayed on my feet and remained conscious enough to hear my mother angrily shout, "Get him, Sam!"

And I did.

I lunged at him and tackled him to the ground. He grabbed me in the infamous headlock and began squeezing the life out of me, except he made one mistake: His hand slipped across my mouth. Fearing he might squash me, I shut my eyes and bit his hand so hard I tasted salty blood. I heard a scream that would have embarrassed a howler monkey. Edgar immediately clutched his hand. I lit into him, arms flying like an off-kilter helicopter propeller. I hit him every which way I could. I wasn't going to let him strike back, not because I was so angry, but because I didn't want to get socked again.

My mother pulled me off of him and separated us. It surprised me to see Edgar look appreciative as he held his hand, his cheeks tear-stained.

"Okay boys, that's enough fighting for the day. The rest of you, go on home! You've seen enough."

All the kids scattered, awed by what they had just witnessed. Terelle and Jamelle, faces glowing with pride, were the last ones to walk away.

"Okay you two, think you've got it out of your system?" my mother asked, holding us by our shoulders. "I don't want to see or hear about any more fighting between either of you *ever* again—is that understood?" Both of us quickly nodded our heads. "Now, shake hands."

Edgar gingerly put out his wounded hand and we shook, both of us eyeing the ground. My mother gave us a sharp reminder pinch before letting go. I had no idea she was so strong.

I was relieved to see Edgar so agreeable. Funny, he no

longer looked so big and menacing. Don't misunderstand me, he was still a giant, but he looked kind of shy now. He held his head down and shuffled his feet.

He was just a kid.

I heard my mother ask, "What's your name? Edgar? Come on inside, Edgar. Let me clean you up and spray some Bactine on that wound. You'll also need a bandage. After I fix you up, we are all going to learn how to be friends."

Now my mother had gone too far.

Kid or no kid... Edgar wasn't civilized!

Still, my mother treated his cut and fed him a grilled cheese sandwich with milk and Oreo cookies. We didn't say much to each other while we ate, mainly because my mother lectured us on how it's easier to be friends than enemies. Edgar's eyes darted around as he nibbled on his sandwich like a nervous stray dog. Soon he relaxed and chomped away.

After we finished our meal, my mother and I walked Edgar to the door. "Thank you for the food, Mrs. Cole," Edgar murmured, still looking uneasy. He searched the ground for words. Finally, he looked up and said, "Uh, see you tomorrow, Sam!" Then he sprinted off to God knows where.

Whoa! Shockingly, he acted almost... well... almost... *friendly*.

"Samuel Scott, I don't think that big bad bully will ever bother you again."

Maybe... I still had my doubts.

"Samuel, I'm so very proud of you. You defended your-self like a big boy today." She leaned over and kissed me on the good cheek. "Ohhh, your poor cheek swelled up like a rock. Let's get some ice, young man."

We headed into the kitchen. I just couldn't stand it anymore: "Mom, why did you treat Edgar so nice? You even gave him a sandwich. I mean, you get mad at me if I start fights at school."

She tenderly caressed my face. "You're right, Samuel... but sometimes you need to be kind to your enemies, too."

Now I was even more confused.

"Samuel, I get the feeling that Edgar's not a very happy kid."

"How can you tell?"

"Hold this ice to your cheek, baby. It's going to hurt a little bit, but trust me, it will feel better after a while. Anyway, you can tell by the clothes he's wearing that his family is having a difficult time. Maybe he bullies people and starts fights because no one pays attention to him. I think Edgar needs a friend."

Uh oh...

"So, I want you to be real nice to him. Don't look at me that way. Next time you see him, let him know he's welcome at our house any time."

I went outside and sat on the stoop, cradling the icepack against my face. I stayed there until sunset. This was all very baffling to me. I had a lot to think about.

I soon found out my mother was right.

A few days later, Edgar ambled up to me, head down. My body instantly tensed. When he raised his head his lips did a funny thing. It looked like a snarl... but he was trying to smile. I guess that was a real exercise for him.

"Hi Samuel."

"Hi Edgar."

Meet Edgar. My new buddy.

But just because he was my friend didn't mean he had to be pals with anybody else. As a courtesy, Edgar was nice to Terelle and Jamelle, meaning he made no attempt to beat them up or extort money from them. Although, I heard rumors that this practice still existed.

Sometimes my mother slipped me extra change to give to Edgar in case he was hungry. He never asked, but gratefully accepted it when offered.

Edgar still seemed to appear out of some invisible portal from the *Twilight Zone* when he'd join us on our walks to school. The twins continued to keep a wary eye on him. They didn't fully trust him, but they also recognized he'd be our best ally if there ever were a full-scale assault from the mole men.

Edgar barely talked, but I honestly believed he liked being around us. He just wasn't used to participating in normal conversation. Over time we got used to his silences as we talked about monsters, dinosaurs, horses, and dogs. He even participated in our weekly pee contests. We competed in alleys to see who could piss the furthest. Jamelle usually won. He'd perfected a special jerking technique to achieve a greater distance.

The only time I saw Edgar retrieve that killer look in his eyes again was after Terelle asked him about his parents. Terelle, being no dummy, changed the subject and Edgar's scowl faded. It never came up again. Except, one day out of the clear blue sky Edgar blurted out he had two mothers. We knew that was impossible, but nobody dared to dispute him.

Edgar escorted me home every day after school and then routinely sped home. He always greeted my mother with a huge smile and wave. Occasionally, she invited him in for a snack. And even though he ate like it was his last bite, I got the feeling he relished the company even more than the food. His entire face beamed with gratitude. Whenever the sun started to go down, my mother reminded him it was time to go home before his mother started worrying.

And he'd always say, "She don't mind, Mrs. Cole."

"Doesn't, Edgar."

"Yes, Ma'am."

One evening Edgar stayed over a little too late playing

games. My father hadn't left for his part time janitor work yet, so my mother offered to take Edgar home in our car.

"Oh no, Mrs. Cole, that's all right. I walk home lots of time in the dark."

"Nonsense, Edgar. You're not walking alone in the dark. It's not safe."

"I'm not afraid, Mrs. Cole."

I believed him.

"I don't care. Come on, Samuel, we're giving Edgar a ride home."

Edgar sat beside me in the front seat, pointing his way home.

My mother asked in astonishment, "Edgar, you walk this far every night?"

"Yes, well, I usually run."

"My goodness!" she replied and said no more.

"Here's my house, Mrs. Cole."

Edgar pointed to a small brown bungalow. The cracked and chipped building was greatly in need of a paint job. About a dozen kids darted in and out of the wide-open front door of the house. On top of a front yard choked with weeds sat a huge black Chevy, hood open, with a man in greasy overalls stooped over it. He looked like Jonah peering into the mouth of the whale as one of his hands scrambled around inside the toolbox next to him. Wrenches, screwdrivers, and rags were scattered throughout the yard. In the driveway, three other empty cars were huddled up, jaws opened. Hearing the car pull up next to the curb, the man raised his head, eyes squinting.

Edgar bounced out, slamming the car door. The man cautiously eyed us and then sauntered towards our car. A beat-up engineer's cap slumped on his head. The patches of oil on his face looked like war paint.

"Boy, you know better than to slam them people's car door! Ain't you been taught no better than that?"

"Yes, sir. Sorry, Mrs. Cole."

"That's okay, Edgar."

"You thank them good people for bringing you home?"

"Thank you, Mrs. Cole. Thank you, Samuel."

"Now that's some good manners. Irma's got some food sitting in there with your name on it! Get on gone!"

"Bye!" he yelled, running past the man who playfully swatted his butt.

"Bye, Edgar!" I yelled back.

"How y'all doin'?" the man said as he rubbed his oily hands on his overalls. "You got to scuse my appearance."

"Oh, please, you're working, that's fine," my mother replied.

He squatted down on the passenger's side of the car. His smile revealed a colossal gap between his front teeth. He reeked of gas and oil, making me feel a little nauseous. My mother introduced us. He looked at me like I was a celebrity.

"Oh, you is Edgar's best friend! He talks about you all the time! Y'all want to come in and sit a spell?"

"Oh, no thank you, Mr. Bradshaw. Besides, I can see you're busy and I've got to get Samuel home and finish up supper."

"Okay, next time. I thought at first y'all might be another one of his teachers... cuz that's all seemed to come by here for him... that and trouble. By the way, call me Jimmy, Jimmy Turner. I'm Edgar's uncle. Me and the missus, Irma, we took Edgar and his sister, Edena, in a couple of years back. Irma is Edgar's mother's sister."

"Oh."

"See, we don't know where Iris... Edgar's mother, is. Last time we seen her she was still hanging out with those Negroes on Central Avenue doing God knows what."

"You haven't heard from her?" my mother frowned, deeply concerned.

"No, Ma'am, been awhile..." He glanced over his shoulder. "We're not even sure right now if she's even... you know..."

He swallowed and turned his head away for a moment.

"I understand," my mother replied, stroking the back of my head.

"Now Edgar's father..." he spat at the ground, "that no good nigger, scuse me, son."

"He's okay, Jimmy."

"He ain't nothing but a con artist. Last we heard of him, he got locked up in prison in Leavenworth County, Kansas. Good riddance, I say. Weren't no good, never will be. You see, now Iris, she could sing, and I mean REALLY sing!"

"No kidding?"

"Oh yeah! That gal was so good, she make your heart dance and ache at the same time. Both Iris and Irma sang in the church choir all their lives... but Iris was the one. And this fool sold her a bill of goods. Told her she'd make it to the big time with her voice, singing rhythm and blues... be another Dinah Washington. Of course, the catch was, he'd be her manager. The two of them planned on making a ton of money, except, whatever little bit of money they made, he got most of it."

"Aww, that's too bad."

"Sho nuff! Iris was a big woman. She didn't meet many men. So when this slickster smothered her with all this fancy talk about bright lights, big houses, and wealth and fame, Iris ate it up. Boy put a mojo on her! Lord knows Irma tried to talk some sense into her but you know how it is... people only hear what they wanna hear. She acted like that nigga's shadow, following him everywhere. She saw a little bit of the country, but most of it she spent singing in joints a dog wouldn't pee in. The only thing she got out of it was two kids and a whole mess of hurt."

He paused, shook his head, and spit again.

"I couldn't stand watching her chase that fool all over town while he scurried around making bad deals and fathering half brothers and sisters. Iris was a giving, big-hearted, beautiful lady. But last time I saw her you wouldn't recognize her."

Mr. Turner got a faraway look in his eyes as he sucked on his bottom lip.

"Black circles under her eyes, hair all messed up, makeup sloppy, and lipstick smeared on. She was stick thin... and I don't mean in a healthy way. A damn shame... the man ruined her."

My mother's eyes tightened.

"My wife, she just fell apart. Tried every way possible to help her sister, but you can't help nobody who don't want it. Iris was too far gone. When the nigga got thrown in jail, she just sunk deeper and deeper. Iris tried to pretend she had it all under control... swore she could do it all by herself... but she didn't know nuthin' about no music business. Them people swallowed her up. Later, she fell into a bad crowd... started drinking, smoking, whatever... you know what I mean."

"Uh, huh, I do."

"The sad part is, the only help Iris asked for was if Irma could take care of the kids for a day or two while she pieced her life back together. Them days became weeks... then months... and here we is today. Irma's just sick about it. She stays glued to that Bible, keeping faith her sister will show up or call one day. I don't think that's ever gonna happen. I can't shake this feelin' in my bones."

"I feel so bad for Edgar and his sister."

"Yes, Ma'am, we did too... That's why we kept the kids, even though we already got a slew of our own. Irma ain't about to let her sister's kids wander around out there in this big bad world or end up in some doggone orphanage. Edgar, him being the oldest, took it real hard. He knew his mama better than his little sister. Iris used to cuddle him in her lap and sing to him all the time. Edgar, he don't say a whole lot, kinda keeps to himself. Irma thinks he'll break out of it someday. Me, I don't know, that's why we was sure glad to hear he and your son became friends. He ain't never brought nobody home before."

"Samuel likes Edgar a lot, too. They've become good buddies." My mother snuck a wink at me. "You and your wife are such good people for taking the kids in."

"We ain't got a whole lot of money, but you do what you gotta do."

"That's right."

Knees crackling, he slowly stood up. "Didn't mean to talk your ear off. Let me let you get on your way."

"Oh that's all right, Jimmy. Thank you for sharing that with us."

He admiringly rubbed his hands along the body of our car. "This here's a brand new Buick Electra 225, ain't it?"

"Well, 1959... We got it last year."

"Shoot... new enough. This is nice... real nice. What's this color?"

"They call it 'twilight blue.'"

He chuckled. "Uh, huh, that fits. This 'deuce and a quarter' is the top-of-the-line. Got yourself a real fine car here." He patted the car admiringly.

"Thank you. We paid enough. It's my husband Grant's pride and joy."

"I bet... two-door, hardtop, blue and white interior, power steering, and it's got a 401, V8 engine... a smooth engine with lots of power! Tell you what... if y'all ever need some repairs, just holler. I'll hug it, kiss it, and give it some TLC. Plus, I'll give you a much better price than the dealer! And don't worry about callin'. Just bring this puppy on by,

I'd be honored to work on it, ya hear?"

"Will do. Thank you, Jimmy. You be sure and tell your wife hello for us."

"Will do, Jolene. Y'all take care now. Bye Sam."

His grin showcased a gap so wide I could have run a football through it.

"Bye," I shouted, the only thing I added to the conversation. The rest of it was hard for me to grasp. On the way home I asked, "Edgar, he don't have a mother?"

"Doesn't, Samuel. Edgar does, but they don't know where she is. Let's just be happy that Edgar and his sister have the Turners as family."

I gazed ahead, confused by all this. We rode in silence till we got home. Suddenly, I felt nervous and fearful.

"Mommy, you're not ever going to leave me, are you?"

My mother put her arm around me and kissed me on the forehead. "No, Samuel. I will always be there for you... always... you hear me?"

I did... but all I wanted to do was snuggle in her arms and never let go.

About a week later, my mother was invited to lunch with Edgar's Aunt Irma at their house. His aunt told her that Edgar's droopy mouth came from a mistake by something called forceps being used on him when he was born. That's why the lower right side of his face didn't move when he tried to smile. Sometimes the corners of his mouth dropped into the shape of an umbrella. Never saw it too much, though, because smiling was still uncomfortable for him.

Chapter 6

"I hear you knockin' *but you can't come in, woooooo!"* warbled Daddy in chorus with the Little Richard record spinning in circles on the hi-fi as he peeked through the cracked front door.

"You best let me in or I'll take my records and go home!"

"Rufus, you can just leave the music at the door. I'll get it later!"

"Fool, is you crazy?" Rufus yelled. "It's dark out here! Open the door, man, before I drop you like a Floyd Patterson left hook!"

Daddy opened it and Rufus burst in wearing an iridescent lime green suit. He struggled to carry an orange crate loaded with 33, 45, and 78 RPM records.

"Good God! Somebody get me a pair of sunglasses!" Daddy exclaimed.

"Shut up, fool, you know I'm lookin' good!" Rufus boasted as he put the crate beside the hi-fi stand.

"About time you got here! Glad you could make the party!"

"Home skillet, don't you know by now a party ain't no party until the prince is here!" he declared, wiping the sweat off his face with a handkerchief and excitedly checking out the crowd in the living room.

"What did you do... rub up against a lemon tree?" my father joked, tugging on Rufus' coat.

"Negro, don't touch the threads!" Rufus boxed his hand away. "EC, you got 'em packed like sardines in here!"

"Yes, sir."

"I thought Evans offered the front house for the party?"

My father popped a beer open and handed it to Rufus. "He did. But I figured we started out in this shack... might as well ride it to the end."

"Uh, huh... makes sense."

My father rubbed his hands. "Did you bring me some good noise, man?"

"Cole, please don't insult me... don't I always have your back? I'm gonna take care of you, partner. I got you some Hank Ballard and the Midnighters, Sam Cooke, The Drifters, The Cadillacs, Ray Charles, Etta James, Fats Domino, Lloyd Price, Little Anthony, Ruth Brown... You name it—I got it! We even got some Elvis Presley, Jerry Lee Lewis, and Bobby Darin jumpin' off in here!"

"So what you're really telling me is you robbed Phil's Records."

"B-O-R-R-O-W-E-D! I work there! So as long as I bring them back before Phil opens the store by noon tomorrow, everything's cool. And that ain't gonna be no problem cuz we gonna party all night!"

"You talking loud, but you ain't sayin' nuthin'. You gotta show me!"

"Can't party on an empty stomach. What you got to eat?"

"Do I look like a concierge? You know where the kitchen is, Banks! We decided to make it a potluck and folks brought enough food to feed an army—ribs, fried chicken, mac and cheese, potato salad, black-eyed peas, greens, baked beans, sweet potato pie... So go on and make yourself at home... like you usually do."

"You ain't got to tell me but once!"

Rufus playfully elbowed Daddy in the side before making his way through the crowded living room towards the kitchen.

"Hi, Rufus!" I yelled with a wave.

"Look out there, youngsta," Rufus hollered back as he cut to our kid's card table. He threw a couple of combination punches at me.

"What y'all doin'?"

"Playing fish."

"Who's all your little friends here?"

"Um, this is Edgar, Terelle, Jamelle, and that's Vicky. She's a girl, but it's hard to tell cuz she's always wearing boy's clothes."

"Shut up! No I don't!" she barked as she lowered her Dodger baseball cap.

"Pleased to meet y'all." He grabbed the snack bowl off our table. "Looks like y'all need more chips. I'll bring some more on my way back."

"Thanks!"

"Man, you gettin' bigger every time I see you!" He poked me in the side.

"But you saw me yesterday, Rufus."

"That's right, Jughead Jones! And you done sprung up about two more feet since then," he teased. "What are you—25 years old now?"

"No. I just turned 12."

"Twelve? You growin' so fast, in another week you'll be as big as Wilt the Stilt! But I'll still be able to whup your flat little behind in basketball."

"No you won't!" I laughed. "Hey, Rufus, Daddy said he's gonna put a hoop up on the garage at our new place!"

"Yeah? Well, I..." he paused, head cocked like a puppy. Leaning down he whispered, "Hey Sam, who is *that* in the blue dress sittin' by your mama at the adult card table?"

"Huh? Oh, uh, that's Althea."

"That right? Althea, huh? So tell me a little something about Miss Althea."

"Um, she's visiting from Kansas City. She's Betty's little sister."

"You mean Betty who works at the grocery store with your mother?"

"Yes."

"Uh, huh… Visiting, huh? She married?"

"I don't know." I shrugged. I could feel my face getting flushed.

"No, uh, uh… I don't see nuthin' on Miss Althea's finger. This lil honey ain't half bad," he mused. "Who she with?"

"Betty had to work the late shift, so Mommy invited Althea to the party. She didn't want her to sit at home all night by herself."

"Uh, huh… well, neither do I!" Rufus mischievously grinned and straightened his coat. "Ha! I need to talk to your Daddy. This goodbye party is about to turn into a HELLO party! Hey, what y'all kids giggling about?"

"Nothing," we giggled.

Rufus Banks was Daddy's best friend. He moved to Los Angeles from Shreveport, Louisiana about a year after my parents. And like Daddy, he was intent on mining the gold fields of California—except, Daddy always joked, Rufus spent more time enjoying the female riches of the state. So I wasn't surprised to see Rufus stroll quickly passed us, flashing his grand smile, and toting our newly filled bowl of chips to the adult card table where super competitive games of Bid Whist and Spades were being loudly played.

Rufus swooped down on an empty seat next to Althea. At first she coolly ignored his attempts to woo her, but as they drank more beers, before long they were sitting elbow-to-elbow, faces close together.

At least Mattie didn't forget us. She brought out a revolving snack tray loaded with popcorn, peanuts, potato

chips, and dip. Her helpers, Jamelle and Terelle, trailed behind her carting sodas. I grabbed a bottle of orange soda,
but set it down in a hurry when I noticed a glint in Terelle
and Jamelle's eyes as they noisily sucked on their chocolate tipped fingers.

"Hey, where did you get..."

"You boys stop teasing him! Sam, there's still icing left
in a silver bowl on the counter. I just put some on the cake
I baked. When you go in there, please do me a favor and
bring the bowl in here for the rest of the kids!"

"Okay!"

"Can we go with him, Mattie?" Terelle begged.

"No! Y'all have already been in there. You can sit right
here and wait."

You'd have thought someone shot me out of a can-
non the way I flew into the kitchen. I instantly spotted the
silver bowl with chocolate icing. But I decided to do the
twins one better and sneak a glob of icing from the actual
cake. I found the cake covered with tin foil in the refrigerator. I lifted the foil, but froze. What if blue-eyed Jesus was
watching me?

"What are *you* doing, young man?"

Oh, God! I spun around. The refrigerator door closed
with a guilty slam.

"Hi, Mommy." I grinned sheepishly.

"Hi, Samuel."

Her hands were planted on her hips, but she wasn't
mad... not with that gushy smile on her face. Obviously,
she'd had a couple of drinks. Her hair was attractively
curled, and she wore a fancy ruby-colored dress and black
high heels.

"Why are you just standing there by the refrigerator?"

"Uh... uh, I wanted to see the cake Mattie baked."

"Oh? Let's take a look." She opened the door and carefully lifted the foil.

Her perfume smelled so good. I hugged her arm.

"What's it say, Mommy?"

"It says, 'To Grant, Jo, and Sam, Congratulations! We will miss you!'" She looked around, hastily covered the cake, and shut the door. She placed a forefinger on her lips.

"We didn't see this, right?" she said, her voice slightly cracking.

"Right!"

"Come on, let's get back to the party." She grabbed my hand and we left the kitchen. But not before I snatched the bowl with chocolate icing.

Later on, after Mattie presented the cake, the mood in the room turned a little sad, but that quickly changed once Daddy put on Ray Charles' "What'd I Say." Fingers started popping and the card tables were quickly folded up and jammed into the closet. Folks needed some room to get busy and dance.

Our farewell celebration may not have been a Holy Ghost party, but it contained an equal amount of spirit. All the kids huddled under the refreshment table and watched the grownups dance. Jamelle reached up and grabbed a paper cup off the table he thought was Kool-Aid.

"Ugh! This is beer! I don't want this," Jamelle yelled, his face wrinkling up.

Edgar stuck his hand out. "Here, give it to me."

Jamelle gladly handed him the cup.

"Anybody want some?" Edgar asked, his eyes wide. We shook our heads.

"My father let me taste beer one time. It's nasty," I remarked.

"Yeah," he said, then gulped it all down. Our mouths dropped. We waited to see if he was going to throw up. Nope. He only grew quieter than usual as he stared at the dancing adults. Minutes later he grabbed the front of his pants. His face looked more in pain than Larry Talbot before turning into the Wolfman.

He ran out from under the table, hitting his head in the process. I saw a wet spot spread across his pants as he half-hopped, half-ran to the bathroom. In the meantime, the adults screamed and hollered when the hottest record of the year, *Twist with Chubby Checker*, came on. People twisted in the living room, in the kitchen... some even danced outside the front door.

People twisted slow, fast, double-time, triple time, on one leg, on their knees, in the air, in circles... whatever style came to mind. It got so crazy in our tiny living room that Rufus yelled, "Y'all stop bumping into the record player. I've got to take those records back. I'm serious! You scratch it, you own it!"

We kids joined in, too, because you could dance by yourself on the twist. My mother and I twisted holding hands, which was really fun because she spun me around until I got dizzy and fell down laughing, but I kept on twisting.

After Edgar returned, my father said, "All right, Edgar, show me what you can do!"

Edgar showed him, too.

Usually kids giggled when they danced—not Edgar— he was intense. He twisted like he was sawing lumber.

Even Mattie was dancing, but not for too long.

"I'm too old to be doing this," Mattie finally said, huffing and puffing as she reached for a chair. She rapidly fanned herself with a magazine.

"I don't know, Mattie, you were lookin' pretty good out there," my father teased. "I like that little hip move you threw in," he added, imitating her.

"Yeah, Ms. Mattie got her mojo working!" Rufus chimed in.

"Y'all leave Mattie alone," my mother said, standing behind Mattie and massaging her shoulders.

"Jolene, I'm not paying them no mind," Mattie chuck-led, grasping my mother's hand. "If y'all had seen me and Mr. White, before I got spiritual, you'd have stayed off the floor—unless you wanted to get your feelings hurt."

"Well excuse me, Miss Mattie," my mother laughed, patting her hand.

"Oh, yeah, baby... all those great nightclubs... Central Avenue was our yellow brick road, believe me!" Mattie sighed.

"Ooooh, Mattie, I'm scared of you!" my father joked while dancing around her.

Blushing, Mattie shooed him away with the magazine.

"Let me show you what Mattie's talking about," Mr. Evans piped in, grabbing Mrs. Evans playfully by the waist. A second ago the Evans looked too drunk to walk the 50 feet to their house, now they jitterbugged and swing danced across the floor like they had guzzled water from the fountain of youth.

"Go on Lavay! I didn't know you had it in you!"

"He better or I'd have never married him," Mrs. Evans yelled.

The real fun came when my father removed a mop head from its pole. Two adults held the pole horizontally and we had a limbo contest. I made myself hoarse scream-ing DAY-O when Daddy played "The Banana Boat Song." The competition between the adults got pretty fierce as people shimmied under the stick. I was surprised that the best limbo dancer was Ike, the barber. Even though he was in his fifties, he could still dance backwards while bending his knees under the lowered stick, with his back looking like it was waxing the floor.

"Harry Belafonte ain't got nothing on me!" Ike crowed as he poured more Scotch into a paper cup.

"Except hair, looks, and money," Daddy shouted.

"My baby's got hair," his wife, Cora, joked as she sweetly kissed him on his bald spot.

"That's right. Y'all just jealous," Ike snorted.

Everyone laughed and clapped along when Rufus put on Elvis' "All Shook Up" and did an amazing Elvis Presley imitation—until a voice disrupted his performance.

"Man, get that Elvis Presley stuff out of here!"

Uncle Stewart casually leaned against the kitchen doorway munching on a fried chicken leg.

"Oh, did I forget to introduce my little brother? Ladies and gentlemen, this is Stewart 'Party-Poop' Cole!"

"Oh, I'm sorry Grant... am I supposed to admire someone who said, 'All a nigger can do for me is buy my records and shine my shoes'? Uh, huh... yeah, that's what Presley said when they asked him if colored musicians influenced him."

"I heard he said that, too!" Ike echoed.

"Oh shuddup, that's just a rumor. Did you actually hear him say that?" Daddy asked.

"No, but a southern cracker from Mississippi? You can put your foot on it!" my uncle staunchly replied, licking his fingers.

"Man, Elvis ain't said no shit like that!"

"How do you know, Grant?"

"Because I read in *Jet* that one of their top reporters couldn't find one interview where he said that. And when the Negro reporter asked him about it, Elvis said, 'Anybody that knows me knows I wouldn't say nuthin' like that.'"

"Man, what else is he gonna say to him? Hey, boy, drop that pen and paper and start polishing my shoes?"

"Stew, I heard him with my own ears say that colored folks have been singing it and playing it just the way I'm doing now. Elvis loves us! Some of his biggest hits were written by a brotha named Otis Blackwell."

"Okay, okay, big brother... don't bang your gavel down on me. I'll leave your white nigger alone. I'm just tellin' you what I heard," Uncle Stewart snickered, shoving the chicken bone into a wastebasket.

"What you oughta be doing is gettin' your facts straight!" my father barked as he headed to the bathroom.

When he got back Uncle Stew, Ike, and Rufus stood beside the hi-fi. Rufus held the arm of the phonograph poised to drop on a spinning record. The room was a little *too* quiet.

"What's going on?" Daddy asked suspiciously.

Ike cleared his throat and in his most formal voice said, "Grant, we dedicate this next song to you. You may not be around this holiday season, so we want you to think about us when you're hanging out in your new home."

"Uh, huh." My father crossed his arms and tapped his foot impatiently.

The sound of Bing Crosby singing the song, *"White Christmas"* broke the silence. The instigators gave each other some skin, sliding their hands across each other's palms, and cackled as my father shook his head.

"That's cold... You Negroes are pathetic," Daddy mumbled, but broke into a big grin as the entire party serenaded him good-naturedly.

My mother barely smiled. I wondered what she was thinking.

It was time for us kids to leave the living room when lights blinked off and only one lamp was left on while they played slow music. "A Woman, a Lover, a Friend" by Jackie Wilson wasn't really fun to dance to so we were headed into the bedroom with Mattie. We had our pajamas on anyway and Mattie promised to read stories to us.

I felt like I wore infrared goggles the way Rufus' loud suit beamed in the darkened room. He stood in a corner with his back to us. I almost ran up to say goodnight until I saw Althea's hands cupping the back of his head.

I smelled the alcohol on my parents' breath when

they kissed me goodnight. Before I left, I saw them slow dancing. Their faces carried the same gooey-eyed expressions movie stars get before a big screen kiss. I thought about busting in between them, but figured it was more important to let them enjoy this moment together.

It wasn't all romance in the room. Ike and Cora slumped on the couch, passed out arm in arm, Cora's head on Ike's shoulder. One guy sat on the floor, head bowed, snoring, and still holding his drink. I needed to pee badly, but there was a woman in the bathroom vomiting. She gagged the same way I did after eating Brussels sprouts. She finally stumbled out of the bathroom, her makeup looking like it had been put on by Bozo the Clown.

When she saw me, she patted her hair down and straightened her clothes. "Hello! You need to use the restroom?" she slurred.

But then her eyes ballooned and she had that oh-no-not-again look on her face as she quickly covered her mouth with her hand. Her eyes said, *I'm sorry*, before she dove back into the bathroom, slamming the door behind her. I heard her cry, "Oh Jesus, oh God... I'm so sick... please make it stop! Please!"

The next morning, the smell of bacon pried me out of bed. My parents slept like the undead while I tiptoed out of the bedroom. In the kitchen, Uncle Stewart had just finished making scrambled eggs and was frying bacon in a huge skillet.

"Sit down and have yourself a seat, nephew! You want some bacon?"

"Yes, please. Can I have some Rice Krispies, too?"

"Ohhhh, so you want a little snap, crackle, and pop to start off your mornings, huh? Comin' up, partner."

He hustled around in the kitchen, while listening to the radio, wearing a T-shirt on his string-bean body, and tapping his fingers on the countertop to piano notes from "Cast Your Fate to the Wind."

"You and your buddies have a good time last night?"

He reached for the cereal on the shelf and shook some of it into a bowl.

"Uh, huh."

He poured milk into the cereal. "Wait... here you go..." He held the bowl next to my head as we listened to the cereal noise. "Man, ain't that something? Guess they'll have singing cereal next."

"I hope so!"

"I bet you do," he chuckled. He flinched as some bacon grease popped. "You excited about seeing your new house tomorrow?"

"Uh, huh... I get my own bedroom!"

"You should. You're a big boy now."

"Uh, huh. Aren't you coming with us, Uncle Stew?"

"Nah, not tomorrow. But I'll be there to help move the furniture in."

"How come you're not coming with us tomorrow to see the house?"

"Because I think you should see it as a family first."

"But you're family, Uncle Stew."

He seemed touched by this as he nodded his head and forked bacon onto a paper towel. "Of course I am, but I think this is something you guys ought to do together, privately. You know what I mean, nephew?"

"I guess so," I answered, chewing my Rice Krispies.

Uncle Stewart sat across the table from me with his plate of bacon and eggs. He salted his eggs and then sprinkled them with pepper and Tabasco sauce.

"You gonna miss all your friends here?"

"Yeah, but Daddy said I can come back and visit anytime I want."

"That's good."

"Daddy said I'll make a whole lot of new friends there."

"Did he?" Uncle Stew looked at me funny as he crunched his bacon.

"Uncle Stew, you think those kids are gonna like me?"

"If they don't it won't be your fault... It'll be something wrong with them." Uncle Stewart paused like he wanted to say more. Instead, he lit the cigarette he withdrew from behind his ear.

"Your Daddy's pretty hot on moving to this new place. And, man, when Grant Cole makes up his mind to do something, nothing gets in his way, no matter what you say."

"You sound like Mommy."

"That right? Hmmm... I suppose great minds think alike."

He kicked back in the chair, crossed his legs, and thoughtfully blew out a huge puff of smoke.

Chapter 7

I was so hyped my legs were trembling and I couldn't stop tapping my feet in the car. Ordinarily this was irritating to my folks, but neither one turned around and screamed at me to cool it. They were too deep in their own thoughts. Finally, I'd get to see the house... and my own room, and front yard, and backyard, and garage. "The opportunity of a lifetime," my father kept repeating.

The journey to Fisher Place was like viewing the world through a gigantic kaleidoscope and seeing all kinds of shapes and colors. I could barely gaze out the car windows in the deep seats of the huge Buick, unless I pushed up on my hands or stood up. But I didn't want to be yelled at, so I remained seated and took in all I could see from the upper half of the car windows.

"Theme from A Summer Place" played over the car radio while blue skies, slivers of gray clouds, treetops, palm trees, streetlights, and street signs swished by. Sometimes flocks of birds zoomed past or I'd see a lone bird that turned out to be a plane. More planes appeared as we neared Century Blvd, which Daddy said goes straight to the Los Angeles Airport.

Daddy cut the Everly Brothers off in the middle of "When Will I Be Loved." The sudden quiet felt scary. Daddy veered slowly to the right, hitting a bump that made me bounce high. We rolled to a stop.

"Champ, we're here!" my father cheerfully announced.

He looked at me in the rear-view mirror, eyes bright, and his dark face beaming. As soon as he pulled the seat forward, I hurriedly stepped out of the car onto the driveway to triumphantly greet my new home, new yard, new bedroom, and new friends!

There I stood on a warm July morning, frozen in place like an icicle.

My father was right about the house. It was large and beautiful with a Spanish red tiled roof, a huge front picture window, and the greenest front lawn. Big palm trees along with other trees lined up and down the block on a long strip of grass nearest the street and separated by the sidewalks from the front lawns. All the houses looked brand new. Each one showed off perfectly trimmed hedges. The streets were twice as wide as my old neighborhood. Gray street lamps stood on the sidewalks like soldiers at attention. Everything was amazingly clean, not a candy wrapper in sight.

And I hated it.

Did anyone even live here?

I got my answer when five or six kids wandered out of their homes like the munchkins in the *Wizard of Oz* after the house fell on the Wicked Witch. They posted themselves on a wall between one of the houses. Other kids soon joined them, gawking at us as if we'd stepped out of a spaceship instead of a car.

Every single face on the block was White. Adults and children peered at us from the refuge of their front doors, parted curtains, back fences, hedges, and even from behind "For Sale" signs. A few curious people stepped onto their porches. Others stood defiantly side by side on their front lawns, arms crossed, and whispered out of the corners of their mouths.

Hadn't they ever seen Negroes before?

It was the first time my dark skin felt uncomfortable

on my body.

Maybe if they had only been smiling...

"Sure didn't take them too long before they got those 'For Sale' signs up," my mother said on the sly to my father.

"Their loss," he replied nonchalantly. "Jolene, why don't you go inside and check it out while we men bring in the boxes."

While my mother hesitantly went into the house. My father began hauling luggage out of the car trunk.

And me? I retreated back inside the car.

I didn't want to be here. I wanted to go back home and be with my friends.

"Hey, Superman, whatcha doin' back in the car? Aren't you going to use your super strength to help me?"

I stationed myself behind the steering wheel and pretended to drive. My father put down his carton and rubbed his hands together as he leaned against the car door. Sweat pellets lay on his wide forehead and the muscles bulged from his short sleeve shirt. I felt him studying me.

"You all right, Sam the man?"

I bobbed my head like I was listening to the radio, eyes straight ahead.

"Must be a little warm in there, huh?"

I shook my head no.

He grinned as he pulled out a handkerchief and wiped his face and neck.

"Okay... but you know what, Champ? We shouldn't leave your mother alone for too long in there. She might need some big strong men like us to help her. Whatcha think?"

I remember thinking, I'll never talk again until we leave this horrible place. And I refused to cry, even though warm moisture stalked the corners of my eyes. Daddy came over to the passenger side where I now huddled. He eased the car door open and offered his hand. I dodged it, shaking my head and edging away from him. I didn't get very far. He gently grabbed my arm and pulled me outside of the car into his massive arms. He held me in a hug against his chest until I tired of struggling to get away.

"Sam, wait till you see the inside of the house," he said, facing me with both of his big hands cupping my shoulders. I'm glad he did that because my legs were wobbly.

"It's exactly like I told you, Champ... great big old yard, kitchen, your own bedroom *and* closet... all kinds of things. Oh, did I forget to tell you it's even got a fireplace? Oh c'mon... don't shake your head—you've always wanted one!"

I couldn't talk... too busy rubbing my itchy eyes.

"I know this place seems foreign to you, but you're gonna love it!" he said with a big smile and a wink.

Sometimes I really didn't get him. Here we were in this strange hostile place and he smiled when no one else smiled back.

"I know it's hard for you to understand why we moved here. One day it will all make sense, you'll see... I promise. We'll be better than okay in the end."

I barely remember anything else he said because the little pioneer was crying. He put his arm protectively around me as we walked inside.

I hated to admit it, but the house was even more beautiful than Daddy described. The fireplace pulled me toward it like a magnet. It sat against the wall in the middle of the spacious living room. I got soot all over my hands from peering up the chimney and trying to figure out why I ever believed a big fat roly-poly man with rosy cheeks and a bright red satin suit could slide down such a narrow passageway without a trace of soot on his clothes.

The kitchen showed off several windows. My mother loved that and the alcove for the washer and dryer. My bedroom was twice as large as the bedroom we slept in at our old place! Still, it was days before I would sleep in it alone. I had to make sure this place didn't come with a bogeyman. I know they now say I'm too old to believe in one, but you never know. Terelle and Jamelle told me when you stop believing that's when he gets you!

Daddy took us out to view the backyard and patio area. We had avocado and lemon trees in the yard and also a gardening area. My mother got real excited about what type of vegetables she could plant there. I did get excited about the garage because Daddy promised to put a basketball hoop on it!

Later, I stood in my empty new bedroom and from my window watched my parents in the backyard chattering eagerly about all the plans they had for the house. My mother was finally into it. Sadly, I realized I'd lost my best ally.

It was a great house. Daddy called it "moving up in the world!" and he was happier than I had ever seen. He said we could afford it because he had gotten a full-time permanent position at Sonbar with benefits. The company, in downtown L.A., made sodas and fruit drinks. My father at first worked there "on call" as a forklift driver, until they made him a "permanent" employee. After that, he quit his part-time job as a janitor. In the kitchen he popped open a bottle of champagne to celebrate. He gave me a sip. My parents laughed when my face bunched up like a pug dog.

I left them giggling in the kitchen and trod into the living room. Gazing out the large, front picture window, I saw that most of the people had gone back inside their tombs posing as homes. Some kids were still sitting on the wall. They all pointed when they spotted me standing at the window. I wished I could shut them out, but we had no curtains yet.

A black station wagon with wood paneling on the side

drove by at a snail's pace and came to a stop at the curb in front of our house. Many cars had slowed down when they saw us standing on our front lawn. I guess word had gotten out that there were Negroes living here. Now I knew what the caged animals at the L.A. Zoo must have felt like.

But this was different. No one had stopped to park in front of our place. I couldn't see the man driving, yet on the passenger side I noticed a woman staring intently at our house. She looked very unhappy. Her face was kinda ghostly looking. The driver wrapped his arm around her shoulder as she fished out a handkerchief. I wasn't sure, but I thought she was crying. She dabbed her eyes with the handkerchief.

Maybe she really wanted to buy this house and we beat her to it. I wanted to run up to her car and say, "I bet if you talked to my parents they'd sell it to you. We're still unpacking! You might be able to move in today! PLEASE talk to them! We both could end up so happy!"

My fantasy ended when the woman's eyes grew bigger. She'd seen me standing at the window. She stared so hard through her puffy eyes that I felt like she had Supergirl's X-ray vision and looked right through me. She smiled and just as quickly disappeared. She moved into the driver's arms and squeezed his hand resting on her shoulder. They sat with the car idling awhile longer before finally driving away.

I tried to catch a better look at them but the stained glass oval in the middle of the window messed up my view. But it also captured my attention. I gazed through the blocks of color as the world turned into yellow, red, blue, and green. It was kind of fun. I felt powerful peering through this stained glass prism and changing the outside world into my choice of colors.

The official move-in date was tomorrow. The Sonbar Company loaned my father a truck to speed up the move, saying they were anxious for him to begin working full time. My father found it flattering. He declared, "Most companies don't trust Negroes with a paperclip... so you know they gotta be *real* high on me!"

And Daddy was high on our new place. He wanted us to get a real feel for our new home so we stayed until evening. There was no furniture, so we sat in the middle of the floor admiring the house.

"Feels good, doesn't it?" Daddy remarked, proudly surveying his castle.

"It does." Mommy looped her arm through his. "Don't you think so, Sam?"

I acted like I didn't hear her until she shot me a look that made me nod like one of those bobbleheads.

"I don't know, honey, Sam looks like he's pouting. His lip is stuck out so far you could stick a plate on it."

I sucked my lip back in. "No it's not."

"You know what, Champ? It may be awhile before people accept us here, just like on my job. Took those folks several years to hire me full time—more than it should have. The Caucasian guys got permanent status right away. I'm the only Negro in that position. It took some time for them to get used to me and learn to trust me. The people here will learn to trust us, too. Remember what we talked about, Sam? It's all about building trust. You just gotta be patient."

I hoped the shadows would hide my lip sticking back out. And I wished that my parents would soon dislike being here as much as I did and return to our old neighborhood. I even prayed on it. Maybe this time God would hear me.

The next day, I'm sure God and the world heard Uncle Stewart fussing about the "PO-lice" as usual. A few of my father's buddies helped us move, and their cars were filled with boxes of our belongings as they followed behind my father driving the gigantic Sonbar truck. The caravan of automobiles was stopped twice on the way. Everyone was ordered by gunpoint to get out of their cars and put their hands up in the air to be searched. Uncle Stewart said, "Those dirty dogs treated us like we were Communists carrying drugs and weapons!" While Uncle Stewart complained, the group successfully carted the rest of the furniture into the house without any more problems.

My father was thrilled to show me all the shelves where the soda pop and fruit drink boxes were stacked on the truck during deliveries. The company really did like him because they supplied the loaner truck with complimentary cases of soda. My father even offered a choice of an orange, strawberry, or grape soda to this redheaded, pigtailed girl watching us over the hedge.

She reached out for the soda, but a woman's voice screamed out the window, "Patsy, get in here!" Rolling her eyes and frowning, she trudged back inside. It wasn't long before the curtains parted and I caught sight of a pair of green alligator eyes peeping over the window ledge.

I made one last effort to stay awake all night to protest the move, but I was so tired I fell right asleep that first night. In the morning, we were shocked to discover a picnic basket stuffed with homemade cookies on our doorstep. Clipped to the basket was a handwritten note:

Welcome to the neighborhood!

Daddy grinned, eyeing us like—See? What did I tell you?

I grabbed a cookie. It was my favorite, chocolate chip, loaded with chunks of sweet chocolate and pecans. It tasted so good I wanted to hug myself, leap into the air, and float back down to earth holding my stomach and sighing like Snuffles the cartoon dog. I reached for a second one. But instead of a sigh, I let out a yelp when my mother whacked the cookie out of my hand! I looked at her to see what I did wrong, but she wasn't even looking at me. Her troubled eyes were on my father.

"Grant? What is it? What's wrong?"

My father had walked out to the driveway to grab his toolbox from the trunk of the car. Now he faced us. I had never seen him look this way. His hands shook and his face was very pale. Behind him, his pride and joy, the Twilight Blue car, had been egged all over it. But that wasn't the worse part... NIGGERS had been scribbled in big, bold Crayola letters across the front and back windows.

Chapter 8

It was horrible what they did to our car, but the good news was, I was sure we were going to now leave this awful place and load our stuff back on the Sonbar truck and go back to our old neighborhood where people loved us.

Mattie was right: The Lord does work in mysterious ways. God had answered my prayers.

I studied my face in the bathroom mirror. How long would it take before I dropped dead from eating the poisoned cookie? Snow White fell into a deep sleep from taking a bite out of the poisoned apple. And she needed a kiss from the prince to awaken her. If that happened to me, the best move would be for Daddy to pick Sheri up from Perry Avenue Elementary and bring her to my bedside for a kiss. The only problem might be that she ups her fee from a nickel to a quarter. It's a big job awakening someone from a coma with a kiss!

Balancing myself by holding the sides of the sink, I leaned closer to the mirror to inspect my pupils. My eyesight wasn't fuzzy, my gums weren't bleeding, and I didn't feel like I was going to flop to the floor clutching my belly and throwing up like they did in the movies. The only thing that came up was a loud burp from chasing the cookie down with an Orange Crush soda.

It's a miracle!

I was still alive!

Or at least so I thought...

Maybe I was already dead and didn't know it yet. Maybe I had turned into a ghost and now it was my job to haunt this house.

I nearly screamed when the bathroom doorknob jiggled.

"Samuel? Are you in there? Why is this door locked? You all right?"

"Yes, Mommy."

"You've been in there for 20 minutes. What are you doing?"

"Nothing."

"Open the door, please. I need to come in!"

I jumped off the step stool and fumbled to unlock the door. My mother rushed in and hurriedly pulled down her skirt and panties and squatted on the toilet.

I watched as she ran her fingers through her hair, smoothing it out. She had what they called, "good hair," which means it was straight like Caucasians' hair—no naps. Mommy had told me her great grandmother was a quarter Indian. The first time I heard that, I roamed around school claiming I was a Chiricahua Apache and Geronimo was my great-great grandfather. But my mother corrected me and said her ancestors came from the Creek Nation in Oklahoma, which didn't sound as fearsome. I wanted to grow my hair longer so I'd look more Indian, but my father refused to let me do so. He complained I never brushed my hair, and it wouldn't look like Mommy's anyway because my hair was as nappy as his.

"Samuel, why is the step stool in here?"

"I don't know... um... I guess, cuz I was playing around."

"Fine, can you please take it with you on your way out?"

"Um, okay... Uh, Mommy... is that all you can see... the step stool?"

"Excuse me?"

"I mean... can you see me?"

"Of course I can see you! Why would you ask such a silly question?"

"I don't know... just asking." I grabbed the stool and ambled out of the bathroom.

"Samuel Scott Cole," she yelled, "please come back and shut the door!"

"Oh... sorry."

I was pleased to be alive, but a little disappointed I couldn't return to my old neighborhood as a ghost. Jamelle and Terelle would have flipped out and we could have had some fun adventures. More importantly, invisibility might have turned the tide in the lunch pail wars against the girls.

I skipped into the living room. We'd finally put up some curtains, so I pulled them aside and peeked out the window. My father, hands on his hips, stood like a sentry next to Twilight Blue, waiting for the police to arrive. Daddy was 6'3" but when angry looked like he was seven feet tall. He wore a white T-shirt, and the lotion and hot sunlight made his muscular arms glisten like my comic book heroes. He intently watched passing cars, a few slowing to a crawl. It was hard to tell what they stared at more—the damaged car or the Negro standing beside it.

I went outside to keep my father company. The police were going to be here soon and I didn't want to miss that. I expected to see about 20 siren-blasting squad cars hopping the curb, with police jumping out, guns drawn, and ready for a major shootout. Anybody who tried to destroy an automobile and then wipe out an entire family with poisoned cookies deserved the worst kind of punishment.

"Hi, Daddy." I skipped up to him and grabbed onto his arm that remained locked at the hip.

He glanced down at me. The sun behind his head blacked out his face. "What you know good, Champ?" Even though he tried, his usually upbeat tone had vanished.

"Nothing."

And nothing more was said as we watched the cars drive by.

One of those cars was the black station wagon carrying the woman with the sad face. It crawled by as they stared at our house again. The man already had his arm around her shoulders and the woman had her hands pressed to her cheeks. She must have really wanted to buy the house. This time, the car didn't stop. Her eyes remained fixed on our house until they rounded the corner. I wanted to say something to my father about seeing them again, but he clearly had that don't-talk-to-me expression as he watched impatiently for the police.

After a while, the silence became more unbearable than the heat, so I asked, "Daddy, aren't you gonna clean the car? I'll help you wash it."

His arm weakened as he patted me on top of my head.

"I appreciate that, Champ... but not right now. We can't touch the car until the police check it out for evidence."

His face remained in silhouette, but at least, I heard a smile in his voice.

"Damn! About time!" he sighed, rubbing his hands together.

One lone squad car eased up to the curb.

What? You've got to be kidding me. That's it? No blaring sirens? No cars crashing onto the sidewalk? No shotgun fire?

Daddy's faraway voice returned. "Son, why don't you go sit on the porch."

"But, Daddy, I want to stay with—"

"You heard me," he responded gruffly, lightly smacking my behind.

I plopped down on the porch steps, elbows resting on my knees and hands against my cheeks. I heard the kitchen curtains rustling and caught a glimpse of my mother's anxious face in the window.

The two policemen in the squad car didn't jump out right away either. They stayed inside talking for a long time. As Daddy waited beside Twilight Blue, his face was as blank as when he plays poker. But his chest heaved up and down when the doors of the police car finally opened.

The policemen lazily walked towards my father like they were facing a dental appointment instead of investigating a crime scene.

"Officers, I appreciate you coming by," my father piped up as he politely stuck out his hand. The younger officer shook it. His white-haired partner with the beach-ball belly only nodded. Neither officer looked him in the eyes, which Daddy said was always important when you talk to people.

"I'm Officer Thomas and this is Officer Mackey."

"Grant Cole... glad to meet you. We moved here a couple of days ago."

"Who is *we*?" the one named Mackey curtly asked as he circled our Buick, squeezing between the three-foot high hedges that ran alongside our driveway and divided the houses.

"*We* is my wife and son."

"Uh, huh."

"So, Mr. Cole, what can we do for you?"

My father's eyebrows lifted slightly. "Well, as you can see... somebody put a hurting on my car."

"Yeah, they did do a number on it... that's for sure," Mackey grunted.

"So, I'm hoping you'll find out who did this and arrest them."

Mackey scratched his neck. "You know... if you really look at it... there's not that much serious damage. I mean, yeah, it may take a little elbow grease to scrub the paint off the windshield, but once you get rid of all this egg crap, wash the car, and give it a few swipes of good ol' Turtle wax, the car will look brand new again," he responded authoritatively, hitching up his pants.

"Uh, huh... and what about those deep, foot long scratches across the hood and sides of the car somebody created with their keys? I don't think a wash and wax job will make it all good again. Do you?"

It was the first time Mackey's eyes met my father's. He had the same bullying glare I used to see in Edgar—except Mackey carried a gun.

Red streams pooled into Mackey's already pink face as he brushed past his partner and bumped his belly against my father's waist. "You gettin' smart with me, mister?" He rubbed the head of the billy club inside his belt.

My father's eyes returned Mackey's glare and for a second I thought he might slug him. I wished he had. The veins in Daddy's forehead looked like they were about to burst through his head. But then he looked away. I wasn't sure why. My father wasn't afraid of anybody or anything. But when his eyes fell on mine, I got my answer.

Officer Thomas grabbed Mackey's arm and whispered something in his ear. Mackey's eyes skirted around. Grumbling, he retreated to the other side of the car and lit a cigar he pulled out of his breast pocket.

He must have backed off because of all the gawkers who'd come outside to see what was going on.

Mackey waved at a man directly across the street who was washing his bright red sports car. The man cheerfully waved back. The only time I'd ever seen him was when he was outside washing and waxing his car with great care.

"Mr. Cole, don't get us wrong. We understand how the damage to your car pisses you off and will cost you some bucks. We're sorry about that, but put yourself in our shoes. Who do you arrest?" Officer Thomas asked.

"Yeah. My guess is that this is just some dumb child's prank!" Mackey bellowed as he paced back and forth on our lawn, puffing his cigar. "You wouldn't want us to throw a bunch of knucklehead kids in jail, would you?"

"I want whoever is responsible to pay for the damages, that's all."

Mackey courteously tipped his hat at a young woman on the sidewalk pushing a baby stroller. He inhaled deeply from his cigar. "Listen, Cole, you seem like an okay guy. I don't know where you come from, but this is a nice neighborhood with good people, and, to be honest, we've never received any calls from this area about any problems until *you* moved here."

My father resumed his poker face.

"I mean... I'm not saying you caused this... I'm just wondering if you said anything to offend somebody here?"

"Hard to do if no one speaks to you."

"Well, you got us there," Thomas chuckled, rubbing his neck. "Listen, Mr. Cole, I hope you don't mind, but may I ask you another question?"

He got Daddy's poker face, too.

"Out of curiosity, with all the possible spots you could have selected to move to in L.A., why did you choose here?"

I wondered the same thing.

My father weirdly grinned as he kneeled down and plucked a dandelion from the lawn. He blew softly on the puffball and watched the seeds float through the air before talking. I saw another dandelion and wanted to blow its puffball but forced myself to remain seated.

"Because my real estate agent told me that this is one of the friendliest neighborhoods in the city for raising a family."

Mackey's grating laugh bothered me. "Boy, those cats will say any damn thing to cut a deal, eh, Thomas?"

"Yep," Thomas agreed, shaking his head.

Mackey held his cigar in the air. "Well, Cole, you're here now. My grandfather used to say, all you can do is try to make sunshine out of the rain."

My father nodded while pinching the upper sides of his nose between his eyes, usually a sign he had a headache.

Mackey continued: "My advice to you, Cole, is to go on about your business. Sooner or later all this crap will pass. You may want to try a little harder to make friends around here.... might even find some folks who like you. Then they won't give you such a hard time."

The Holy Ghost must have finally gotten inside of me. I couldn't keep myself from jumping up and yelling, "Don't talk to my Daddy like that! Everybody likes him. He's got a whole lot of friends!"

"Samuel!"

The Holy Ghost must have caused me to lose my mind, too, because I ignored my father.

"Leave my Daddy alone! He didn't do nothing! He's a good person and he will go to heaven one day!"

Sobbing, I ran and stood next to my father.

"Samuel... it's all right... everything's fine," my father softly reassured me, placing his arm around me and pressing me against his body. "The nice policemen and I are just trying to figure out the best way to take care of this. Now, be a big boy and stop crying, Champ." He pulled a hankie out of his back pocket and handed it to me. I wiped my tears and blew my nose.

Surprisingly, Officer Thomas warmly said, "We believe you, son. I can tell your father is a good man. Don't worry, we're not going to hurt him or you. Right, Officer Mackey?"

"Yeah, that's right."

Mackey came over to me, got down on one knee, and drew his club. His breath stank worse than his cigar. His eyebrows were so thick they looked like two caterpillars lived on his forehead.

"Hey, kid... you look pretty big and strong. You want to hold my nightstick? We use this on the *real* bad guys!"

Oh how badly I wanted to hold that club and play with it... but I couldn't forget the way Officer Mackey looked at my father.

"No thank you."

Mackey struggled to get back on his feet. His hacking cough didn't help. He popped the cigar back in his mouth like a pacifier.

"So what do you want to be when you grow up, Sam?" Thomas asked.

About 20 things ran through my mind, but I blurted, "A scientist."

"A scientist?" exclaimed Mackey, easing off his cap and scratching his head. "You've got to be pretty smart to be one of those, lots of schooling."

He didn't need to tell me that. Dr. Frankenstein was a scientist. There was no way he could have created the Frankenstein monster if he was not smart.

"You look more like a football or basketball player to me. Can you shoot?"

"Yes. My Daddy's gonna build a hoop on the garage in our backyard."

"Aha, there you go! When you get that hoop built, we'll stop by and see how you're doing!"

"Okay."

"Anyway, Mr. Cole, I'm betting this is a one-time deal," Mackey stated, rubbing his hand along a car scratch. "I doubt you'll see another car incident."

"And if we do?"

That question stretched their fake smiles.

"Then call us right away. We're here to serve the people," Mackey replied.

"Are you going to talk to some people and find out if they saw anything?"

"Yes," Thomas speedily responded. "I'll write up a report and I promise you we'll patrol the area and keep an eye out. If we find out anything, you'll be notified immediately. Feel free to call us if you discover anything suspicious."

"Oh, don't worry, I will."

Mackey rifled my father another look, but then his eyes zoomed to mine and his grimace formed into a tight smile.

"Nice meeting you, kid. When you guys get that hoop up, I want to see you practicing every day. The next time we come through here I'll expect you to make a hundred free throws in a row!"

Mackey pretended to shoot a ball and clumsily dropped his cigar on the sidewalk. He bent down to retrieve it and stuck it back in his mouth, then lumbered back to the squad car. Thomas shook my father's hand.

"Sorry again about your car, Mr. Cole. I guess this is not quite the reception you were looking for when you moved here, huh?"

"No, not quite."

"Well, good luck to you and your family."

"Thank you, Officer."

Once Thomas closed the door to the squad car, the officers sat and chatted awhile longer. A joke must have been shared because sharp laughter erupted from the car before they revved up the engine and screeched away. They didn't talk to anyone in the neighborhood before leaving.

My father watched the car until it became a speck. The frown on his face disappeared as he turned to me and clasped my face in his hands. "Did I ever tell you you're the best kid in the whole world smush-face?"

"Yes."

"Oh, I did, huh?" He laughed and patted me on the back. "Let's go wash this car."

My mood rose higher than a cloud. After this disgusting episode, I was absolutely positive we'd leave this unholy place and head back to our old neighborhood. It'd be nice to have my own basketball hoop, but I'd be just as fine playing basketball in the park or at school like before.

No more Mackey, no more stares.

"Daddy, do you feel better now?"

"You better know it, Champ!"

My smile lengthened.

"You know... you really are a chip off the old block," he said.

"Yep!" I raised my arms in triumph.

"We showed them that no matter what they do, nobody is going to run this family off this block!"

My smile crumbled and my arms wilted to my sides.

***

Maybe I really had died. But instead of turning into a ghost I was sent to hell instead of heaven.

I blamed Terelle.

He'd dared me to steal that pack of bubblegum from the grocery store. And everyone knows you can't back away from a dare. Should have listened to Mattie instead of Terelle. She'd told me, "God knows whenever you do something wrong."

Now I was paying the price of thievery by being raised in hell for all eternity. I could be a million years old before I became a teenager.

"Samuel, stop messing around and eat those vegetables! Don't you want to be big and strong like your Daddy?"

"Yes, Ma'am." I used the fork like a push broom with the spinach on my plate. If a dab of green landed on my fork I ate it, hoping she'd be satisfied.

"Yeah, remember, spinach is what gave Popeye his strength," my father commented, lifting a huge forkful of that nasty stuff and eating it.

I almost smarted off and told him Popeye popped the spinach out of the can and it flew straight into his mouth, but I left it alone.

"And another thing, Sam... I thought fried chicken was your favorite. All you've been doing is picking at the skin."

This turned out to be a bad time for me to decide to be on a self-imposed hunger strike to protest moving to Fisher Place. Tonight we were also having my other favorites—apple pie and vanilla ice cream for dessert.

My mother and father arose from the table with their empty plates.

"Young man, you can stay at that table until all your food is finished."

"Yes, sir."

While my mother washed dishes she announced, "Your father and I have to run some errands tomorrow and pick up mail in our old neighborhood so we thought you might want to play with your friends until we're done."

"What? Really?"

"Except, you can't go unless you eat your vegetables," Daddy warned.

My Hunger Strike was over. I pinched my nose and downed the spinach in several disgusting gulps. Now that it was out of the way, I could enjoy my chicken and dessert. Man, I was so excited! A trip back to the old neighborhood might bring my parents back to their senses. Now they'd see how great it was to be around our friends again.

I watched my father sort through mail with no labels or addresses on the front.

"Hmmm... more love letters," he grumbled.

The word NIGGER, and other dirty words, jumped out

in bold marker colors across a few of these handwritten letters before Daddy ripped them to pieces and stuffed them into the wastebasket.

My mother closed and reopened her eyes slowly, then toweled the same plate she'd already dried.

"Can't wait to see what's in store for us on our front lawn tomorrow," Daddy said while smiling, except his voice sounded hollow... and very alone.

He snatched the newspaper and tromped into the living room.

Tomorrow before driving to work, he'd scoop up the trash and garbage on the lawn and bags of dog feces on the porch and in the mailbox. He'd do it as calmly as raking leaves off the grass. Sometimes he'd even hum like he was at the beach collecting seashells off the shore instead of doo-doo off the lawn. He'd complain to us inside the house or car, but never outside where he could be possibly overheard by the cowardly gawkers hiding behind their curtain shields. He said he didn't want to give them the satisfaction of seeing him bothered.

Daddy still felt like things were gonna get better, but he was nobody's fool. He parked our car in the garage nightly and draped it with a tarp. He called the police every day about all the stuff thrown on our front lawn and backyard and the hate mail cluttering our mailbox. The police rarely showed up, but he said calling them anyway made him feel better.

Still, no matter how Daddy acted, I know it was hard for him to keep smiling when, every time we crossed Century Blvd on the way home, he was pulled over by the same white handlebar-mustached-sunglass-wearing cop and asked to show his license! My father said it was insulting. He felt like he was being treated like an illegal from another country instead of a citizen born and raised here. He got so used to it he often slapped his wallet on the dashboard before reaching Century Blvd because he knew he'd be stopped.

Sometimes it left him so angry he wouldn't speak for hours. Other times he'd try to find something good to say—like the time we parked the car on a side road blocks away from the airport and watched the planes flying low overhead.

"The more I think about it, the more I realize how right Kennedy is. We're the new generation of pioneers and as a pioneer you may have to give up your safety and comfort to build a new world. We may not be sitting at lunch counters and marching down South like our other brethren, but we are fighting to make a difference in our own way. We're trailblazing a path for Negroes to move wherever they want to."

I didn't hear everything he said because of the earth-shaking roar of a plane passing over us. But I really didn't care what Senator Kennedy had to say. It was his fault we moved here in the first place!

When the plane landed and my father was no longer drowned out, he went on to say, "Hell, we've got it easy compared to the early settlers. Imagine if we had to deal with bad weather, hostile Indians, and wild animals, too!"

But I knew we WERE dealing with *wild animals*... The only difference was *this* kind stood on two legs instead of four.

Chapter 9

I was so excited to play at Mattie's while my parents did errands! Terelle, Jamelle, Vicky, and Edgar were also there and we were having WAY too much fun! I missed being with my friends so much I couldn't stop touching and grabbing them—even Vicky. I was thrilled to be back to hiding behind trashcans and listening for the voice of the child-eating monster.

Usually we argued over who got to be the monster. But when Edgar said he wanted to be the monster we just started running. The role of monster was made for him and he loved it—growling, roaring, and tirelessly chasing us. Edgar deserved a nomination in the Hall of Fame for "best pretend monster." Yes, sometimes he got too rough, but that was okay, it was worth the adventure.

During the screams from the monster, Mattie belted out gospel songs from the kitchen window as she cooked and cleaned. Howling monsters and spiritual music were pure joy to me. I didn't want to ever leave again.

However, it was all ruined when I spotted the talking heads of my parents through the thin curtains of Mattie's kitchen window. That's when a flood of anger rippled through my body. Time for me to go back to that horrible neighborhood where people hated us simply because of our skin color.

My parents strolled into the backyard. "Okay, Sam, let's go!"

Daddy's voice was cheerful, but it greeted my ears like a death sentence.

All the kids stopped playing—except for me.

Squatting behind a trashcan, I peeped around it and saw the monster hugging my mother. I hopped up and down to attract his attention.

"Hey monster, you can't catch me! C'mon, slowpoke!" I even ran in circles around Edgar, shaking my booty in his face. But his werewolf face was gone and he was back to being the nice Larry Talbot as he happily held my mother's hand.

"Edgar, c'mon... let's play... Are you tired? That's all right... I'll be the monster and you guys can start running. Okay? Go! RAAARRRRRRGGGGGH!" I yelled, raising my hands in one of my finest, I'll-rip-your-faces-off monster pose. They all stared at me like I'd escaped from an insane asylum.

My father glanced at his watch. "Okay, that's enough, Champ! I'm sure you're having fun with your friends, but we need to head on home before it gets much later. Say goodbye. You'll see everybody again. Mattie, thanks for watching Sam and inviting his friends over to play."

"Grant, you know better than to thank me. You drop my boy off any time."

Well, *her boy* howled at the setting sun, then pounced on the other kids. I pretended to viciously gnaw on their arms, legs, and necks. Terelle and Jamelle watched me in shock, the same way they had when I came out of the manhole, except, I was at an even greater danger with my father than the mole men.

"BOY, did you hear what I said?!"

I had, but I kept racing around and screaming as if I hadn't.

"All right... don't let me take this belt off..."

My mother touched my father's elbow as he loosened

his belt, in a life-saving effort.

"Can't you see your father's ready to leave, Samuel? Come on, honey," my mother beckoned, extending her hand to me like a life raft.

Mattie joined in: "Samuel, listen to your father. When you come back, I'll cook you Mattie's famous chicken and dumplings. How's that sound?"

Sounded great... but I wanted Mattie's chicken and dumplings NOW! I also wanted to keep playing monster, compete in a pissing contest, pick boogers from my nose and throw them, wait for the ice cream truck, smack some girl with a lunch pail, and do everything I couldn't do on Fisher Place. I felt crazed and unable to stop the words exploding from my lips.

"I'm never going back there again! I hate it! I hate those people! PLEASE don't make me go back, Mommy! I wanna stay with Mattie!"

The world suddenly fell silent, except for the clinking sounds of my father unstrapping his belt.

"No! Don't spank me! I don't want to go! Mattie!!!"

I rushed to Mattie's side and clung to her waist. Mattie softly said, "Awww, bless his little heart..."

My father pried my hands away. I stomped my feet and dove to the ground in a full-scale temper tantrum, crying repeatedly, "Noooo! I'm not going!"

"Boy, you too old to be doing this. If you don't get up, I'll give you something to cry about!"

"I don't care! I'm not going!" I screamed. I lay on my back with my arms stubbornly crossed.

And then it hit me—I hadn't been baptized. If the whupping killed me, I had no guarantee I'd go to heaven.

My father seemed to be wrestling over what to do as he stood over me holding the belt strap limply in his hand.

I prayed the concrete would transform into quicksand and swallow me up.

I gazed into my mother's eyes for sympathy, but she looked away.

I braced myself.

Then I panicked and tried to run, but it was too late.

THWACK! THWACK! THWACK!

Wearing Bermuda shorts, I felt a hot searing pain as the belt ripped into my legs. I thrashed and flapped and rolled around on the ground like a runaway electrical wire to get away from the belt's wrath.

"Boy, STOP screaming... and QUIT moving around! You hear me?!"

I did... but as long as the belt moved—I moved! When the strap whacked the inside of my thighs I grabbed myself and let out a blood-curdling wail that would have made a vampire jealous.

"Daddy, you hit my privates!" I cried.

He stopped.

The truth was, he'd only grazed my privates. Even so, I held onto my penis through my pants like it might fly away!

"Daddy, you hit my pee-pee. It really hurts!"

"Grant... that's it, no more," my mother firmly voiced.

Daddy pulled the belt jerkily through the loops of his pants.

My mother kneeled down and carefully unbuttoned my shorts while I groaned. The welts on my legs rose like yeast, though no marks were found on my privates. Edgar and the twins curiously peeped over my mother's shoulders. So did Vicky. But I was in so much pain I didn't care about her looking.

I could tell my father felt bad. Speaking barely above a whisper he told my mother, "I'll wait in the car."

Mommy nodded and then offered her hand to me. "Ready, Sam?"

I struggled like an old man to stand up.

Terelle begged, "Can we see it again, Sam?"

I turned to pull my pants down, but my mother shook her head and pulled me along.

***

Later that evening, before tucking me into bed my mother gingerly rubbed my still stinging legs with a ton of Vaseline petroleum jelly while I lay on my stomach. After some time she said, "Samuel Scott, you know your father didn't really want to spank you; I think it hurt him more than it did you. Don't frown… just try and understand… your father's got a lot on his mind. He's frustrated about more things than you'll ever know. And you being out of control didn't help.

"Trust me, he feels really bad. He told me he was in the wrong and you were too old for whipping, and even worse, to do so in front of your friends. He swore he'd never ever spank you again. He stated he should have taken the time to pull you aside and express why he was angry with you. I'm sure he'll talk with you about it later before you go to sleep tonight."

He didn't. But the next morning, I awoke to find him standing at the foot of my bed with a mischievous grin. He held something behind his back.

"Good morning, Champ."

Pouting, I murmured, "Morning" as I winced like I was still in pain.

"Feel like shooting some baskets?"

Before I could guilt him by saying *NO*, he pulled out a brand-new basketball from behind his back! He twirled it on his forefinger like one of the Harlem Globetrotters.

"Samuel, you think you can shoot better with an official NBA basketball?"

"Oh, yes!"

I quickly sat up in bed and hugged my brand-new official basketball.

"Thank you, Dad!"

"You're welcome, kid! So, are you gonna stay in bed all day or do you want to go out and play?"

"Yes, but I have to change my clothes first."

"No you don't. Keep your pajamas on. It'll be more fun!"

He picked me up and carried me holding the ball out the open backdoor into the yard. My mother stood in front of the garage, smiling, her hands upturned like one of those *The Price Is Right* models on TV. She stood underneath a basketball hoop and wooden backboard attached to the garage. I must have been in a deep sleep. I never heard my father putting it up.

"Whatcha think, Champ? You like it?"

What pain?

I leaped out of my father's arms and tossed the ball way up in the air. I happily jumped up and down in my bare feet.

Daddy waved his hands like a referee. "Hold on there, partner... You get the honor of making the first shot on our new basketball court." He grabbed me and hoisted me high enough to dunk the basketball. My mother clapped and then made up a silly cheerleader routine that made us fall out laughing!

Afterwards, we passed the ball to each other and played basketball. It was a crack up to watch my mother awkwardly trying to score a basket. It seemed like it took me forever to make just two baskets, but my mother was worse than me. On the other hand, Daddy drilled shot after shot.

Mommy said, "Who does he think he is? Let's get the big showoff!"

We chased him, grabbed him, fouled him, and tried to block his shot, but he still kept making baskets.

I loved watching Daddy guard my mother. She elbowed him every time he tried to steal the ball from her. And they'd flirt, even kiss, and I'd hug them both.

We had so much fun that day! The neighbor's curtains on the other side of the fence constantly parted as we laughed and giggled. I didn't care. I forgot all about hating Fisher Place. It was the best time we'd had since moving there.

I loved having my own basketball court! And the lawn was a part of it. Dribbling around and trying to make a basket kept me from feeling so alone. I'd play pretend games attended by thousands of people who watched me win in the last second with a stupendous shot!

Whenever he could afford it, my father took me to see the Lakers play at the Los Angeles Sports Arena. We usually sat in the "nosebleed" section, sharing binoculars to watch Elgin Baylor and Jerry West create their magic on the court.

Daddy showed me how to hold the ball correctly to help me shoot better. He taught me a two-handed push shot that he said I'd have to get rid of once I grew bigger and stronger. But for now it'd do the trick.

One morning, about a week after my father set up the basketball court, I ran outside eager to practice shooting hoops and almost tripped over my own feet in shock. Separating our backyard from the neighbor's stood a white wall about five feet high, and sitting on that wall munching from a bag of pretzels was a girl with two foot-long, bright red pigtails and a million freckles. I recognized her, or at least parts of her. These were the same green eyes I often spotted peeking through the curtains and the same uncombed tufts of red hair that floated above the hedges.

She smiled at me. "Hello."

"Hi," I replied as I launched a shot that missed the rim badly and banged off the garage door. I wasn't used to this.

Nothing more was said, yet I felt her studying me. After missing about 20 heaves, I finally made a basket.

She gasped, "Wow. You're really good!"

"Uh? Oh, yeah, thanks. I'm better than this, though," I coolly replied as my shots clanked under the bottom of the rim a dozen more times.

"Can I try?"

She jumped down before I could answer, then clumsily patted the ball with both hands in a dribble and flung it at the rim. It went only about three feet in the air. It didn't stop her from trying again. A couple of times the ball ricocheted and bopped her on the head.

She giggled. "I'm really bad, huh?"

"No, not really... I used to shoot that way. Bend your knees more... like this," I demonstrated. I was a little too excited because I put too much arch on the ball and it went so high it bounced on top of the backboard several times, then came down and breezed through the net.

"WHOA, you really ARE good! I wish I could do that!" she marveled.

I shrugged, acting like it happened all the time.

After a few more shot attempts she said, "I'm tired" and sank to the ground, pressing her back against the wall. "You want a pretzel?"

I paused, thinking about the cookie thing.

"You don't like pretzels? You want me to get some potato chips or Fritos?"

"No, no, I like pretzels." I sat on the ball as she handed me one.

"They're good, huh? I love pretzels!" she exclaimed, crunching away.

They were good. When she offered me another one, I didn't hesitate.

"I'm Patsy McGuire! What's your name?"

"Samuel."

"You don't have a last name?"

"Of course! Everybody has a last name, except Lassie." This made her laugh.

"Sooooo, what is it?"

"Cole."

Twirling a pigtail around her finger she thought about it. "Cole… hmmm… I like it! How old are you, Samuel Cole?"

"Twelve!"

"I'm 11! Do you have any brothers or sisters?"

"No."

"Me neither. But I will! My mother's gonna have a baby soon. I hope Daddy comes home to see it."

"From work?"

"Kinda. He's in the army. He's stationed in Germany."

"Oh. Where's that?"

"I don't know… Real far away… I think overseas."

"Oh."

"You're lucky cuz your dad lives here."

"Yeah, but he works downtown. That's really far, too."

"Yeah, except your dad still comes home every night."

"Yeah."

"Do you want a brother or a sister?" She asked me.

"I don't know… I had an older brother… His name was Benjamin… he woulda been two years older than me, but my mother said he died in his crib."

"Ohhhhh, that's so sad."

"Yeah, my mother still cries sometimes."

She got quiet, then said, "Yeah… I still cry about my cat sometimes, too. His name was Comet."

"What happened to your cat?"

"Nobody knows. One day he was gone. My mother thinks he got hit by a car or got lost and found a new home where somebody else is feeding him."

"Oh… I bet he'll come back someday…"

"You do?"

"Sure. Lassie did. He always finds his way home when he gets lost."

"But Lassie's a dog… and *he's* also a girl, not a boy!"

"I know that! All I'm saying is animals know how to find their way back home. They can smell which way to go."

"I hope you're right… I really miss him. Tell me if you see him. You can't miss him. He's an orange tabby with white paws that look like tennis shoes."

"Okay."

"PATSY!"

"Uh, oh… that's my mother. Gotta go."

She struggled to climb over the wall. I pushed her up from behind. Glancing back she said, "Thanks, Samuel. You wanna be friends?"

"Uhhhhh, okay."

"You can have the rest of my pretzels."

"Thanks!"

"Bye, Samuel Cole."

"Bye, uh, Patsy Mac…"

"McGuire!!"

Her red pigtails flapped against her shoulders as she jumped off the wall and landed softly on the grass, followed by a loud slam from the backdoor. I squatted down on the basketball and licked the salt off a pretzel.

Amazing. I made a friend…. My first one on the block.

Early the next morning, I sat on the couch flipping through the pictures in my *Moby Dick* book while I waited for my mother to join me in the living room so we could read another chapter. Lately, we'd read a lot of books together since I didn't have any friends to play with. She called it a "mixed blessing" and said it would be good for me in the new school, which I feared was gonna be as bad as this neighborhood.

Mommy was in the kitchen boiling oatmeal and frying sausage patties when I heard a very soft knock on the front door. I was never allowed to open it alone in this neighborhood, so I yelled, "Somebody's at the door!"

My father jogged into the living room, hurriedly buttoning his work shirt. I liked the picture of the soda bottle bubbling over on the logo of his shirt.

"Who is it?"

Nobody answered.

"I said, who is it?" he asked more loudly.

"Patsy!"

I sat up straight.

"Patsy?" Daddy frowned. He warily eased the door open. His gruff voice suddenly sweetened. "Well, hello... Can I help you?"

This change of tone brought my mother to the door. A smile broke out on her face when she discovered who he was talking to.

"Hello, Mr. and Mrs. Cole. I'm Patsy. Can Samuel come out and play?"

My parents turned around and looked at me like— When did this happen? My book dropped onto the coffee table as I slid off the couch and ran to my father's side.

"Hi, Samuel Cole!"

"Hi, Patsy McGuire."

"You wanna play basketball?"

"Yeah."

"Yes," my mother corrected. "Patsy, is it okay... with your parents?"

Patsy pointed. "Sure. That's my mom in the window."

I don't think her mother expected to be called out. Her face got red as she opened the curtains she was peeking through and enthusiastically waved.

"Samuel, I think you should eat something before you..."

"Jo, Sam can eat later. Let the kids play. It's such a

beautiful morning!"

She caught Dad's tone, smiled, and gently pushed me out the door.

At first Patsy and I stood on the porch staring at each other. Then, like two puppies realizing they'd been let loose, we raced to the backyard. Once again, the rim suffered a beating as we tried to score a basket. Like before, Patsy quickly tired out and copped a seat on the grass.

"I'm hungry!"

"Me too!" I echoed, sidling next to her.

"I'm getting something to eat."

"Okay, I'll see you later."

"No. Stay here. I'll be right back."

Patsy ran all the way up to the front of my house and quickly returned with a tin can. She fumbled around, finally opened the lid, and pulled out a cookie.

"Did you get that can from my front porch?" I asked.

"Of course, silly. Oh goody, they're chocolate chip cookies!"

My father must not have seen the can when he rushed to work.

"Wait, Patsy... DON'T EAT IT!"

I tried to snatch the cookie out of her hand, but Patsy giggled, dodged me, and swallowed it in two bites. I reached for the can but she protectively cradled it under her arm.

"I'm not playing, girl. You can't eat those cookies!"

"Why not?" She laughed while nibbling on a second one.

"Because they're poisoned."

"No they're not, silly." She defiantly popped another one in her already full mouth and opened it wide enough for me to see the soggy crumbs.

"Okay, it's your fault if they kill you," I warned, slumping to the ground. She twirled around in circles doing an

I'm-so-happy-eating-cookies dance.

Patsy plopped down beside me, smacking loudly on purpose. She waved a cookie in my face. I shook my head and waited for the poison to take effect. She downed two more cookies while I waited. She even shot some more air balls at the basket.

Nothing.

Was I wrong about the cookies?

Nope.

All of a sudden Patsy's eyes ballooned. She grabbed her throat, struggled for breath, and began hacking as crumbs flew from her mouth. Her body jerked violently and then she lay still.

"Patsy? Patsy? Are you all right? Oh no... please don't die!" I pleaded, trying my best to pry her eyelids open.

I knew what to do to revive her. I hustled and grabbed the water hose. Like a fireman, I rushed over to Patsy and aimed the nozzle at her face.

Her eyelids split open and she yelled, "SAM! NO! DON'T! I'M JUST PLAY—" right before I blasted her with water.

She slowly stood up, arms out, drenched from head to toe, hair plastered against her face, and water streaming down the front of her shirt.

"Why did you do that? I was playing possum!"

"I thought you were dying, knucklehead! Sorry."

Relieved, I put the hose down, water still gushing from the nozzle.

Patsy snatched the hose and aimed it at me! I took off running as she chased me around the backyard spraying wildly. I finally turned the water off at the spigot, but not before I was also a soaking mess. We fell to the ground laughing.

It was a hot day, so our clothes dried quickly. We sat in the sun, rolling the ball back and forth in the water puddles to create miniature waves. I reached for the cookie can lying against the wall.

"You ate all those cookies?"

"Yep. You didn't want any."

"What a pig."

"Oink, oink, oink," she snorted, which led to more belly-aching laughter as we competed to see who could make the best pig snorts.

We played some more, and after a while Patsy went home. The second I stepped inside the house my mother said, "Looks like you guys had a good time! Why didn't you tell us about your new friend?" She pulled clothes out of the dryer and put them in a laundry basket.

"I forgot."

"You forgot? How do you forget something like that?"

"I don't know."

"Well, it's good you made a friend, but for heaven's sake, take those dirty clothes off before you get smacked." She aimed a towel at me like a slingshot.

"No!" I replied, sticking my tongue out.

"What did you say? Why you little... Wait till I catch you!"

I screamed as she chased me while snapping the towel at my behind.

Chapter 10

Squinting, Patsy shielded her eyes from the glaring sunlight with her hand. "You don't know who's putting cookies on your doorstep?"

"Nope."

I hopped on one foot while trying to avoid landing on the hopscotch chalk squares.

"Somebody leaves cookies on your porch every Monday morning?"

"Uh, huh... all kinds... chocolate, oatmeal, lemon, vanilla with sprinkles..."

Patsy rubbed her chin. "I wonder who's doing that?"

"I don't know."

"Betcha I can find out."

"How you gonna do that?"

"Stay up all night on Sunday and wait for them to show up."

"Your mother won't let you do that."

"She'll be asleep. I've stayed up all night before!"

"Me too!"

"I can stay up longer than you."

"No you can't."

"Betcha I can."

"No you can't! I've stayed up almost 1,000 times!" I hollered, losing my balance and stumbling onto the chalk line.

"Ha! Ha! Ha!"

"It's not funny, Patsy! That's not fair! You made me mess up!"

"So! Too bad—that's your fault! My turn!" She threw a beanbag onto a square and leaped forward.

The next Monday morning, I got up early and grabbed the tin can of cookies from the front doorstep before my father found it. I hid it in the garage. As soon as I heard Patsy climbing over the wall, I ran inside the garage and pranced back out, raising the tin can in the air like I'd won a championship trophy. I slid a cookie out of the can and chomped down on it like it was the most delicious oatmeal cookie in the universe. I waved the can in Patsy's face and did my own I'm-so-happy-eating-cookies dance.

"Ha, ha! Betcha want one! Tastes goooooood! Got raisins in it and..."

"Sam, don't take another bite or you'll die!"

"Huh? What? Stop playing, Patsy!"

The look in her eyes told me she wasn't playing.

I coughed and spit out the crumbs on the grass. I flung the can down and sprinted to the hose. I gargled enough water to fill a swimming pool.

"I thought you said the cookies weren't poisoned!"

She shrugged. "I didn't think so until I saw the werewolf!"

"You saw a werewolf?"

"Yes. Right in front of your doorstep. That's not the only monster around. There's a vampire that lives right across the street from you."

"A vampire, too!"

"Yeah, Vernon the Vampire. He drives a red car that I think he flies at night. He doesn't come home until early morning."

"You're talking about that weird looking guy that's always working on his big car in his driveway?"

"Yep. That's him."

"Wait a minute... he can't be a vampire... he can't live in the light during the daytime. His whole body would burn up."

"Well, maybe he has some extra special powers that protect him during the day from bursting into fire. I don't care what you say—I swear he's a vampire," Patsy said haughtily.

I shook my head and left it alone. Obviously, Patsy didn't know much about vampires.

"Okay, so tell me more about the werewolf."

Patsy looked over her shoulder and lowered her voice. "His wife is a witch. She made you those cookies."

"A witch and a werewolf live on our block?" I asked.

I thought about how jealous Terelle and Jamelle would be when I told them a witch and a werewolf and an alleged vampire lived here. They'd move to Fisher Place for sure then.

"Uh, huh... remember when I told you I could stay up all night?"

"Yeah, um, I can stay up all night, too... if I want to!"

"I saw the werewolf put the cookie can on your door-step in the middle of the night."

"Don't be trying to scare me, Patsy... cuz I'm not afraid!"

I was.

"Samuel, I'm not telling a story. I promise it's the truth. I really saw him!"

I believed her. I saw a full moon last night.

"You know what else, Samuel?"

"What?"

"I don't think my cat got hit by a car. I think the were-wolf stole him from our house and they cooked him and ate him," she mumbled sadly.

"I'm sorry, Patsy." I patted her on the shoulder.

"It's all right... You believe me about the werewolf,

right?"

"Yeah… but hold on… why would a werewolf bring me cookies when all he has to do is crash through the window and eat me?"

"Sam…" she sighed, "he doesn't want blood all over the place. Then people would know there's monsters on the block and hunt them down with torches. They want to fatten you up first, then eat you later."

She was right. That's how it usually worked.

"It's like Hansel and Gretel… The witch probably put a spell on those cookies so you'd fall asleep and make it easy for the werewolf to kidnap you and drag you to their house. Then they'd throw you in a big old pot, stick it in a hot oven, and gobble you up once you're well done," she declared, her green eyes bugging.

I trembled with fear and excitement. "Where do they live?"

"A few houses down. You know that one with all the overgrown weeds and big ol' giant bat tree in front?"

"Uh, uh."

She grabbed my hand. "C'mon, I'll show you!"

I jerked it back. "Uh, uh. I can't go."

"You don't have to be afraid. Monsters never come out in the daytime."

"I know that! I'm not afraid!"

I was.

"My parents won't let me walk down the street."

"How come?"

"Because people hate us here and somebody might try to kill me."

"Not me, Samuel. I don't hate you… I…" Patsy stopped talking as she tugged at her pigtails and shuffled her feet.

The awkward silence made me uncomfortable.

"All the kids on the block always ask me about you, Samuel."

"They do? You're lying."

"No I'm not, silly. They wonder if you're a normal kid."

She picked up the ball and shot it. It banged loudly against the garage.

"What'd you say?"

"I told them they're stupid! You're as goofy as the rest of us."

That made me feel good.

She clumsily dribbled the ball on the pavement, patting it with both hands.

"You know, a lot of kids want to come over here."

"For real?"

"Yeah... you're the only one on the block with a basketball hoop!"

I felt like I'd grown a foot taller.

It got quiet again before Patsy abruptly stopped dribbling. "I gotta go."

"Already? Why?"

"Cuz everybody's playing sockball at Jerry Clark's house. Wanna come?"

"I can't."

"Oh yeah, I forgot. I'll see you later then." Patsy held the ball out to me.

I snatched it from her.

"Go ahead and play with your stupid ol' friends! I don't care!"

I threw the basketball as hard as I could against the backboard. Then I grabbed it and started humming and pretending to have a great time shooting by myself. I listened as the front gate creaked open and closed. I waited until the sounds of her skipping feet faded away before I slammed the ball down. I watched it bounce until it hit the grass and rolled to a stop.

About an hour later, the doorbell rang. I was lying on my bed reading a Superman comic book. I listened as my mother opened the front door.

"You're back!"

"Hi, Mrs. Cole!"

I hopped off the bed and went into the living room when I heard Patsy's voice. Surprisingly, another kid stood beside her. He looked like Pig Pen from the *Peanuts* series. He was younger than us. Looked like he was about nine or 10. A cowlick rose from his tousled hair, which also had bits of grass in it. He had mud smudges on his cheeks and T-shirt—my kind of kid.

"Hi, Samuel."

"Hi, Patsy."

"This is Billy."

Billy timidly raised his hand, fingers wiggling.

"Nice to meet you, Billy!" my mother spoke for both of us.

He grinned, eyes bouncing around excitedly.

"Looks like someone is waiting for his new teeth to grow in!"

His gap-toothed grin broadened, pleased my mother noticed.

"Mrs. Cole, can Samuel come out and play sockball with us at Jerry Clark's house... pretty please?" Patsy clasped her hands and hopped up and down. So did Billy.

"Can I, Mom?" I also begged, making it a threesome.

"No, I don't think that's a good idea right now... We haven't met Jerry, yet, and..."

"I'll go get him," Patsy quickly offered, ready to zoom away.

"No, that's okay, Patsy. We want to be sure Jerry's parents don't mind."

"Oh, they don't mind," Billy assured her. "He's got a big front yard! We play there all the time."

"And maybe one day Sam will too, but not today."

"Yes, Ma'am," Patsy replied, sadly shuffling her feet.

"Well, bye, Sam."

"Bye, Sam," Billy echoed.

I stomped into my bedroom and slammed the door—
and immediately realized my mistake as I heard angry
footsteps trailing behind me.

"I *know* I didn't hear that door slam!"

"Sorry, Mom."

I winced after banging the door against my foot in my
hurry to reopen it.

"Sit your little behind down NOW!"

"Yes, Ma'am."

I nearly missed the chair in my effort to obey her.

"Samuel, I know how much you want to go outside
and play sockball with them. I really do, and I wish I could
let you... but I can't," my mother announced, her eyes shift-
ing from anger to compassion. She sat across from me on
my bed.

"Look, we know Patsy, but we don't know the other
kids or their parents, and with all the stuff that's been going on since we moved here, it makes me nervous. Do you
understand, Samuel?"

I did. I only wished I could stop the tears gathering in
my eyes from overflowing.

About twenty minutes later, the doorbell screamed
like a fire alarm.

"What in the world..." my mother uttered from the living room.

I heard the curtains being pulled aside before she
opened the front door.

"Patsy, dear, you only have to ring the doorbell once...
oh... oh..."

Oh? What did "Oh" mean? My legs started jiggling.

"Sorry, Mrs. Cole." Patsy huffed and puffed, like she'd
been running.

"That's all right. SAMUEL!"

I bolted out of the chair and to the front door. I expected to see Patsy but not the seven or eight kids standing behind her in our driveway. One lanky kid held a big fat red sockball. Billy happily waved like we'd been friends forever.

"Since Samuel can't come over to Jerry's, can we play in YOUR front yard?"

Even Shirley Temple didn't have a smile as bright as Patsy's.

"Patsy, you're something else," my mother said, shaking her head. Then she turned to me. "So, what are you waiting for? Go on outside and play!"

"Yay!" Patsy hollered, grabbing my hand and pulling me outside.

I was excited to join them but also suddenly felt shy. So much so that I wanted to run back inside. These were the same kids who for weeks had stared at me but never talked to me. But they must have felt funny, too, because they all kind of stared at the ground when Patsy introduced us. We chose sides and started playing sockball. At first there were no screams or arguments; everyone played nice and boring.

This changed pretty quickly once they saw what a great sockball player I turned out to be. I caught every ball, tagged people out, scored points, and smacked the sockball past kids and over their heads into the next couple of yards.

Jerry Clark, playing on the other team, hadn't seemed too enthused from the get-go about us playing in my yard instead of his, judging by the way he'd glared at me. I could tell he was sick and tired of listening to all the ooohs and aaahs whenever I made terrific catches. He was used to being the best sockball player on the block until I showed up. He hit one ball as hard as he could at me, a line drive, and I caught it. OUT! What made it worse was that some kids clapped. I don't think he was well liked. He angrily kicked the hedge.

"Shuddup, you dummies! That was luck! I'm way better than him!" Jerry shouted. I guess he wasn't used to people catching any of the balls he hit.

After that he shifted into turbo gear, diving after balls and swatting them as hard as he could. Jerry was taller and huskier than me, so when I socked the ball and raced around the bases, instead of tagging me out he tackled me with the sockball as I sprinted for home base.

He didn't say I'm sorry or anything as he pushed up off of me.

I jumped to my feet like it was no big deal.

He eyed me up and down as he swaggered with the ball. I didn't care. It broke the ice. My initiation was over, and I was officially accepted as another one of the kids who had to put up with Jerry's crap. Soon Billy, Tina, Sharon, Bradley, Patsy, and all of us argued, laughed, and played noisily like most kids do.

Thanks to Patsy, I went from one friend to 10 in a single afternoon.

Daddy was surprised when he turned into the driveway and waited for the kids to part so he could drive forward and park the car in the garage. Afterwards, he stood on the front porch and watched us play. I swear he might have been happier than me seeing kids romping around in our front yard. So pleased he only cringed a tiny bit when the ball caromed off the front window.

"Hey y'all, be careful... Try not to bang the window!"

"Okay!" we all shouted, used to parents saying stuff like that.

Must have been that kind of day because we met Patsy's mother for the first time when she came around the hedge and introduced herself. She seemed really shy at first, but relaxed after my parents joked around with her.

Unlike Patsy, she was a brunette, but I saw Patsy's face in her smile. I kept staring at the pregnant stomach that bulged from someone so skinny. The shape of her body reminded me of a tetherball attached to a pole.

As the days passed, more adults came by and said their hellos. Others, not so ready, at least waved if we were in our front yard or drove by.

The best part was, the graffiti, rotten food, ugly letters, poop in the yard, and smelly mailbox packages stopped coming.

I guess Daddy was right about being patient and letting people get used to you. Life on Fisher Place was starting to get better—with the exception of Jerry's two crew cut and leather jacket wearing older brothers.

At times I'd peep through the curtains and find them standing in front of our house scowling. Even when Jerry and all the other kids were in our front yard playing, the two of them stood on the sidewalk glaring, arms folded like a sandwich. They never talked to me, but their sneers, sideward glances, and ear hustling spoke loudly enough. When my parents came outside, they'd coolly walk away.

The roar of their souped-up jalopy burning stinky rubber down the streets at all times of the night often woke me up. I'd find it hard to go back to sleep. My father suspected it was the Clark brothers who'd scribbled bad words on our driveway and left those disgusting gifts on our lawn and in our mailbox. He also thought they were the ones who had messed up his car when we first moved in. He couldn't prove it though.

The only thing that didn't change was the number of "For Sale" signs that posted in yards like sentries, block after block.

Despite that, I was grateful to Patsy for bringing kids over to play and single-handedly improving our living situation. I thought she deserved a Nobel Peace Prize for her efforts, but I don't think they give those out to kids. My parents even gave me permission to play at other kid's home, as long as I never crossed the street or played on another block.

Even so, that still didn't keep me from being subjected to danger.

Now that I could play at Jerry's house, he was a teeny bit nicer to me and we got along better. One day, Patsy, Billy, Jerry, and I played catch as we walked to Jerry's house to play sockball. As usual, for his own amusement, Jerry intentionally threw the ball too hard to Billy, who was about the size of an acorn with hands to match. However, Jerry stopped laughing when the ball ricocheted off Billy's head, bounced on top of the fence, and dropped to the other side.

I peered through the slats in the wooden fence. All I saw was a jungle of a yard cluttered with weeds, ivy, shrubs, flowers, and a giant oak tree. And a house that rose from the ground like a bulb from a flower.

"Ohhh nooo... You STUPID dodo bird!" Jerry yelled harshly. "Look what you did! How am I gonna get my ball now? Gaawwd, you are so clumsy!"

"I-I-I'm sorry, Jerry!" Billy cried, nervously picking at his cowlick of hair.

"Forget SORRY, you dumb retard! You BETTER buy me a new ball!"

Jerry's face was as pale as a possum's in headlights. Patsy was quiet.

"Stop yelling at him! Let's just go get it!" I suggested.

I strained to push the gate open. It parted just enough to slip inside.

"It's open, c'mon!"

The gate suddenly shut with a BOOM and latched itself. The three of them fearfully backed away.

"G-G-Ghosts!" Billy stuttered, grabbing Patsy's hand.

"No, that's just the wind, c'mon," I encouraged.

"Uh, uh... not me... I'm not going in there," Jerry stated firmly.

"What are you guys so scared about?"

"Tell him, Patsy!" Billy's eyes never strayed from the gate.

Patsy whispered, "Samuel, that's the werewolf's house. If you walk inside that gate, you'll never come out again."

I stepped back away from the gate, but tried to act brave.

"Stop being fraidy-cats! He won't hurt you."

"How do you know?"

"There's no full moon."

"Yeah, but his witch wife doesn't care about a full moon, stupid!"

"Don't call me stupid, Jerry!"

"Shhh... listen." Patsy cupped her ear. "You guys hear the strange music?"

Billy and Jerry nodded, exchanging fearful glances. The music drifting out of the house sounded like a demon angrily raking a piano with its talons.

"That's their signal," Patsy said, rubbing her chin. "I bet they're calling for a secret meeting between monsters. Let's go before they smell our blood."

"Yeah!" Billy cried. "I don't care if you think I'm a fraidy-cat, Sam... I wanna go home." On the verge of tears, he shook more than Jell-O.

I noticed a wet spot spreading on the front of his pants and then pee running down from his ankles.

I wrapped my arm around him. "It's okay, Billy, we'll leave right now."

"Thanks, Sam," Billy said gratefully, wiping his eyes.

"Hold on, Sam... since you're not scared, why don't you get the ball?" Jerry challenged, a smirk on his pencil-thin lips.

"Hey, you know what? I've got two balls at home (I only had one). I'll give you one of mine, Jerry—for free!"

"No! I want MY ball! I thought you said you're not a fraidy-cat?"

"I'm not! But my parents said I can't go into anyone's yard without permission or I'll get a spanking!"

"Awww, you're just saying that!"

"No I'm not!"

"He's not lying, Jerry, he told me that before," Patsy argued.

"I *dare* you to go get it!"

I was screwed—you DON'T turn down a dare.

I jumped when Patsy touched my arm. She looked more afraid than I felt.

"Sam, you don't have to..."

I waved it off and stepped forward... then hesitated... The werewolf's gate loomed even larger than before. Crisscrossing red bougainvillea crawled along the fence. Patsy had claimed the vines were once green but turned red after the werewolf watered them down with the blood of all the people he and his witch wife had massacred.

I worried that the witch might turn the vines into guardian snakes as soon as I entered their realm. I thought about turning back, until I saw the sneer on Jerry's face. I convinced myself that all I had to do was find the ball, grab it, and get out of there.

Jerry gave me a boost and I reached over the fence and unlatched the gate. I pushed but it didn't budge this time. Lowering my shoulder, I pressed against it like a fullback. The stubborn weeds tried to hold their ground but the gate partially opened, squealing like a tortured pig. I stepped inside, kneeled down, and squeezed a wad of bubblegum wrapper underneath the gate to keep it open. When I glanced back, Patsy and Billy looked terrified.

Jerry shook his head and gaped at me like I was a dang fool.

All at once a gust of wind made the bubblegum wrapper pop up and fly away followed by the gate slamming shut with a horrific click of the latch. I heard the echo of my friends' footsteps as they fled down the sidewalk.

Chapter 11

Like a popsicle, I stood there frozen—surrounded by plant chaos and haunting piano music wafting overhead. Be that as it may, I looked around and saw some of the most beautiful and striking flowers I'd ever seen. The witch must have tended these flowers. Patsy had warned me the witch used the prettiest flowers to lure unwitting victims into her trap. One whiff of the flower's scent and a hypnotic spell made you fall into a deep sleep. Once that happened, you'd be dragged into the house, seasoned, and thrown into a gigantic pot of boiling water.

I tried not to think about that as I searched for the ball. I kept a wary eye on the vines in case they transformed into poisonous snakes.

Yes! At last! There it was—on the porch—the red ball—as noticeable as a clown's nose—and only a few feet away.

All I had to do was pick it up and go.

It sure looked easy enough... maybe a little TOO easy.

The front door of the broken-down house with its split and peeling walls was open. Furious music blew out of the house along with the tempting smell of chocolate chip cookies. Maybe Hansel and Gretel wasn't a fairy tale after all.

Meanwhile, the ball just sat there on the porch teasing me like a shiny red lollipop.

Right then and there I should have said, FORGET IT

and gone home.

But I didn't.

I crept up on the porch. Once I got close enough I reached out and grabbed the ball. Things looked good until the music abruptly ended. My heart pounded when I heard padded shoes clomping my way.

I turned to run but froze when I heard the screech of an oven door opening. Most likely the witch was checking on her cookies. Patsy had sworn the chips weren't chocolate. They were the burnt eyeballs of babies the werewolf and witch kidnapped.

I remained still, waiting for the right time to make my move. I figured I'd get only one chance. I propped myself up onto the ball. My first step on the very old floorboards made a thunderous crackle. Seemed like the floor was coming alive with the panels turning into gnarly teeth.

I leaped to the ground, cradling the ball like a football, and raced down the narrow pathway towards the front gate. Almost there, I tripped over one of the vines and the ball flew out of my hands. Although, I was sure the vine grabbed me by my ankle and pulled me down. I was trapped in the arms of the bougainvillea and every time I tried to wrestle away its claws ripped deeper into my flesh leaving scratches all over my body.

Things got worse when I heard: "Land sakes alive! It's the young Mister Cole! What are you doing here?"

Helplessly, I raised my eyes to see a slightly hunchedback, elderly man standing over me. He searched around in his oversized pullover sweater and withdrew a pair of spectacles. The werewolf held them to his eyes like a magnifying glass. He spoke English with a very thick foreign accent.

Even scarier—he called me by name.

"Ohhhhh, I see now, Master Cole... you came to get your ball."

Why had I let a dare turn me into an idiot?

"Oh my, what did we do to ourselves today, Young Mister Cole?" The werewolf scratched at his sketchy crown of white hair.

Held captive by his ivy soldiers, I didn't know what to say. The only sound that came out of me was my stomach growling from missing breakfast.

"Are you cold, son? You're shaking."

He carefully untangled my feet and arms from the vines. Surprisingly his fingernails appeared to be human, He didn't have claws soaked or stained with blood. But then again, Larry Talbot looked normal during the day, too!

"Let me see..." He examined my arms through his oval glasses.

A werewolf with glasses? Maybe his eyesight was weak during the day.

"You managed to give yourself a couple of scrapes and a skinned knee, still, I think you'll live. Nothing a little Mercurochrome won't cure," he diagnosed.

Mercurochrome stung worse than an angry wasp. Though, he might use Mercurochrome to season his meals like we used Tabasco sauce.

He helped me to my feet. "You all right, son?"

I nodded, trying my best to avoid looking at him, but my curiosity made me gaze into the gentlest blue eyes I'd ever seen. This might be part of his spell! On the surface he appeared to be a frail old man, but that could be just his mortal disguise for a demon hiding a bushy tail inside his pants.

"Stay right here, Mister Cole, I'll be back."

He turned and walked away. I should have run, but my legs were paralyzed—again, from the spell. His plants would have stopped me anyway. I just stood there, fearing he'd return with the witch to devour me raw. Instead, he came back holding Jerry's ball.

"Here you go, Mister Cole."

I cautiously reached out for the ball. "Thank you, sir."

"If you're not in a hurry, come on inside and have some milk and cookies with us and listen to some more Thelonius Monk. You ever heard of him?"

Us? You and the witch? And who was Thelonius Monk? Sounded like it could be another monster. Uh, uh... forget it... it's got to be a trap.

"Uh, no thank you, sir. I better go home before my parents get worried."

"Okay, suit yourself... but you'll be missing the greatest jazz music in the world on top of my best batch of chocolate chip cookies!"

What? HE made the cookies? Ooooh they... smelled so good... but then Patsy's warnings came to mind... burnt eyeballs.

He squatted down, eyes narrowed as he studied my face. "Okay, but I hope it's not because you believe I'm a werewolf."

I shook my head from side to side so fast I got dizzy.

"Good! Sometimes I hear the kids talking outside my gate. I get so tickled they believe I'm a werewolf. Yes, now that I think about it... Nate the Werewolf sounds much cooler than Nathan Wolfberg. People have been trying to get me to drop the 'berg' from my last name forever. Maybe I should give it some thought," he chuckled.

I didn't know whether to laugh, cry, or run like a cheetah.

"Aw heck... I'm too old and stubborn to change now to try and 'fit' in."

He made the comment more to himself than to me.

"Okay, young man, you don't need to listen to the ravings of some old German Jew... I'm sure your family hasn't had it easy here either."

This confused me.

"Did you like the cookies I made for you and your family?"

"Uh, huh... thank you." So Patsy really had stayed up late and seen him.

"You're quite welcome. Are you absolutely sure you won't change your mind and have some milk and cookies with my wife and me?"

"My parents won't let me go inside a stranger's house."

"I see... but inside a stranger's yard is okay?"

I didn't know what to say and I didn't feel good about it.

"Well, your parents are right."

He laid his hand on my shoulder, releasing the spell on me. My legs came back to life and he walked me to the front gate.

"Okay, off you go! I need to clean up around here. These weeds are getting ridiculous!" He pried the gate open and shooed me out.

"Thank you, Mister Wolfberg," I uttered.

"You're welcome, Master Cole. Maybe one of these days we'll no longer be strangers, huh?" he replied, offering a soothing grin.

I wandered down the sidewalk, not sure what to think.

There were close to 20 kids gathered in front of my house, looking like they were attending a memorial service. Patsy screamed when she saw me and led the charge as they circled around me, firing questions my way. I handed the ball to Jerry.

Not even a thank you. It was okay, I had greater things on my mind.

I tried my best to convince them that I didn't think Mr. Wolfberg was a werewolf; he was just a very nice old man. Nobody wanted to hear that. They argued Larry Talbot was a nice guy, too, until he turned into his snarling and hairy alter ego—the Wolfman!

An irritated Jerry didn't want to hear any more. He stomped away expecting to be followed, but he was on his own. The kids were too busy begging me to tell them over and over again about my meeting with the werewolf.

If Terelle and Jamelle had been around to tell it, they would have built the story to epic proportions. Still, my adventure with the werewolf was about to become as legendary on this block as the mole men story on the Perry Avenue schoolyard.

***

The smell of fried chicken in the car drove me crazy as we pulled into our driveway. Daddy and I had picked up food from one of our favorite restaurants—Chicken Delight. I couldn't wait to dive into that chicken and squeeze the little rectangle bar of cranberry sauce from its plastic case into the stuffing. Sometimes we asked for extra packets. I'd pull the seal on the packet and eat the sweet cranberry by itself. The cherry pie dessert topped it off.

My father opened the door and I skipped into the house swinging the bag of chicken dinners; but I stopped—and the bag kept on swinging.

Sitting on our couch chatting with my mother was the werewolf!

He sprang from the couch and greeted my father with a warm handshake.

"Grant, this is our neighbor from down the block, Mr. Wolfberg."

"Grant, it's a pleasure, but please call me Nathan, Nate, or even Wolf." He gave me a sly wink.

"Nate, the pleasure is mine."

"Hello, Master Samuel!"

"Hi, Mr. Wolf... berg... um, I mean, Mr. Wolfberg."

"Guess what? Nathan is our mysterious cookie donor,

Grant," my mother remarked, nibbling a cookie.

"Is that right?"

"I mentioned how we were afraid to eat them, but after sampling his lemon cookies I regret that decision."

"No need for regret. More will be coming your way."

"Wonderful! I'm excited."

"And I was so excited to welcome your family here that I didn't think about how it might be perceived. Please forgive me. I can understand your reluctance."

"You don't have to apologize, it's really okay," Daddy remarked.

"I usually stay up very late, and I didn't want to disturb you at such ungodly hours, so I left the cookies on your porch. I assumed I'd get by eventually during the day and introduce myself. It took young Mr. Cole dropping by to remind me."

"Dropping by?" my father asked, shooting me a look.

"His ball accidentally landed in my yard, so I retrieved it for him," Mr. Wolfberg quickly mentioned, giving me a knowing smile.

"Oh, I see... well please, Nate, sit down, and make yourself at home."

"No, no," he said patting my father's hand. "You good people are about to eat dinner. I certainly don't want to disturb you."

"Not at all," my mother said. "We've got plenty of food."

"Smells delicious, but no thank you. I need to get back to Esther before she begins to worry."

"Then we'll have to get together for dinner one night."

"That would be delightful. I'm sure Esther would love that."

"Well, bring her by one of these days. We'd love to meet her."

"Might be a little easier for you to come by our place, Jolene. You see, Esther is paralyzed, so she spends most of her time in bed."

"Oh, I'm so sorry to hear that."

"Thank you. We've dealt with it for quite a while. There was a time she was able to sit in a wheelchair, but I'm afraid her condition has worsened."

It seemed to take the air out of the living room as his eyes turned blank.

"I hope you don't mind me asking, has she always been paralyzed?"

"No, Jolene, not always... The first time I saw Esther playing piano at a classical music concert, I fell in love with her. The music was fantastic, but I couldn't take my eyes off her as she sat on the piano bench like it was a throne. She was beautiful, vivacious, talented, excuse me—and still is! Ha!"

"I'm sure."

"I never thought I'd ever have a chance with her. I wooed her every way I could with flowers, romantic music, and love letters. She finally agreed to marry me. Although, if the truth be told, I think my cookies sealed the deal."

"I believe it. These are so good you ought to open up a shop!" Jolene commented while munching on another cookie.

"Thank you, Ma'am... I did. I owned a very successful bakery in Germany. Unfortunately, in the late thirties, it was very dangerous to be a Jew there. German children weren't allowed to play with ours."

He glanced at me.

"I will never forget *Kristallnacht*... what we call the 'Night of Broken Glass.' Hitler's Gestapo bullies took to the streets and destroyed businesses, burned synagogues, and murdered Jews. They set our bakery on fire while we were still inside, and beat us to the ground as we ran out of the burning building."

"Oh my God," my mother gasped.

"Yes. Women... children... it didn't matter. All I remember is seeing Esther lying so still and quiet..."

He paused, but his silence was loud.

"When I heard her groan I can't begin to tell you how grateful I was to see her still alive. But she had suffered a spinal injury. We were lucky to escape before being killed. Sadly, I cannot say the same about so many of our family and friends.

"We had enough money to make it to America, but not enough to give her the proper medical treatment she required. Esther believed she could do without it and refused to go into the hospital and compile more debt. It seemed like she'd recovered, but it got worse and by then it was too late to do anything. Her faith and spirit have taken her this far, but I know one day..."

Mr. Wolfberg seemed to drift until my father gently cupped his shoulder. It jolted him back from wherever he'd gone.

"All in all, she is still my Esther today, and I treasure each moment as it comes."

"Bless you, Nathan," my mother added.

The air felt very heavy so I added my thoughts.

"My friend Edgar, he used to be a bully, too, huh, Mom? But he's changed. He's a good guy now."

"Wouldn't it be nice if everyone could change like your friend, Edgar, Samuel?" Mr. Wolfberg said with a smile.

I didn't understand everything they talked about, but I knew by the pain in Mr. Wolfberg's eyes that he and his wife had faced something more horrible than any monster stories I knew.

"Nathan, be sure to tell your wife 'hello' and let her know we'll be coming by to visit her soon."

"She'd love that, Jolene. Okay, time for me to go... Your dinners are getting cold," Mr. Wolfberg said as he opened the door.

My father shook his hand. "That's why we have ovens, Nathan, so we can heat them back up. Listen, we really appreciate you stopping by with cookies."

"Oh, please, I'm so glad you and your lovely family moved here. This will add a little class to the neighborhood. I just hope you won't get tired of two lonely old people taking up your time."

"I seriously doubt that," Daddy said.

"Don't be so sure... I took note of your record collection and you've got some pretty nice jazz. I might try to steal some of your music."

"Say what? You into jazz, Nathan?"

"Into it? I live for it! Esther and I used to follow the performances of your American jazz artists throughout Europe before anti-Semitism invaded Germany and we were no longer free to move about. I owned a major collection of jazz music before those Nazi pigs burned us out."

Daddy shook his head. "That's a damn shame."

"That's okay, I'm rebuilding it. You must come by and go through my records and bring some of yours along with you!"

"You ain't said nothing but a word—I'll do just that."

"Oh, Samuel, before I leave, there's something in your ear." Mr. Wolfberg tugged my ear and a quarter fell out.

"Look at that! It must have been hiding there the whole time!"

I stared in awe at the quarter in my hand. "Thank you, Mr. Wolfberg!"

"Don't thank me. It came out of *your* ear not mine."

I picked at my ears to see if any more change might fall out.

He laughed. "Goodbye, my friends. God be with you."

"What a nice man," my father declared as he closed the door.

***

The Wolfbergs didn't waste any time. They invited us over for lunch the following Sunday. Mrs. Wolfberg was a small woman and not much taller than me, propped up in her wheelchair. Her hands placed in her lap didn't move, but her smile was like a warm hug. She wore her bright silvery hair in a bun and her eyes sparkled. I studied the photos in their bookcase of her as a young and lovely blonde woman playing piano in front of an orchestra. She now had more lines in her face, but I still found her beautiful.

"What a handsome boy!" Mrs. Wolfberg said in a startling voice that sounded more like she was singing than speaking. She may not have been a concert pianist anymore, but the music remained inside her.

"Come and give me a hug, Samuel. I've heard so much about you!"

Usually I was shy about things like that, but there was such a joy and cheerfulness about her that made it easy to hug her. I did notice, when I held her, a smell coming from her body that could not be hidden by her perfume... She smelled of old age.

My mother and Mrs. Wolfberg talked like they had known each other a zillion years. Mommy didn't hesitate to take over for Mr. Wolfberg and wheel her around the house. While they gabbed, my father and Mr. Wolfberg were going over his album collection.

"Oh my God, you've got this one by Miles? And Dizzy Gillespie? And Cannonball Adderley? Man, stop it! You might not ever get me to leave!"

A beaming Mr. Wolfberg didn't seem to mind as he whipped through more albums for my father to be thrilled about.

"So Esther, I hear you were an amazing musician!" my mother commented as she wheeled her next to the piano in the living room.

"Amazing? Hmmmm... I don't know about that... but I think I did okay."

"OKAY?! She was a superb pianist!" Mr. Wolfberg exclaimed. "She played like the angel she is!" He got off his knees, still holding an album he planned to show my father and kissed her tenderly on the forehead.

"I wish I could have heard you," my mother sighed.

"Oh, my goodness, Jolene, you would have loved it! She was a virtuoso!" Mr. Wolfberg dreamily eyed his wife like she was in a concert performing at that moment.

Mrs. Wolfberg smiled before quickly changing the subject. "Grant, you're obviously a big music lover, do you play an instrument?"

"Not really... I used to mess around a little bit on the piano, learned a few chords, mostly by ear, but no formal lessons."

"He can do okay. Grant, give them a taste of some boogie-woogie!" my mother suggested.

Daddy gave Mommy a look. I looked at her like she was crazy, too. I could probably bang on the piano better than my father.

"Yes, please, Grant, let us hear something!" Mrs. Wolfberg begged.

"Y'all are not gonna make me embarrass myself, not with that beautiful grand piano of yours, Esther."

Mr. Wolfberg marched over to the shining piano and pulled the lid up over the keys. "Pianos are meant to be played, Mr. Cole! And, if you're any good, I may reward you with some of my finest Sherry!"

"Yes, sir," Daddy replied, saluting him. "But don't say I didn't warn you!"

As soon as my father sat down to play, I covered my ears. Everyone laughed. My father toyed around with the keys a few seconds then pounded out some "get down" boogie-woogie music.

I eyed my mother like Mickey Mouse's wizard from Fantasia had suddenly appeared in the room. My mother, bouncing up and down, said, "Uh, huh... you didn't know your father could play so well, did you? He used to play all the time in high school and we'd dance like crazy!"

"Well come and dance with me, Jolene!" Mr. Wolfberg grabbed her and spun her around the living room.

"Your father is very talented!" Mrs. Wolfberg exclaimed, nodding happily to the music.

Afterwards, we had cookies and ice cream and my parents drank some of Mr. Wolfberg's Sherry while I gulped a cherry soda.

Later, I saw Mrs. Wolfberg blinking and fighting to stay awake while everyone talked. She lost the battle, closed her eyes, bowed her head, and fell asleep. I overheard her gentle snoring.

As Mr. Wolfberg walked us to the door, my mother said, "Nate, I hope we didn't overstay our welcome."

"Are you kidding? Esther had a great time! She had more red in her cheeks than the Sherry we drank. Thank you so much!" He gathered each of us in a hug. "The door to our home is always open to you."

***

My mother often stopped by their house in the mornings, since she no longer worked part-time, and kept Mrs. Wolfberg company, often reading to her. Sometimes she'd bring me along and I'd read Mrs. Wolfberg animal stories.

Most times Mrs. Wolfberg stayed in bed while I read to her. If she was feeling really good, she'd tell me German fairy tales she'd learned as a child. I'd stay with Mrs. Wolfberg until she began nodding off to sleep.

One time Mr. Wolfberg pulled me aside and thanked me for coming by. He said that since Esther was unable to have children, she cherished my visits. There was a deep sadness in his eyes when he said it.

Mr. Wolfberg really appreciated our visits with his wife. I guess it was a kind of a break for him. He'd take a walk and sometimes go down to the local market to pick up food. Other times he'd sit on the porch in his rocking chair, reading or pretending to read—still holding the paper, but eyes tightly shut, and snoring. If he heard me coming, his head would jerk up and he'd raise his paper and flip a page like he'd been reading it the entire time.

When he did take off for a walk, I liked watching him because he'd hobble down the sidewalk like one of those fairy tale elves strolling through a forest. His pants looked huge on him, like they were meant for a taller person.

Like my Dad, he smiled at the neighbors. It wasn't always returned, which I found odd considering the Wolfbergs had lived here for a long time and were White. And I never saw any of the neighbors visit them. I wondered if the adults were afraid of them, too.

I did my best to convince everyone that the Wolfbergs were human. I knew it was more fun to believe monsters exist, even though it can lead to sweaty nightmares, but I liked the Wolfbergs too much to let people run around telling horrible lies about them. Sad to say, I found I needed to do more than talk.

Chapter 12

It was close to sunset and we were playing dodge ball in my front yard. Jerry and I were the only ones left standing. It was my turn, and I fired the ball at Jerry who dove to his right. The ball glanced off his leg and over the hedge. Jerry argued I missed him. Everyone knew he was lying and backed me up.

"I'm taking my ball home, you bunch of cheaters!"

He marched home with his ball. No one really cared about him taking his ball since the game was over anyway. We sat on the grass and yakked about the newest summer movies. Jerry came back with two of his friends no one knew. We ignored him and kept talking.

Except, Jerry wasn't in the mood to talk about *One Hundred and One Dalmatians*. He jumped to his feet and jabbed his finger in my face.

"You don't know what you're talking about, Sam! You're stupid!"

Huh? I hadn't said a word because I hadn't seen the movie yet.

"That old man... maybe he's not a werewolf, but he's still a monster!"

"No he's not!"

"Is too!"

"So why didn't he eat me, Jerry?"

Jerry didn't know what to say.

One of his friends said, "Cuz colored people taste like

poo-poo!"

Jerry slapped his thigh as he and his buddies laughed. How stupid... werewolves don't care about color!

Then Jerry said, "My Dad said people like them are evil! They're greedy, and they lie, and they kidnap children, and they killed Jesus!"

"No they didn't! The Wolfbergs didn't kill Jesus!"

"Yes they did!"

"No they didn't!" I yelled, quickly rising to my feet.

Jerry chest bumped me.

"You calling my father a liar?" His eyes cut from side to side as the kids circled us.

"You wanna fight?" he said, balling up his fist.

His eyes told me he really didn't want to fight, but his friends were goading him to. I didn't want to fight either, but not because I was afraid of him.

I was afraid of my father! Daddy had warned me I better not get into any fights or he'd beat me blue.

"No," I answered and backed away.

Jerry stepped back too and seemed relieved, until one of his buddies yelled, "Little Black Sambo is scared of you!"

"Yeah," chimed the other boy, flapping his arms. "What a big *black* chicken! Squawk! Squawk!"

"Come on, Samuel, let's play in your backyard," Patsy said, nudging me.

"You gonna go watch his eyes bug out like a baboon, Patsy?"

Jerry and his buddies stuck their lips out and made their eyes pop out. I tried to ignore them, but it's hard to do when kids laugh at you. Jerry arched his shoulders and waddled like a gorilla, making ape noises and picking at his butt.

"Leave him alone, Jerry!" Patsy yelled, stepping in front of me.

He pushed her aside and got nose to nose with me

again.

"Hoo, hoo, hoo... isn't that what you colored people do in the movies? Hoo, hoo, hoo... your eyes get all big and buggy and your hair sticks up. He licked his hands and pulled strands of his hair up. He cocked his head from side to side and made his eyes balloon again.

"Come on, Sam," Patsy grabbed my hand, but I jerked it away.

I balled up my fist. "You better shut up, Jerry!"

"Awwwww, wassa matter, NEEEGROOOO? Ya gettin' mad? Whatcha gonna do about it... huh, NEEEGROOO?"

My father's words were becoming very faint, but I turned my back on Jerry. I walked down my driveway with Patsy even though his friends chanted over and over, "He's a Big Black Chicken!"

But Jerry, feeling his oats, ran up and cut me off. "You gonna get some watermelon and fried chicken to eat, NIG-GER?"

He turned around to laugh with his buddies. When he turned back to me, I smacked him so hard I heard a loud crunch.

He clutched his nose and crumbled to the ground like he'd been shot. Rocking back and forth he cried, "Why did you hit me? I was just playing. Golly, can't you take a joke?"

Blood oozed between his fingers. Jerry kept his head up as he pinched his nose to stop the bleeding. Red spots sprinkled on his T-shirt.

"Look what you did! I hate you! You just wait... I'm gonna tell my Daddy and my brothers and they'll beat up you and your whole nigger family!"

I moved towards him but he took off running, holding his nose like it might fall off. Some kids followed him and others went home. Only Patsy and Billy stayed.

My fists remained tightly clenched. My body wouldn't stop trembling.

"It's all right, Samuel," Patsy whispered, easing her hands onto mine and gently un-balling my fists. "Jerry's always picking on people. I'm glad somebody finally punched him!"

Billy looked around first before he said, "Me too!"

I couldn't talk.

"Samuel, is it alright if I come with you the next time you visit the Wolfbergs?" Patsy asked. "They sound like really nice people."

I may not have answered her. All I was thinking about were the fireworks in store for me once my parents found out I got into a fight.

Later that evening, there were no fireworks.

Worse.

My father, grimacing, with his hands on his hips and that vein popping out of his forehead, stared out my bedroom window for the longest time without saying a word. My mother sat on my bed, arms folded. I was balled up in my red chair, head bowed, awaiting sentencing.

"Do you hear how much that phone is ringing?"

"Y-Y-Yes, Daddy."

"All because YOU hit that boy. We can't even answer the damn thing!"

"Grant, please... your language..."

"I'm so furious, I don't know what to do! What-did-I tell-you-about-fighting?"

It felt like someone had set fire to my chair as I scrunched around. Now I knew exactly what it meant when people said, "He's on the hot seat"!

"SAM?!"

"You said, 'Don't get into any fights with nobody.'"

"Anybody," my mother corrected.

"And you did WHAT?"

"Punched Jerry in the nose."

"So after all our talks you STILL got into a fight?"

Tears burst from my eyes.

"I'm waiting..."

"Yes," I sobbed.

"Did he hit you first, Samuel?" my mother asked, rubbing her elbows.

"Your mother asked you a question!"

"No, but Daddy, he said all kinds of mean things about Mr. and Mrs. Wolfberg! He called me a monkey... and pushed me and stuff."

"So what! Do you remember what I told you about sticks and stones?"

"Yes, sir."

"And, how does it go?"

"Sticks and stones may break your bones, but words will never hurt you."

I buried my head in my hands, realizing I was my own worst witness.

"Then why did you hit that boy?"

"I don't know."

"You don't know? You better give me something better than that."

"Because..."

"Because what?"

"He called me a nigger."

"Called you a what?" My mother unwrapped her arms and stood up.

"A nigger," I repeated more strongly.

"Did you hear what that little weasel said, Grant?" My mother's eyes were lit up as she ran her fingers through her hair.

My father rested his hands on top of his head.

"I heard, Jolene."

He dropped his hands when something caught his attention out the window.

"Well, here we go... someone just tossed some dog

shit in the backyard."

My mother joined him at the window. Disgusted, she sat down on the bed, once again folding her arms protectively.

Daddy turned and faced me. He rubbed the bridge of his nose like it pained him.

"Okay, Samuel, I agree, he had no business calling you that."

"No he did not! That comes from an ignorant person!"

"Jolene's right, but Sam, I guarantee you this won't be the last time some idiot calls you a nigger."

"Uncle Stewart told me to never let *anyone* call me a nigger... and if they did to knock 'em upside their head!"

"Thanks, Stewart!" my father snorted.

"Mommy said it too, Daddy!"

"Jo, you shouldn't have told him—"

He never finished after my mother rifled him a look I'd never seen before. He hesitated before speaking again.

"Sam, you can't punch every single person that calls you a nigger."

"Like how you and your friends call each other that in the barbershop?"

"Uh, well, no... that's different. We're just joking around."

My mother rolled her eyes. "Yeah, funny! Ha! Ha!"

"Jolene, please... I'm trying to educate him. Son, we're talking history here. It's more serious when a Caucasian person says it. Our ancestors were slaves... whipped, chained like livestock, separated from their families by their slave masters, and sometimes beaten to death. Your mother and I went to segregated schools. We had to go into separate bathrooms and drink water out of fountains marked for coloreds only. We couldn't drink out the White ones."

"Even if you were really thirsty?"

"I don't care if you were dying! It was the law! You could get arrested!"

"Just for drinking water in the wrong fountain?"

"That's right. That's how bad it was."

"IS," my mother corrected.

"Yeah, it's still going on in some places. But Sam, what I'm trying to say to you is, I got called horrible names all the time. If I received a dollar for every time I got called a nigger, I'd be as wealthy as Rockefeller."

"Don't forget to tell him about all the fights YOU got into, too, for being called a nigger, Mr. Rockefeller. Remember, we grew up in the same town."

"Jo, that was then... Times have changed."

"Really? Then somebody forgot to tell it to that little brat down the street."

Daddy scooted next to her and folded his hands.

"Sam, I understand why you got mad, but you can't let some bonehead get the best of you by calling you names."

"Well, they've got some other names in case that one doesn't get to you... like darkie, tar baby, spear-chucker, jigaboo..."

"Jolene..."

"Grant, he's bound to hear them sooner or later."

"Then let it be later... Right now I'm trying to make a point. When a Caucasian person calls you a nigger it's worse than a Negro saying it."

"It's bad when anybody says it," my mother retorted, tapping her foot impatiently.

"Like I was saying, Samuel, I told you guys before we moved here it wasn't gonna be easy. Like it or not, WE are the new pioneers. Some of these folks have never seen a Negro in their entire life except on television and in the movies. Some of them have never talked to a Negro before, let alone lived next door to one. Some of the idiots really do believe our eyes look like ping pong balls when we get scared, and they call us shiftless, lazy, liars, thieves, and violent."

"That's not true!" I yelled, my eyes welling up again.

"Of course not, Champ... but you sure didn't help our cause today."

My chair heated up again as the tears rolled down my cheeks.

"Some people are just plain ignorant, Sam. That's why you cannot react to kids calling you names or teasing you. Once they figure out that's your weakness, they'll take advantage of you. You've got to be bigger and better than that. We not only have to constantly prove we're as intelligent as them, but we have to be smarter just so we can be treated like equals.

"You hear me talking all the time about the Negroes down South fighting for our civil rights. They're getting beat up, sprayed with fire hoses, police dogs sicced on them, houses bombed, shot, and killed... but they're fighting back—not with their fist, but legally. They're using the law to win their battles. In the long run we may lose a few battles, but we'll damn sure win the war!"

I got up and sat on the bed between my mother and father. "Are they gonna bomb us because I hit Jerry in the nose, Daddy?"

"*Going* to bomb us," my mother corrected.

Daddy smiled and rubbed my head. "No, son, they're not going to bomb us. But the stuff we dealt with before is bound to happen again."

"I'm sorry, Daddy. I didn't mean to start any wars."

Daddy wrapped my mother and me in his big arms. "Don't worry about it, Champ. We'll get through it... just like before."

The bonging of the doorbell followed by pounding on the door made us all jump. My father's chest heaved up and down. He gathered himself and slowly stood up like he had a 300-pound barbell on his shoulders.

"I'll come with you, Grant."

"No. Stay here with Sam."

"NO," she said. "Samuel, why don't you go outside and play basketball."

I stepped out the backdoor and got hit by flashing, multicolored lights through our open front gate. I didn't expect to see two police cars parked in the driveway and another one on the grass in front of the house! I thought about hiding in the garage as my heart whomped against my chest.

I heard people can bleed to death. Had Jerry died from his nosebleed? I'm too young to go to prison! My imagination went wild as I saw myself in a witness chair facing a mean old White judge:

"But your honor, I didn't mean to hit him so hard!"

"Why did you hit sweet little Jerry in the first place?"

"He's not sweet... he's mean! He called me a nigger!"

"That's no excuse, young man. It's against the law to hit White people!"

"I'm sorry," I cried.

"Sorry? It's too late for sorry, young man! I'm ready to make my ruling: I pronounce you GUILTY of hitting Jerry and sentence you to life in prison!"

"LIFE? But I'm only 12!"

"Age doesn't matter when you commit a crime, son! Officers, take this nigger away and lock him up forever," the judge yelled, banging his gavel.

Officers Thomas and Mackey grabbed me by the arms and slapped handcuffs on my wrists and chained my ankles. As they walked me through the crowded courtroom, Jerry's family leaped up cheering and applauding like they were at the World Series.

Terelle and Jamelle, Edgar, Patsy, Billy, Mr. and Mrs. Wolfberg (in her bed), Mattie, Uncle Stewart, and Mommy and Daddy tearfully waved goodbye. As I passed by them I heard Mattie scolding my parents, "See? I told you he should have been baptized!"

***

"Sorry you had to stop by officers!"

My father's voice saved me as the police vehicles crept back out of our driveway. I ran inside and the entire house rocked after Daddy slammed the front door.

"That man had the audacity to call the police on US? And, Jerry's dad wants to file criminal charges? The boys had a spat, not a knife fight! Yet, OUR car gets messed up, we get dog shit in OUR mailbox, NIGGER written on OUR garage and mailbox, crazies calling OUR house day and night cussing and screaming stuff that can't be flushed, and not one person on this block is questioned. But Jerry's dad makes one phone call and they come at us like we bombed City Hall!

"That cowardly son-of-a-bitch didn't even have the balls to bring his sorry ass here and discuss it man to man! Tell you the truth, Jolene, the more I think about it, the more I'm glad Samuel decked that boy. If he's as big an asshole as his father, then he deserved to get his ass whupped! I just wish..."

"Grant..."

Mommy steered his gaze to me in the hallway scratching my head.

"Sam, I thought we told you to stay outside and play basketball?!"

"I'm sorry, Daddy, I got bored and..."

"Bet you won't get bored if I take a belt and..."

I was outside before he completed that sentence. Still, I felt a little better when I heard my father say he wanted to deck Jerry's dad, too.

That night, my parents argued in their bedroom, but

I couldn't hear what they were saying. Once it got quiet, my door creaked open and hall light invaded my bedroom. Pretending to be asleep, I peeped through the slits in my eyelids and saw my father's silhouette. Seconds passed before the door clicked shut. It's one of those rare times I welcomed the darkness.

As Daddy predicted, hate mail was back in our mailbox along with plastic bags of dog poop. Strangers never had to figure out where the Negro family lived. The word NIGGER was spray painted on our front sidewalk and in our driveway and across our garage door.

Daddy once again made calls to the police, and as usual, they took forever to show up and investigate the new damage to our property. When they rolled up, once again, they looked like WE ruined THEIR day. Our neighbors no longer offered us a courtesy smile or wave. All the kids were back playing in Jerry's front yard, except for Patsy, and sometimes Billy.

One day Patsy and I were creating mud pies when Billy came into my backyard. He didn't join in, he just watched us.

"I'm not supposed to be here."

We ignored Billy as we shaped the crust on our imaginary cherry pie.

"Momma said Negroes are born with hot tempers... and that's why they always act so crazy and violent."

He waited for a response but got none.

"Momma said that's why you hit Jerry."

I wanted to hit him but he was just being Billy.

"That's dumb, Billy! I'm not a Negro and I've always wanted to clobber Jerry!" Patsy barked. She decorated the pie with a leaf.

Billy shrugged, stuck his hands in the mud, and started his own mud pie. Guess he'd said what he needed to say.

Motor-mouth Billy later mentioned that his mother said they sold their house and were moving to the Valley because the neighborhood was getting bad now that people like us moved in.

A couple of weeks later, Billy and family left without even a goodbye... at least to me.

If not for Patsy, I would have been alone... again.

On another day as I watered the front lawn as part of my chores, Jerry and friends roosted on his wall, coldly eyeing me. He almost buried his head in the ear of the kid he whispered to, creating a chain of whispers from ear to ear. Soon they leaped off the wall with mischievous looks and raced into his backyard.

It didn't take long for me to find out why.

They came back with mud smeared on their faces and chalky-white lips. They pounded their chest and howled and screamed like monkeys.

Jerry's father waddled out of the house adjusting his tie and slapping on his sports coat. Seeing I was the target of their bullying, he smiled and leaned against the car to enjoy the show. After a while, he squeezed his roly-poly body into his car. He gave me a hard look as he screeched past me.

Choosing to be my friend was also bad. Jerry and his troop of suck faces were cruel to Patsy. They'd say, "Hey, Patsy, you're a nigger lover." Or, "Do you need a banana for your pet monkey?" Patsy either ignored them or gave Jerry a stare that made him shut up.

Patsy told me she got so sick of Jerry teasing her that she warned him she'd tell her Dad to come home with a machine gun and blast Jerry with a thousand bullets like *The Rifleman* did to the villains on TV. And since her father was in the army, the police would never arrest him for killing Jerry either. That cooled him off real fast.

Patsy also told me her father had called her and

said he was proud of her for being friends with me. He'd formed lifelong friendships with Negroes in his platoon and viewed them as brothers in arms. I'd never met him but I already liked him.

One Monday morning while Patsy and I were dancing in the backyard to music from my transistor radio—actually, Patsy hopped around more than danced—she stopped and said, "I'm hungry. Are there any cookies on your porch?"

Mr. Wolfberg still dropped off cookies now and then.

"Let's go see—race ya!"

Patsy ran behind me laughing and tugging on my shirt.

"Yay!" I shouted grabbing the tin can on the doorstep. It was heavier than usual.

"He must have put a lot of cookies in this one!"

"Hurry up! Open it!" Patsy jumped up and down.

My mother peeked out the door. "What's going on?"

"Mr. Wolfberg left us some cookies!"

"Awww, that Nate, he really is a good soul. Patsy's right—hurry up! I want a couple, too! You need some help?"

"No, I've got it!" I finally popped the lid off, but a foul smelling liquid splattered us. I dropped the can like I'd been stung. Soggy cookies floated in a pool of yellow liquid.

"Ewwww... somebody PEED in that can!" Patsy cried.

My mother's grin twisted like wrinkled paper. "Sam, you and Patsy change your clothes and rinse off!" She snatched the hose and wetted down the porch, cursing under her breath.

Patsy ran home still crying, "Ewwww." I ripped off my shirt and threw it on the ground before I went inside.

Daddy mentioned the incident to Mr. Wolfberg and that was the end of our Monday morning cookie deliveries.

Chapter 13

"Samuel, I'm going over to Esther's for lunch. You want to come?" my mother called out from the open bathroom door. The scent of perfume was in the air as I heard her busily brushing her hair.

"No thanks."

"I'll be gone for a couple of hours. You sure you'll be okay by yourself?"

Aquaman used his telepathic powers to build a fish army of octopi, flying fish, dolphins, swordfish, and barracudas to battle the evil sea creatures.

"Samuel Scott Cole!! Stop reading and answer my question!"

"Yes, Mom! Patsy's coming over. We're going to play hide and go seek."

"Okay, good. If you guys get hungry there's plenty of bologna, cheese, mayonnaise, mustard, and Wonder Bread in the refrigerator to make a sandwich. There's also some Fritos and potato chips in the cabinet."

"Okay."

"Don't leave the kitchen looking like World War III."

"Okay."

After I finished reading, I grabbed my basketball and headed outside to shoot some hoops. Before long I heard tennis shoes as Patsy ran down the driveway, pigtails flying, ready to play hide and seek. She lost the flip for heads or tails and immediately started counting to 100 while I searched for a place to hide.

I ran on tiptoes to the front gate and tried to open it without a squeak. As I hid behind the hedge someone yanked me up by the collar of my shirt.

I found myself staring into "Mudge" Clark's frightening face as my legs dangled uncomfortably in the air. He let me go and I tumbled awkwardly to the ground, while his brother, Jeff, cackled loudly.

Once I got to my feet, the Clark brothers with their identical crew cuts closed in, pressing so hard against me I felt like a piece of meat in a sandwich. Their stinky breath didn't make it any better.

The oldest brother, Mudge, was built like a tank due to all his weight lifting and playing football at the local high school. He looked even bigger wearing his leather motor-cycle jacket. Jeff was stocky too, except he had a fat belly.

Mudge's real name was Matt. I suspect his nickname had something to do with his pancake-shaped face and pig-like nose.

"Where ya running off to, squirt?" Mudge demanded to know, thumping me hard underneath my chin and forcing me to look up at him.

"Uh... I-I-I was t-trying to hide."

Meanwhile, Patsy happily counted, "75, 76, no 74, wait... 75, 76, 77, 78..."

"Jeff, give Sammy some room to go and hide."

"Here you go, Sammy!" Jeff stepped back a fraction.

I peered through the slit of space between them. Across the street, the guy the kids called Vernon the Vampire washed and waxed his car as usual. I saw him looking, but he didn't seem to care.

Patsy yelled from the backyard, "Ready or not, here I come!"

My throat felt like cotton when I asked, "What are you guys doing here?"

Mudge smacked his gum loudly. "Hear that brother? Goofy wants to know why we're here."

Jeff snickered.

"We saw your mother leaving and thought you might be lonely."

"My mother's coming back real soon—you better go!"

Jeff patted my shoulders. "No, I don't think so, Sammy. Not with all that food she was carrying. Bet she's having a nice long lunch with the witch."

"Don't call her that, brother. You know Sammy's friends with her. I heard he doesn't like people calling her that. What's her real name, Sammy?"

"Mrs. Wolfberg."

"Oh yeah, that's right, Mrs. Wolfie Berg. That better, Sammy?"

I hated how he said my name—it sounded like a curse word.

"Hey, Sammy, since you're alone... we'll keep you company and play with you."

Mudge's smile was more menacing than any frown I'd ever seen.

"You don't have to. I'm not alone—Patsy's here."

"Patsy!" Jeff belched. "She's a girl! What if some really bad guys tried to beat you up?"

Mudge clapped his hands to my face. "Yeah... you think Patsy's gonna jump in and help you fight?"

The latch of my gate lifted up. Patsy burst through and came to a stop when she spotted the Clark brothers.

Mudge waved. "Hey, Patsy,"

"What are you guys doing here?"

Mudge shook his head. "I don't get it, Jeff... why does everyone keep asking what are we doing here?"

"Don't know, man," Jeff said, creeping up on Patsy and playing with her pigtails.

"Stop it Jeffrey!" She flipped her hair away and stood

next to me. Jeffrey gave her a look like she'd killed his mother.

Vernon stopped waxing. He held the cloth over the roof of his car, as he now seemed more interested in the goings on.

"Isn't this where all the cool people hung out and played basketball?"

"Not anymore, Mudge."

"How come, Sammy?" Mudge demanded to know, lips curled in a snarl.

I shrugged.

"Aw c'mon... you really don't know, Sammy?" Mudge asked facetiously. "Maybe it's cuz you punched my little brother in the nose and almost broke it? And now nobody wants to play with you except a stupid little girl!"

"Don't call me stupid, Matt!"

He gave her a dirty look. NO ONE called him Matt.

His attention returned to me after I cried, "I didn't mean it, Mudge... honest! Jerry called me names and he wouldn't stop..."

Mudge gave his brother a sly look. His scowl flipped to a smile.

"Hey, it's cool, Sammy. We know you didn't *mean* to hit him."

"You d-do?"

"Yeah, man. We really want you guys to make up and be friends again."

Patsy eyed him suspiciously.

"Jerry told us he really misses playing with you."

The shock on my face must have resonated.

"It's true. Doesn't Jerry want to apologize to Sammy, Jeff?"

"Yup! He sure does." Jeff grinned.

Patsy snapped her hands to her hips. "How come he's not here?"

Mudge ignored her. He put his arm around me.

"Sammy, that's because my brother is really shy. Jerry asked us to invite you over so he can apologize to you face-to-face, like a man."

Patsy frowned. "Jerry's not shy!"

Mudge gave Patsy the stink eye, then turned back to me.

"Don't listen to her. She doesn't know Jerry like we do. You believe me, don't you, Sammy? Trust me, Jerry really wants to make up with you."

"Yeah, man, my brother wouldn't lie to you."

I wanted to believe him, no matter how stupid it seemed. I thought about how proud and happy my father would be if I made everything right again.

"Ya coming with us, Sammy, so we can make everything right?" Mudge asked nicely.

Patsy's voice cut through as I wrestled back and forth about what to do.

"They're lying, Samuel! Don't trust them. If you go with them I guarantee they'll do something bad to you!"

My sanity returned long enough for me to respond with, "I better not, my mother told me not to go past Patsy's house."

Mudge rested a hand on my shoulder.

"Look man, I promise... we are not going to do anything to you. We'll bring you back home before your mother even knows you were gone."

He stood close enough that I thought I smelled alcohol on him; it could have been rubbing alcohol and not the other kind—after all, he did play football.

"Don't do it, Samuel!"

Jeff snapped his fingers. "Hey Sammy, Mudge forgot to tell you how much we want you to be a part of our boys' club."

"Oh man, Jeff's right. I forgot all about that!"

"They're lying, Samuel! They don't have no club!"

"Our club is a secret! Why would we tell a girl about a boys' club?"

It was the strongest argument Mudge made to me. I liked the idea of a secret organization.

"Let's go, Sammy," Mudge said, patting me on the back. "You're hanging out with the big boys today!"

The Clark brothers stood on each side of me like bookends as I reluctantly walked with them... wanting so badly to believe.

"Samuel, STOP! PLEASE don't go with them, they're gonna hurt you!" Patsy wedged herself between Jeff and me. She clutched my arm. "Remember the pee in the cookie jar? I betcha *they* did it!"

"Shut up, you dumb stupid chick!"

Jeff pried her fingers away and shoved her so hard she fell. She immediately got up rubbing her behind. He looked ready to do it again.

"Don't hurt her!"

"It's all right. She's fine, Sammy. Jeff's didn't really hurt her, Patsy's a tough girl."

Mudge shot Jeff a look and he slowly backed away, still glaring at Patsy.

What bothered me more was how Patsy looked at me. She seemed more hurt by me not listening to her than the pain from being pushed down.

Mudge leaned into me. "Patsy's just jealous, Sammy, cuz she can't be in the club."

"No I'm not! YOU DON'T HAVE ONE!"

"C'mon, Sammy," Mudge said, shielding me from Patsy by smashing me closer to his smelly jacket. "I swear, we'll bring you back in a few minutes way before your mother comes home. Then you guys can go back to playing hide and go seek. Right now, we men have some business to take care of."

"Patsy, we'll be back soon with Sammy, I promise," Mudge said, smiling and with a tone of sincerity.

"No you won't," she replied tearfully.

"Don't you worry, Patsy, we'll take real good care of your little Sammy."

Jeff's voice was devoid of any of Mudge's sincerity. It made me start second-guessing my decision to join them, except I was now at their house. I felt like a zombie as they escorted me into their backyard. I heard Patsy screaming my name in the distance.

Then it all got quiet.

As we walked along the side of the Clark house into the backyard, Mudge's gentle hold on my arm began to feel more like an iron claw.

"Owww, that hurts."

I attempted to pull my arm away but Mudge tightened his vise-like grip.

"Stop crying, punk!" Mudge barked, no longer smiling as he pushed me roughly ahead of him.

"I want to go home. My mother is probably back."

"Too late now, Sammy Sambo," Jeff said.

I was such an idiot! Why hadn't I listened to Patsy?

At that moment I heard behind us the patter of my favorite tennis shoes—Patsy jumped in front of the brothers.

"You better let me stay or I'll tell my mother AND your mother on you!"

"You better get out of here, Patsy or I'll..." Jeff balled his fist up.

"Naw, forget it, Jeff... let her come. It won't change nuthin'. Sammy's still gonna get what he deserves."

Mudge the Thug was back.

Patsy latched onto my arm as we walked into their backyard.

Jerry swung back and forth on a tire attached to a

rope tied to the branch of a tree. He didn't see us at first as he fired his toy pistol at some unseen bad guys—except in Jerry's case, it was probably the *good* guys.

Jeff shouted, "Jerry, look who we brought with us to play with you!"

Jerry was so stunned to see me, he dropped his gun and got stuck in the tire swing trying to get down.

"What's HE doing here?"

Mudge snickered and planted a hard elbow to my shoulder. "How's it feel when someone else asks, 'What are you doing here,' Sambo?"

Jerry stomped. "Get him out of here! I don't want to see his ugly face!"

Patsy gave me an I-told-you-so look.

Mudge grinned at Jerry. "We're not leaving until YOU say, 'I'm sorry.'"

"What? *Me* apologize? But he hit me, Mudge!"

"He doesn't have to apologize," I said. "I'll still be friends with him."

"I don't want to be friends with you!" Jerry yelled, cupping his nose.

A disturbing smile crept across Mudge's lips.

"Oh no, you misunderstood me, little brother. I would never make you become friends with a nigger! What you will do is tell this mud duck that you're sorry you're gonna have to kick his ass!"

I tried to run, but Mudge grabbed me in a headlock. He snagged my chin roughly and raised it so I'd have to stare into his hardened face.

Stupidly, I said, "I thought you wanted me to be in your boys' club?"

"Oh, yeah, I did say that... didn't I, Jeff?"

"Sure did, Mudge."

"Okay, let's take him out in the alley. Jerry, open up the secret entrance to our clubhouse out in the alley."

"But Mudge…"

"You heard what I said."

Jerry shrugged and walked over to the back fence, pulling up two planks in the fence that we'd have to walk under to get to the alley behind their house.

"I can't go into the alley, my parents…"

"You don't have a choice, blackie."

Mudge carried me kicking and screaming underneath the raised wood into the alley along with Patsy who kicked and screamed in Jeff's arms.

Trashcans were lined up on both sides of the dusty alley road where few cars traveled. Mudge held me in a headlock. He leaned over, still holding my arms, and picked up a piece of wood with rusty nails in it. He handed it to Jerry. I noticed Jerry didn't seem as excited as his brothers to punish me. I saw something different in his eyes.

Jerry let the wood drop.

"I don't want to fight him," he said, staring at the ground. "Just take him back home! And don't ever bring him back here again. I hate him!"

I could live with that.

Too bad the Clark brothers couldn't.

Mudge dragged me closer to Jerry.

"Are you going to be a big sissy about this? This is your chance to get revenge. Bust him in his nose and make it flatter than it already is!"

Jerry wouldn't look up.

"Are you scared of him or something?"

"No."

Jeff grabbed Jerry and pushed him up against me.

Mudge pinned my arms behind me with one hand and whacked me hard on the back of the head with the other.

"See, do it just like that! I've got his arms, so go ahead and smack him in his charcoal face so we can see if he cries real tears or black oil!"

I gritted my teeth. My eyes welled up, but I was not going to cry when he hit me.

Jeff was foaming at the mouth.

"Leave him alone!" Patsy screamed. "Or I'm gonna tell!"

"No you're not!" Mudge barked. "And even if you do, it won't matter. All we have to do is say he ran over here and started another fight with our brother again for no reason. You know how violent they are. Jerry had to defend himself and beat him up! Do you really think they're gonna take a nigger-lover's side?"

"My mother and father will... and then they'll tell the police!"

She tried to run away but Jeff snatched her by her pigtails and swung her to the ground. This time Mudge didn't stop him. Jeff pulled her back up by her hair and wrapped her in his arms as she kicked and tried to bite him.

"Whew! She's a little wolverine!" Jeff chuckled.

"Let me go! My father is gonna machinegun you when he gets back!"

"We'll be moved by the time your father gets here from the army! And since our little brother is acting like a scared chump, we'll have to show him how we treat darkies that want to live with White people."

"I didn't want to move here!" I truthfully cried.

"Shut up! And Patsy, if you say one word to anybody, we'll show you how we treat White traitors who want to be friends with these spear-chuckers!"

Jeff jerked Patsy's head back by the pigtails, causing her to wince in pain. He slapped his hand over her mouth to muffle her screams.

Mudge pushed my head down so that all I could see was a trail of ants streaming into a trashcan.

An explosion nearly burst my eardrums.

Chapter 14

The ground shook and all of a sudden it seemed like a roaring and fire-breathing dragon dropped down out of the skies as a cloud of dust swept over us along with heat and the smell of gasoline. Mudge loosened his grip enough so that I could raise my head. In front of me sat a bright red and shiny Chevrolet Impala. The engine angrily idled. A raspy voice hollered:

"Get your filthy fucking hands off of her!"

The commander of this fire-breathing demon was Vernon the Vampire! I'd never seen him up close so when he stepped out of his car wearing overalls, I understood why the kids called him a vampire. It wasn't just because of his blood red car or that he was often seen slinking into his house at sunrise...

Half his face was burned and scarred on one side. Yellow snaggleteeth sticking out of his mouth looked like a butcher had worked on them instead of a dentist. He had eyes like a chameleon with the left eye roaming all over the place. If Mattie saw him, she'd probably say he was "uglier than sin." But right now, both eyes glowered at Mudge and Jeff. I could easily see him pouncing on them and sucking the lifeblood out of their bodies.

"We're just funning with them, Mister Doru," Mudge said, letting me go.

Patsy slipped out of Jeff's arms. "Uh, uh... that's not true!" She pointed at them like they were suspects in a police lineup. "They planned to beat Samuel up and me, too, if I told on them!"

"She's lying!" Mudge barked.

"Patsy does not lie," Vernon snapped.

"Mr. Doru, honest... we weren't really going to hurt Patsy. She's just like us... SHE belongs here."

"I'm not like you, you liars! I'd never hurt Samuel... he's my best friend."

"Don't worry, they won't put another hand on you or Samuel ever again." Vernon the Vampire opened the car door and said softly, "You guys get in."

Both of us hesitated before Patsy said, "Come on, Samuel."

I'm not supposed to ride with strangers, but he lived across the street and just rescued us. He put a hand on Patsy's shoulder when she passed him to climb into the car. She flinched like a horse bugged by flies.

Vernon locked his good eye on the Clark brothers. "If you EVER threaten or touch them again, we'll have a different talk, and I guarantee you it won't be nice—got it?"

The way he said it was scarier than a crazy person cursing at you.

"Okay, but what's going on between that bush baby sitting in your car and us is really none of your business," Mudge replied, still trying to act tough.

"*Today* it is!" Vernon glanced at Patsy and grinned reassuringly.

The veins in Mudge's neck grew and he thumbed his nose like a boxer. Jerry always bragged about how he got into fights in other neighborhoods all the time. You could tell he was thinking about taking on Vernon.

Vernon may have been thin, but he had Popeye arms, and the gleam in his good eye seemed like he wished Mudge *would* start something.

Jeff pulled on Mudge's taut arm. Mudge slapped his

hand away and gave Vernon a hard stare. Vernon uttered a raspy laugh and hopped into his Chevy. Patsy and I practically sat on each other's lap as Vernon fired up the Chevy and floored the gas pedal. He sped past the Clark brothers who ducked from the dirt spewing out like a tidal wave from underneath those humongous tires.

I had never been inside a car that moved so blazingly fast. I was both scared and thrilled. We blew around the corner as if we never touched ground. Vernon's car leaped onto his driveway. We climbed out, and Vernon grabbed our hands and walked us across the street like a crossing guard.

We stood in front of my house in an uncomfortable silence until I finally mumbled, "Thank you, Mr. Doru."

"You're welcome, Sam!"

"You all right, Patsy?" he asked tenderly. Except his voice did not match the way he gazed at her.

"Uh, huh, thank you," Patsy answered, keeping her head bowed.

"Hey Patsy, you don't have to be shy around me. It's Vernon... come on, you know me... we're old friends. I can remember when you were born, girl. I think I was probably about 15 at the time."

Patsy grabbed my hand. "You want to play basketball, Sam?"

"Um, yeah, sure."

I don't know why Patsy seemed so ungrateful about Vernon saving us. Maybe she still thought he was a vampire.

I no longer believed he was one of the undead. If he was really a vampire, not only half his face would have been burned by the sunlight, it would have been his whole body. I'd learned my lesson with the Wolfbergs. We thought they were monsters and they turned out to be the nicest people in the world.

Sure, Vernon was scary looking, but so was Quasimo-do.

Although, Quasimodo did end up killing his brother...

"Patsy, it's a good thing we saved Samuel from those punks, huh?" Vernon asked.

"Uh, huh."

"I can't stand chumps like that... always playing big shots with someone they know they can bully and push around. I should have bust them in their mouths... picking on a nice colored kid and even worse—a girl! That takes no heart... But don't you worry, it won't happen again—I promise you that!"

I don't think Patsy realized how hard she was squeezing my hand. She bunched my fingers together so tightly I winced from the pain.

Another uneasy silence fell, then Vernon said, "Well, I guess I better finish cleaning Mama."

My father often joked that I needed a safety pin on my lips because I'd always pop off before thinking.

"You have to clean your mother?"

Vernon flashed his snaggletooth grin. "No, man... Momma died when I was little... I'm talking about my ride—the Red Hot Mama!" He pointed to his car. "It's one of the fastest cars in the City of Angels, man!"

"Wow! You ever win a racing contest?"

"Win?" I ain't never lost a race yet, buddy, and I've raced some of the best cats in the city. I street race all over the place... Mulholland Drive, Wilmington, Long Beach.... You name it—I've done it. Man, the second I get off work at the airport, I hop inside Mama and take off to the races."

"You fly planes, too?" I gasped.

He chuckled. "Only cars. I'm a baggage handler at Trans World Airlines."

"Will you take us racing with you one day?"

Patsy shot me an are-you-INSANE look.

"Your parents aren't going to let me do that. I race after I get off work."

"What time do you get off work?"

"Sam, I don't get off work until after midnight. Sometimes I have to work the graveyard shift and then I don't get back home until five or six in the morning."

This got Patsy's attention. She asked, "Y-You work in a graveyard?"

"Yep, along with all the other ghosts."

He may have expected us to laugh with him, but instead, we looked terrified.

"I'm kidding! The graveyard shift means you work all night until morning."

"Oh," I said. This explained why he came home at dawn.

I thought Patsy would be relieved, but she shuffled her feet uncomfortably.

"Sam, can we go play now?"

"Wait, hold on… Can I sit in the front seat of your car one day, Vernon?"

"Hell yeah, man… I'll even let you start it up and turn the steering wheel."

"You will?" I focused on the one eye to see if he was serious.

"Yeah! And I've got tons of car magazines and comics I'll let you borrow."

That sealed it. As far as I was concerned, he could do no wrong.

"Hey Vernon, you ever seen cars crash?"

Vernon rolled his good eye. "Have I seen cars crash??? Man I've…"

Suddenly Vernon straightened his posture and quickly took his hand out of his pocket and reached past me. His voice changed from Mr. Cool to Mr. Polite.

"Hello, Mrs. Cole. I'm Vernon, it's a pleasure to officially meet you."

"Oh, hi Vernon... YOU'RE the car washer! You don't miss a weekend!"

I hadn't heard my mother walk up. Amazing how parents can do that.

"Yes, Ma'am, that's me. Gotta keep the Red Hot Mama looking good!"

I could tell my mother was amused by the name of his car.

"You do a great job! It shines so much I need to put on sunglasses!"

"Thank you, Ma'am!"

My mother's smile dropped and she eyed me suspiciously. "So what's going on, Sam. Everything okay?"

Suddenly I was at a loss for words. I thought if I didn't hurry up and speak, Vernon might say he'd rescued us in the alley from the Clark brothers. And no matter what I'd say thereafter, I'd still be in trouble for disobeying her orders.

"Everything is A-okay, Mrs. Cole. They were playing on the grass and their ball rolled across the street so I brought it back to them and we got to talking... I hope that's all right with you."

"Of course! I was only afraid Sam was up to something he shouldn't be."

"Oh no, we've been talking about cars and comic books."

Saved again! I was so grateful. If he was a vampire I would have DONATED a pint of blood to him.

"You hit the nail on the head. Cars and comic books are his favorite subjects!" my mother replied.

He laughed. "Mine too. I was just telling Sam that one day, if I have your permission, he can come over and I'll raise the hood of my car so he can see my big racing engine and later I'll show him my collection of over a thousand comic books."

"Over a thousand?" I gasped. "Whoa!"

"I'm sure we can arrange it at some point. So you race cars?"

"Yes, Ma'am, that's a hobby of mine."

"He wins all his races!" I added.

"Sounds like more than a hobby. Congratulations!"

"Thank you. But sometimes winning comes with a price. That's how I got this beauty mark on my face."

My mother was an expert at acting like she'd never noticed.

"What? Ohhh... I see... well you're still handsome... How did it happen?"

"A stupid amateur racing accident... I thought would never happen to me."

"In the Red Hot Mama?" my mother asked.

"No, it happened on the Lions Drag Strip on a raceway in Wilmington. Street racing is my thing now, but when I first got into racing I started out on a drag racing track. At the time, I owned this beet red dragster called 'Vernon's Bloody Thrill.'"

I could feel Patsy's eyes boring a hole through mine.

"...I was flying past all these cars, knowing I was about to beat Duke Favors, one of the top drag racers in the country. I got too greedy on the curve and gunned the engine. My car overturned three times and my fuel tank exploded. They pulled me out of the car, but not before 40% of my body was burned... part of it you see in my face. If I took off my shirt you'd see all the burns on the right side of my body."

"I'm sorry to hear that. But I have to ask—why in the world would you want to keep racing after all you've gone through?"

"Can't really say, Mrs. Cole. I guess it's in my blood... the thrill... the danger... feeling the rush of the wind as you zoom down the track... I love that!"

"As Chuck Berry said, 'Getting your kicks on Route 66,' huh?"

"Now you got it!" he laughed. "Well, time to get back to Mama. A pleasure talking to you, Mrs. Cole. See you, kids!"

"Good talking to you, too. Take care, Vernon!"

My mother bumped me. "Say goodbye!"

"Bye Vernon!"

Patsy kinda waved.

As soon as Vernon got across the street he went back to polishing his car.

"Vernon's a little strange, but he seems like a good guy; don't you think?" my mother asked Patsy and me.

"Uh, huh," I replied, for both of us.

"Esther told me he's been living in that house alone for years. Oddly enough, his parents died in a car crash when he was only four. He ended up here because his grandparents took him in. He inherited their house after they died a year apart a few years ago. He was 18. Ester thinks his obsession with cars has a lot to do with his parents dying in a car crash. I wonder if he has a girl..."

I never heard the rest. I chased after Patsy who ran into the backyard and started shooting hoops.

Patsy angrily clanked shot after shot off the rim, under the backboard, over the hoop, and over the wall into her yard. Each time I went and retrieved it, and she'd go right back to her horrible shooting.

"What's wrong with you?" I questioned.

"Nothing."

"Are you mad at me?"

"No."

"Then what's wrong?"

"Nothing." She clenched her teeth as she aimed the ball at the basket and shot an air ball.

"You're a liar, Patsy!"

Patsy frowned. "No I'm NOT!"

"Yes you are, you're acting stupid!"

"DON'T CALL ME STUPID!" Patsy raged, marching towards me with one fist balled up. She tried to hold the basketball crocked in her other arm, but dropped it several times.

She pushed me. "TAKE IT BACK—NOW!"

I pushed her back. "Or what?"

I really didn't want to fight her... not just because my father would get mad... because she was my only friend on the block.

"Or... or... I'm going home and I'm never ever-ever coming back again!"

"So don't!"

"I won't!"

She whipped me in the face with her stinging pigtails as she turned. But she walked as slow as a snail to the front gate. She unlatched it, then whirled around and ran back up to me.

"So you like Vernon now because he helped us?"

"Yeah. Why shouldn't I?"

"Because he's a vampire."

"No he's not, Patsy!"

"Yes he is!"

"Everybody thought Mr. and Mrs. Wolfberg were monsters, too!"

"He's for sure a vampire!"

"Why would a vampire save us from the Clark brothers?"

She slid down onto the pavement with her back against the wall. She picked up the basketball and hugged it like a teddy bear. I sat next to her.

"I don't know. He looks at me real funny."

"He can't help that. He has a bad eye."

"No... it's something else. He looks at me like he wants

to eat me."

"Vampires don't eat you, they suck your blood."

"Yeah," she murmured and then looked at me hopeful-ly. "But don't you think he's weird?"

"Yeah, I guess so, but..."

"Oh goody! We can be best friends again!" She dropped the ball and grabbed me in a rocking hug.

I pushed her away... which didn't bother her a bit... Patsy was Patsy again.

Chapter 15

Patsy happily jumped up and down like she had swallowed a pogo stick. She waved for me to toss her the ball. As usual, it popped out of her hands. Patsy picked the ball up and cradled it in her arms. She paced back and forth.

"What's wrong now?" I asked.

"We have to prove Vernon is a vampire."

I rolled my eyes and grit my teeth.

"Why?" I asked.

"If we don't do something, I could be his next victim. You saw how he looked at me."

Vernon had given her odd looks.

"So how are we going to prove he's a vampire?"

She sat down on my basketball and rubbed her chin in deep thought.

Finally, she raised her forefinger and shouted, "I got it!"

This couldn't be good.

"We'll break into his house!"

"What? We can't do that! I'm not getting arrested and put in jail!"

"It's the only way, Samuel. We need to find evidence in the house he's a vampire... like a coffin, a black cape, pet bats, a dead body, anything..."

"Uh, uh... I'm not doing that! That's too scary!"

"No it's not. I thought you weren't a fraidy-cat?"

"I'm not!"

"Then why are you afraid of vampires?"

"I'm not *afraid* of no vampires!"

I was.

"Okay, so I DARE you to go inside Vernon's house with me."

Oh, no... not the *dare*!

"Fine, I'll go!" I sighed.

"Good. But we need to do this as soon as possible."

"Wait! I just remembered... I can't."

"Why not?" she asked.

"Things are still bad. My parents don't want me going across the street!"

Patsy grabbed me by the shoulders and pressed her forehead against mine as she gazed into my eyes.

"Samuel, do you want your parents to die?"

"No!" I said pushing her back a little.

"Well it's our fault if Vernon kills our parents and everybody here! Samuel, we have to be superheroes, like Wonder Woman and Batman."

"I wanna be Superman!"

"Okay, you're Superman and I'm Wonder Woman."

"But what if we have to fight him?"

Pretending can only go so far.

"No, silly, once we find some evidence, we'll let people know. Then our fathers can drive a stake through his heart and burn up his coffin and house."

"How are we going to get into his house?"

"Don't worry. I've got a plan..."

She clasped her hands around my head and whispered into my ear. I couldn't help giggling because her lips tickled. We were the only ones in the backyard, but Patsy smartly didn't want to be overheard since vampires and bats have a powerful hearing range.

It was a pretty good plan. My mother had started working part time again at the store and was dropped off at work by my father on his lunch break. We convinced her to let me stay at Patsy's and her mother would babysit us. Mrs. McGuire's babysitting was telling us to go play in the backyard or watch TV. Since she was close to giving birth, she slept all the time—officially napping around 3:00 pm, the same time Vernon usually left for the airport.

The next day we sat at Patsy's front window and watched Vernon get into his car, back out of the driveway, and head to work. Once we were sure it was safe, Patsy turned the volume up on the TV so her mother would hear it through the closed door of her bedroom. Then we tip-toed out the front door, shutting it softly.

We waited for what seemed like a century for no cars to appear before carefully crossing the two-way street. Most people worked during the day, so I don't think any-body noticed us turning the knob of Vernon's small side gate and sneaking into the backyard. The first thing I saw in Vernon's yard was a huge patio with a barbecue grill. But no graveyard or coffin in sight. I smirked at Patsy, but she ignored me and pointed at the grill.

"Look, ashes! Bet he burns the bodies here so nobody can find them." She rubbed a finger across the grill and held it up so I could see the black smudge.

"No, vampires are afraid of fire. C'mon, Patsy, let's get back to your house before your mother wakes up and finds out we're gone."

"Uh, uh, he's too smart to keep his coffin outside... it's in the house."

I groaned. "Patsy, did you hear me? Let's go! There's nothing here."

"No, Samuel, we need to find out what's inside. And then, cross my heart, we'll leave and I'll never talk about it again... Girl Scout's honor!"

"But you're not a Girl Scout... you're not even a Brown-ie."

She yanked on the backdoor. "It's locked!"

"Okay. So can we go now?"

"Not yet. Let's see if we can climb in through the window."

I looked at her like she'd lost her mind.

"They're too high. How are we going to get up there to break in?"

"Easy." She motioned for me to follow her.

She led me to what looked like it might be the bedroom window. It was lower than the other ones. From our angle it looked like it was cracked open.

"We can't get up there without a ladder. I bet it's locked in his garage."

"Yeah..." She chewed on her lip as she thought about it.

"Okay, then let's go right now... I don't see any cars in the street."

"Hold on. I've got an idea!"

Oh, no! I cupped my face with my hands.

Patsy trotted over to the patio and grabbed several orange crates she spotted. She excitedly put each crate on top of the other and pushed them against the wall below the window.

"Okay, Samuel, you can stand on these to get up there. Go ahead."

"Me?"

"Of course, silly! You're stronger and taller than me. I bet you can reach the windowsill."

Patsy motioned for me to climb the crate ladder. I just stared at it. What if I opened the window and a vampire bat flew out? They suck blood, too.

"Superman would not be scared!"

"Superman can fly."

Finally I gave in and hoisted myself onto the crates. I shakily stood up.

"I can't reach the windowsill, Patsy."

"Yes you can! Just pull yourself up, silly."

Guess she could tell my hands were overlapping the ledge.

I pulled myself up with my elbows planted on the ledge. I could see the window was cracked enough for me to push it open all the way.

Below, Patsy loudly whispered, "See anything?"

"Just a water hose."

"In the house?"

"Yeah."

The bright glare of the sunlight made it hard to see, but I saw a very thick water hose coiled in the corner of the window. It had really interesting colors, too—grayish with dark brown and red patterns. I eased my fingers underneath the window. Just as I was about to push it up, the hose moved!!!

What I'd thought was a spray nozzle on the hose rose up and floated in the air facing me. It took me a moment to realize I was staring into the muddy eyes of a giant snake. Its jaws opened wide, showcasing rows of curved, needle-sharp teeth.

I was so frightened I tried to scream but nothing came out. Patsy did scream as I spun around and fell off the ledge and crashed into her. We fell onto the grass and I got hit on the head by the orange crates falling on top of us.

"What in the world happened?" she asked, pushing the crates aside.

All I could do was point at the window. Patsy screamed again after seeing the huge snake flattened across the window.

"It's the Devil's serpent!" Patsy cried.

We scrambled to get out of the backyard. As we tried to squeeze out the narrow gate at the same time, we ran smack dab into the arms of Vernon the Vampire!

"Hey! What the hell are you guys doing here?"

"Get out of my way!" Patsy yelled.

"Yeah, there's a big snake chasing us!" I frantically explained.

"What? Freda got out?"

He looked worried—but not for us—for the snake. He angrily gripped both of us by the arm and jerked us into the backyard.

"Let me go!" Patsy yelled. "Or I'll scream REAL loud!"

"Go ahead—do it—scream your lungs out, so I can tell your mothers how I found you in my backyard without permission! For all I know, you were trying to break in and steal my stuff!"

Vernon eyeballed the window and saw the snake's head hovering again. "Oh, good… lucky for you guys, Freda's still inside. She must have gotten out of her aquarium again. Everything's fine."

Except us. Nevertheless, he did let go of us.

"Stay right here!" he commanded as he walked over to the window.

"It's okay, my little baby, Daddy will be there in a minute to feed you," he cooed sweetly, kissing the window before shutting it completely down.

I was sure Patsy and I were thinking the same thing—feed her what?

But neither of us tried to run. Vernon came back.

"What am I going to do about you cornballs? Tell your folks?"

"No, please, don't… we're really sorry," I pleaded.

Patsy nodded in agreement.

"So what are you guys doing in my backyard? The only reason I came back is because I forgot my wallet."

Patsy and I looked at each other. Ordinarily, Patsy was the fast talker, but I had more at stake. I wouldn't be able to sit down for a lifetime if my parents got the news I crossed the street AND tried to break into Vernon's house.

So I started yakking.

"We didn't know your car was gone... we thought it was in the garage or something... and we really wanted to see your comic books... so when you didn't answer the front door we came to the back... and I started pounding on the window and that's when I saw your snake... and..."

"Okay, forget it... I believe you," he said, cutting me short. He gave Patsy that sickening grin again.

Patsy didn't see it because she was looking at me in amazement like—Wow, that came out of you?

"Okay, I'll let you see my comic books, but it will have to be a quick tour because I've got to go to work. Let me put Freda in her aquarium first. I'll be right back," Vernon said excitedly.

The second he stepped inside his house, Patsy tugged on my arm.

"C'mon, let's go!"

"Uh, uh... I can't."

"What do you mean, you can't?"

"If he tells on us I'll get a whipping!"

"I thought you told me your father said he would never spank you again?"

"This might be bad enough to make him change his mind."

"I'm not going into his house with that monster snake inside!"

"You're the one who said we need to find out once and for all if he's a vampire or not."

"That was before I saw the snake. Aren't you afraid of snakes?"

"NO," I lied, trying hard not to blink.

"Yes you are! You told me you have nightmares about being stuck in a cave filled with a thousand snakes!"

"Not anymore!"

The backdoor opened and Vernon giddily waved for

us to come in.

I trudged to the door like I was walking the plank with a sword at my back.

"You're really going in there?" Patsy whispered, astonished.

I unsurely nodded.

Patsy sighed, "Okay... wait for me."

She grabbed my shirttail and followed from behind as we walked into Vernon's house. The second we stepped inside, a horrible odor hit us. Patsy frowned and pinched her nose behind Vernon's back. I wanted to do a U-turn but it was too late.

The sun shined brightly outdoors—but you'd never know it inside Vernon's living room. We didn't have to look for the coffin anymore, the coffin was his house. The curtains were drawn so tightly I felt like I was inside a dark cave. Clothes were thrown everywhere: on the floor, on the couch, on the dining room table. Food crumbs made their home all over the carpet, and half of an old pizza sat on the coffee table. As we followed Vernon through the kitchen, I saw dirty food-stained dishes piled high in the sink and stacked on the countertops.

"Bet your parents would have a heart attack if they saw this, huh? Maybe I can get you guys to help me do the dishes later, whatcha think?" he chuckled.

Not funny, but we laughed anyway to get on his best side. I hoped he wouldn't blackmail us and force us to wash his dishes as a tradeoff for not telling on us. He led us into his bedroom. Surprisingly, it turned out to be the neatest and cleanest room in the house. To me it was comic book heaven—mountains of comics everywhere and cardboard cartons filled to the top with comic books. His bookcases were loaded with books and magazines on cars and auto mechanics. Comic book superheroes and classic car posters hung from his bedroom walls.

"Feast on all the comic books you'll ever want to read, Samuel. Whatever you want—I got!" he boasted.

I reached out for one.

"Uh, uh... wash your hands first," he ordered, pointing to the bathroom. "I don't want them to get dirty, might turn out to be real valuable one day."

"Okay."

"I'll go wash mine too," Patsy said, still holding on to my shirt.

I could tell she didn't want to be in the bedroom alone with him. He kept gawking at her with that strange smile. It wasn't just because of his paralysis.

While we washed our hands, Patsy whispered, "I want to go home, Samuel. This is creepy."

"All right. Let me look at some of his comics first, so he doesn't get mad and then we'll leave!"

"Hurry up!"

He had every comic book in the world: *Archie, Superman, Batman and Robin, Captain America, Flash, Richie Rich, Aquaman, Captain Marvel, Green Arrow, The Hawkman, Wonder Woman...* and new ones like *The Fantastic Four* and *The Atom*. I was in awe of all the comics he had. I didn't know where to begin.

Like a leaky faucet, Patsy tapped her foot as she nervously sat on the edge of the bed while I sorted through Vernon's comics. "Samuel, we're going to get in big trouble if we don't leave pretty soon!" Patsy insisted.

"Okay, okay, one more second." It was tough to put down *Green Lantern*.

"Wait, before you guys leave, you want to meet Freda?"

"No! I don't want to. We have to go, NOW!" Patsy insisted, shuffling her legs like she had to go to the bathroom.

"Just take a peek. I put her back in her aquarium. She

can't hurt you."

"You promise?"

"Sam, I promise! You guys will be safe. Come on. She's in the other room."

Despite Patsy's protests, I was really curious. I'd never seen a snake up close, especially a big one, except at the zoo.

"Patsy, you can stay here alone, if you're scared." Vernon winked at me.

"No, I'm coming."

"Good. You don't have to be frightened. You're a big girl. You don't need your Mommy. I bet you're old enough to sleep alone in your own room now, huh?"

Patsy acted like she didn't hear him.

Chapter 16

Vernon's second bedroom was like a natural history museum. Millions of things were on his bookshelves: stones, sculptures, seashells, rings, and bracelets. Even so, my eyes were glued to the huge glass aquarium.

"There's my sweet girl," Vernon announced lovingly as he proudly caressed the glass tank. "Isn't she beautiful?"

At first I didn't even see the snake because it was so well camouflaged against the log inside the tank. Freda slithered slowly forward when she heard Vernon's voice. I was fascinated the way her muscles looked every time she moved. My eyes zigzagged to the top of the tank to make sure the lid was shut.

"You guys can move a little closer. You can't see her way back there."

When I finally got the nerve to inch forward, Vernon said, "Boa constrictors are pretty good escape artists..."

I stepped six inches back.

"Where you goin', Sammy? All I'm saying is, when I first built this tank my baby got out all the time. See, boas are strong and crafty. I forgot to lock the top before I left. She was out sunning, trying to get a tan like you, Sammy. Ha! Ha!"

I was so on edge, I jumped like a cricket when he patted my head.

"Whoa, easy, man... it's okay, everything's cool. Move

closer so you can really see her. You too, Patsy, you don't need to hold up the bookcase. Ha!"

Patsy shook her head no.

"Oooh, Freda's moving again," I said.

"She's just exploring, checking you out, Sammy. I think she likes you."

"Are you serious?"

"Yeah, man. Don't be afraid, because then you'll make her nervous."

I'm not gonna lie, I was afraid. Still, it was so interesting to watch Freda move along the tank like a giant muscle.

"How big is she?"

"Hmmm, about 10 feet long. She'll get even larger. The Red Tail Boa can grow up to 14 feet and live over 20 years."

"Wow!"

I even got comfortable enough to press my face against the glass; I could see my breath every time I spoke. Inside Freda's tank there was a bowl of water and tiny lights covered by a screen on the underside of the tank top. I guess the screen was to keep Freda from burning herself. She flicked her tongue in my face and I jumped back. I glanced back excitedly at Patsy.

"Hey Patsy. Come here. You should see her tongue!"

"Yeah, Patsy, you should," Vernon echoed.

Patsy ignored us and examined the things on Vernon's bookshelves.

"You know why she flicks her tongue don't you?" Vernon asked.

"Uh, uh."

"Her tongue acts like your eyes and ears. She uses it to take stuff out of the air, and then she can put it on the roof of her mouth and tell whether you are a prey, a mate, or an enemy. If she thought you were dangerous, you'd be in trouble."

"Does she know I want to be her friend?"

"Oh yeah, man, cuz you're with me. She may be a cold-blooded reptile, but she's very affectionate."

"She is?"

"Uh, huh... I can take her out and show you," Vernon replied eagerly.

"NO!" Patsy said. She held a clear rock into the sunlight from the window.

"That's one of my rock crystals... beautiful isn't it?"

Patsy quickly placed the rock back on the shelf. When Vernon turned away, she mouthed to me—LET'S GO!

I mouthed—Okay—but I had to ask a couple more questions.

"When was the last time she ate?"

"Two days ago."

"She's not hungry?"

"Probably not. They're not like us. It can take a constrictor four to five days to digest its food. She may not eat again for another week... maybe even a month."

"Would she eat a human?"

"They have killed people—but it's very rare. They'll only do that when they feel threatened or no other food is available. When they do eat their prey, they kill it by constriction, meaning they squeeze it to death. Boas are carnivorous, they like to eat meat, so I usually feed Freda rats and mice I get from the pet store."

"Where I used to live she could have eaten all kinds of mice!"

"Yeah? I find some in the alleys every once in a while. In the wilds, boas eat rodents, birds, lizards, bats, and bigger mammals like a wild dog or an ocelot."

"Isn't an ocelot a cat?" Patsy suddenly asked with her back to us.

Vernon's eyes narrowed to slits. "Yep, that's right... an ocelot is part of the cat family. You're a pretty smart girl,

Patsy."

"I knew that," I lied.

Patsy kept her back to us as she fiddled with items on the shelves.

Vernon talked some more about boas until there was a loud CLANG!! Turning around we found Patsy gaping at a bracelet lying on the hardwood floor. It didn't look broken, but she looked horrified.

"Pick it up, silly," I teased.

Patsy stared more fearfully at the bracelet than she ever had at Freda.

Vernon scooped up the bracelet and placed it back on the shelf.

"Hello... calling Miss Patsy... are you there?" He wiggled his fingers in her face. "You don't have to worry about the bracelet. It's not broken."

Patsy nodded, but she didn't look up.

"Oh, you're probably wondering why I have a girl's bracelet. It's a birthday gift for my cousin's daughter. Actually, I'm glad you dropped it. I forgot her birthday is this weekend. I need to get it gift-wrapped. You know how to do that?"

Patsy moved her head from side to side in slow motion. When she finally looked up, the expression on her face shocked me. Her usually rosy cheeks were pale. Her eyes darted around the bedroom as if ghosts were floating out of the walls.

"I think I'm gonna throw up, Samuel."

She ran over and locked onto my arms like handcuffs. Her skin was super-hot, sticky, and wet. Ordinarily I'd push her away so she wouldn't vomit on me... but something told me not to. I felt like she really needed me.

"Yeah, Sammy's right. You don't look so swell, Patsy... maybe you're catching a cold or the flu. Here, I'll walk you kids back home," Vernon offered sweetly. Yet his eyes looked like he was drilling a hole through her.

My hands sweated as we crossed the street. That look was evil. Patsy refused to hold the hand Vernon offered, brushing it away, while crunching mine.

Once we got across the street, Patsy took off like a lion was chasing her. She fumbled to open her door and rushed inside.

Vernon curtly stated, "That was rude. She could have said goodbye."

"I think she had to throw up."

"Uh, huh. Sammy, keep in mind, this visit is our little secret. I don't want you to tell your parents or anyone else about Freda. Some people don't understand how reptiles can make great pets. You got me?"

"Okay."

"Tell Patsy she needs to keep quiet, too. Long as you kids are cool and don't say nothing, I won't either. If you do talk and your folks come at me, I'll tell them everything."

"I won't say nothing."

Vernon had spoken softly, but his words were as loud as thunder. His eyes were fixed in a weird way on Patsy's house. It made me very uneasy.

"Why was Patsy acting so funny at my house?"

"I think she was sick. She really is afraid of snakes. She's not like me."

"I don't care if Patsy was sick! You be sure to go inside and make sure she gets my message to keep her mouth shut!"

"I will."

"Shit!" he glanced at his wristwatch, "I shouldn't have let you kids into my bedroom. That's what I get for trying to be nice!"

I tried to lighten things up.

"Thanks for letting us see your comic books and meet Freda!"

Vernon rolled his eyes like I had said something really dumb. He crossed the street, ignoring the cars skidding to a stop and honking at him. He yanked his keys out of his pocket and got inside his car. He slowly backed out and then abruptly maneuvered the car to our side of the street, again, not caring who was honking and cursing at him.

He sat in front of Patsy's house with the car idling. I offered a friendly wave that wasn't returned. He sneered before stomping the accelerator and jetting down the street, cutting madly between cars, tailgating, and bullying cars to get out of his way. A firework of sparks blazed from his tires.

I leaped over the hedge and ran to Patsy's front door. I lightly knocked even though Patsy had left it wide open.

"Come on in, Sam!" Patsy's mother wearily yelled.

The first thing I saw when I went inside was Mrs. McGuire wearing a beige robe over a flowery muumuu dress. Her curly dark brown hair was messy, half of it hanging in big loopy curlers. One hand was cupped under her medicine ball stomach. Her forehead was planted against the closed bathroom door as she jiggled the doorknob.

"Patsy, are you okay?" she asked through the door.

I heard a groan and a flush of the toilet.

"I'm fine, Mommy." Another groan, an abrupt waterfall, and another flush.

"No you're not!" her mother fired back. She banged louder. "Open up so I can take a look at you. Didn't you hear me yelling for you earlier?"

"No. We were in Samuel's garage reading comics."

At least the comic book part was true.

"Do you know what's wrong with her, Sam? Did she eat something bad?"

"Huh? No, uh, uh, we haven't eaten anything."

"I figured. That's why I've been calling you guys. I made you some hot dogs."

"You did? Yay! Thanks, Mrs. McGuire! With buns?"

My mother would have killed me if she heard me ask that.

"Of course, silly! What's a hot dog without buns? Patsy, open the door!"

Now I banged on the door.

"Patsy, hurry up! Your mother made us some hot dogs!"

"Thank you, Samuel," Mrs. McGuire said.

More shuffling in the bathroom before the toilet flushed again. Water tinkled from the faucet then abruptly shut off. Patsy opened the door, wiping her hands on her pants. Her face was sugary white.

Her mother lifted her chin up and studied her face. "Your eyes are all red and puffy. You been crying?"

"No."

"Hmmm... you already had the measles... I don't see any blisters... doesn't look like chicken pox... you don't have the mumps... You feel like you're catching a cold or the flu?"

"No."

"Maybe you ought to come to bed with me and take a nap."

"No, Mommy, I'm okay now. Probably something I ate last night."

"Like all those See's Candies I told you to stop eating so much of?"

"Uh, huh."

"Yes, that's it! You need some real food in your system—go eat some of those hot dogs I made; that'll make you feel better. I left them in the oven with the temperature on low to stay warm. If your tummy is still upset afterwards, then it's time for a little Milk of Magnesia."

We both made a prune face. "Eeech!"

"It's your own fault for eating all that candy last night!"

"You ate more than me!"

"GO! I'm sure Samuel's starving. I don't want his mother angry with me for not feeding him! I'll be in the bedroom watching TV if you need me. Gotta go!"

Mrs. McGuire dashed into the bathroom hurriedly raising her gown. As she closed the door she complained, "This baby won't come soon enough!"

"You don't want any Oscar Mayer Wieners?" I spread a thick layer of sweet pickle relish over my hot dog.

"No. I don't feel like eating."

I bit into the hot dog and closed my eyes, loving the taste. I broke into a happy hot dog dance as I held it up. Patsy's mood cut my celebration short.

"What's wrong with you? You love hot dogs as much as me."

She stomped her foot. "Stop asking me stupid questions!"

"Stop being stupid!"

"NO, YOU STOP BEING STUPID!"

"Everything okay in there?" Mrs. McGuire yelled from her bedroom. "Are the hot dogs still warm?"

"Yes, Mommy, we're just playing a game!"

"Not in the kitchen! If you want to play, take your food outside!"

"Okay, Mommy. We'll be in Samuel's garage!"

"If I call you, you better answer!"

"I will."

"But I want to stay in the kitchen to eat another hot dog!"

"Samuel, stop whining! We'll take some with us! Here!"

She grabbed two paper plates out of the cabinet and slapped two hot dogs and buns on one. She covered it with the other plate and handed it to me.

"What about mustard and relish and catsup?"

Rolling her eyes, Patsy grabbed packs of mustard and relish and catsup. She cocked her head for me to follow as she marched toward the backdoor.

"Why can't we go out front and eat on the porch?"

"Samuel, why can't you just SHUT UP and follow me?" She grabbed her Barbie purse and held it like there was a million bucks inside.

"YOU shut up!"

Even though she pissed me off, I trailed behind her. I really didn't care where we ate. I just didn't like a girl ordering me around. But then I remembered Vernon and his glare might be waiting for us out front.

Patsy, eyes glazed, sat quietly on the concrete garage floor with her purse in her lap while I finished eating my last hot dog. Even after I was done and licking the catsup off my fingers she didn't say anything. For the time being, I was fine with that. I stalled to avoid talking for long as I could, picking my teeth and sucking on peppermint-flavored toothpicks. After a while, I broke down.

"Vernon's not a vampire, Patsy."

"I know," she replied in a crackly voice.

"What? You do?"

"Yes."

I looked confused.

"He's not a vampire—he's a killer."

The sweet relish between my teeth suddenly tasted bitter.

"Huh?"

"Vernon killed Comet."

"Comet? *Your* cat?"

Her eyes filled with tears. She began wringing her hands.

"Everybody always says Comet ran away or got hit by a car, or lives with a family on another block ... but they're all wrong. Vernon murdered him!"

"You don't know that!"

"YES-I-DO!"

I angrily spit out the limp toothpick.

"Patsy, stop making up stories!"

"I'm not making it up!" she cried. "Vernon stole my cat and killed him."

"But Vernon likes animals," I countered. "Why would he do that?"

"To feed him to Freda."

That shut me up.

Hands shaking, Patsy snapped open her purse and reached inside. She handed me an object that made MY hands tremble.

"Look, that's Comet's collar. I found it on Vernon's bookshelf. And it wasn't the only one I saw."

"Here, get this away from me!" I insisted, tossing the collar back at Patsy like it was diseased. I didn't want to believe it.

"M-Maybe Comet WAS hit by a car and Vernon found the collar and just kept it. He might not have known it was your cat's."

"He knew. He used to come over and pat Comet all the time... he knew."

Patsy sniffed as a ton of tears fell. She tried to wipe them away with the back of her hand but they spilled through her fingers. "As soon as I saw the blue collar with stars on it, I knew it was Comet's. See here on the inside? Mommy helped me write his name there."

I didn't need to look. I believed her.

"I snuck the collar inside my pocket while you guys looked at Freda... That's when I accidentally knocked the bracelet off of the shelf."

Patsy got a faraway look in her eyes then fixed her gaze on me.

"Samuel, you know that bracelet I dropped..."

"Yeah?" I had a feeling this was something I didn't want to hear.

"It was Suzie's."

"Suzie? Who's that?"

"You know… Suzie North… Her mother is the one who drives by."

It hit me like a missile. I gasped out loud. "Wait… you mean your babysitter? The girl who used to live here? The missing one?"

The dam burst. Patsy reached out to me like I was a life raft. She looped her arms around my neck and almost suffocated me. Her tears dampened the neck of my T-shirt. But I was all right with that. I held her, too.

"Oh Samuel," she wailed, "I'm so scared. What am I going to do? He knows I know the truth about him. He wants to kill me."

"No he doesn't, Patsy. Quit saying stuff like that."

"Samuel, I think he killed Suzie. Maybe she found out the truth about him like we did. That's why he has to kill me—and you, too!"

"Why does he have to kill me? I didn't do anything!"

"You were there. You saw the bracelet. He knows I'm going to tell you whose bracelet it is because you're my best friend."

I pushed her away and retreated to the other side of the garage, as if it was safer there. I sat on my father's workbench and clapped my hands to my head.

"We're NOT best friends! I would never let a girl be my best friend."

The grenade I'd lobbed didn't faze her one bit. She came over and sat next to me, smushing her body against mine. This time I didn't push her away.

"I'm sorry I made you do this, Samuel. I really thought he was a vampire."

"It's okay, Patsy." I rubbed my headachy forehead.

When I thought about it, I remembered Vernon's whole face had changed after she dropped the bracelet. His friendly gaze turned into a granite stare. And when we crossed the street and Patsy broke away and ran into her house, I couldn't forget how Vernon targeted her like a space alien with a ray gun. It was obvious to me now that he wanted to keep our visit a secret... for his protection—not ours.

Chapter 17

"You know what, Patsy?"

"What?"

"Vernon is the bogeyman!"

Patsy almost flipped off the bench. "You really think so, Samuel?"

"Uh, huh. The bogeyman is the only one that does evil things to children and their pets. He hates animals like cats and dogs because they can sense who he is. Sooner or later, Vernon was gonna do something bad to us, whether we found out about him or not."

"Yeah, yeah… you're right, Samuel, that's exactly who Vernon is—he's the bogeyman!" Patsy declared.

She seemed kinda relieved by knowing this as she bobbed restlessly up and down on the bench. Her efforts to prove that Vernon was a vampire were not in vain after all. He still turned out to be a monster… Not that it made things better for us… it was just good we figured it out.

"Poor Suzie. Do you think she might be still alive? Maybe Vernon's got her trapped in a basement or a secret room in his house."

"No, I don't think so, Patsy."

All of a sudden she bawled, "I want my Daddy! He'd kill ugly Vernon with a machine gun or run a tank over him."

Sounded like a good solution to all our troubles, but I didn't think he'd get here in time before Vernon killed us.

Leave it to Patsy… she had a backup plan.

"Hey, what about *your* dad? You told me he could beat up a *T-rex*!"

"He can. But I can't say nothing about this."

"How come?"

"If we're wrong, Vernon will tell on us and I'll get a whupping!"

"So let's call the police and get him arrested!"

"Nah, they won't do nuthin'. My father calls them all the time. Sometimes they don't even show up. They'll just laugh and say we're making up stories."

"We have to do something—quick! Vernon HAS to get rid of us now that we know his terrible secret."

I scratched my head like it would stir something up in my brain. We were in a no-win situation. If I told my father I went across the street without permission, he'd whip me before I'd even got to the bogeyman part of the story. Worse, after the beating, I still might get killed by Vernon or kidnapped and taken to some hellish place where the bogeyman hides children and then eventually eats them.

"Hey Samuel, wouldn't Vernon be afraid to get caught if he tried to do something to us? He'd have to go to prison forever!"

"He don't care about that. No one has ever captured the bogeyman. That's why he never got caught dragging Suzie away."

Patsy cried again, "I want my Daddy!"

I touched my finger to her lips. "Shhhhh, you don't want to let Vernon hear you. The bogeyman gets stronger when he knows you're afraid of him."

"Samuel, he doesn't have to murder us by himself… He could sneak Freda into our house while we're asleep and let her swallow us up."

"Boas don't like human flesh."

"Vernon said they will eat humans if they're really

starved!"

"He's not going to sic Freda on us. He'd have to carry her giant body across the street and hope no one sees him."

"What if we never leave the house or backyard? He can't do anything, right?"

I started scratching my head again. "I guess... but we have to make sure everything is locked up real tight in our houses so that he can't find a way to slip inside."

So that was our plan. For several days, Patsy and I played inside our houses and in our backyards. Not once did we roam out to our front yards unless a parent stood out front, too. After the incident with the Clark boys, Patsy no longer played in their front yard, but hardly anyone did. Many of the kids and their families had already moved away.

Once, we peeped through my curtains with binoculars and caught Vernon doing the same thing. He opened the curtain wider and we jerked ours closed. Another interesting thing was, Vernon never parked his car out front anymore. He must have done this on purpose because now we never knew for sure if he was home or not. We figured it was a trap to catch us if we ever tried to sneak into his backyard again. That was NOT gonna happen.

What DID happen was, we were in my bedroom playing the board game Candy Land when we were interrupted by a hard knock followed by the doorknob jiggling. We almost skyrocketed through the ceiling.

"Why is your door locked, Samuel? Open up! You've got a visitor!"

A visitor? I didn't get many of those. My mother said it with such cheerfulness I quickly unlock the door, excited to see who it was. Maybe Edgar or the twins had finally dropped by for a surprise visit.

My mother stepped aside and gestured for the mystery guest to come in. "Look who's here!"

Patsy gagged like she was being choked.

Vernon stood in the doorway. Grinning broadly, his good eye zeroed in on Patsy.

"Hey kids! What's cooking?"

Thanks to my mother—US!

"Nothing," I said, acting blasé.

"Where you guys been? Traveling to France? Italy? Spain?" Vernon asked good-heartedly, although I detected a slight edge in his voice.

"Hardly," my mother answered. "The only traveling they've done lately has been from the bedroom to the backyard to the garage."

"Maybe today they can try something different, Mrs. Cole, with your permission of course," Vernon remarked in his fake good guy voice.

"Tell them what you've got planned. I think they'll be so excited!"

"I was telling your mother, Sam, that I don't have to go to work till a lot later today, so, I wanted to see if you guys would like to come over for lunch? I'm making hamburgers on my grill in the backyard. You can bring your board game with you. I mainly want to show you guys my huge collection of comic books I've been bragging about. What do you think? Want to come over?"

"Are you kidding? Ha! Ha! Samuel LOVES comic books! You don't even have to walk him across the street. He'll fly like Superman to get there!" my mother responded.

My head ached from Vernon's overly loud laughter.

Patsy didn't waste any time speaking up. "I don't think my mother will let me go… she's pregnant and…"

"I already talked to your mother, Patsy, she's fine about it. Vernon stopped by there first. Then she called to let me know it's okay."

Patsy's face might have been comical if it hadn't come

from fear.

"I want to, Mrs. Cole, but I was getting ready to go home. I don't feel good... my stomach aches."

She keeled over and held her stomach to prove it.

I wanted to scream—LIAR! Mainly because she stole my excuse.

"Oh, I'm sorry, Patsy," my mother said, gently rubbing her back.

"Yeah, me too," Vernon said sympathetically, but his Cyclops' eye flashed larger than usual.

Not to be outdone, I echoed Patsy. "Yeah, I don't feel very good either, Mom." I gasped like it was my last breath. I also bent over and grabbed my stomach. "I think both of us ate too much candy."

"My goodness, what is going on here? You guys need some Pepto Bismol?"

"Yes, please," I said, barely raising my head as if a 100-pound weight was strapped around my neck. I hated Pepto Bismol, but if drinking it was going to get me out of this mess, then let it be.

My mother raised her eyebrow. This had to be serious. She knew there was no way I'd swallow that nasty-tasting pink stuff if it wasn't.

Vernon's face did not have the same worried look as my mother's even though he said, "Awww, that's too bad... Maybe you guys will feel better later and come over, even for only an hour, before I head to work."

He continued his fake smile when my mother said, "No, I think we better try this on another day, Vernon. I'm sure you understand."

"Of course I do," Vernon replied. "If you're sick, you're sick. I promise we'll try it again another day. I know how much they want to see those comic books!"

I don't know if my mother caught the tone in his voice, but we sure did. Patsy looked like she wanted to crash head first through my bedroom window and run.

Thankfully my mother said, "Let me walk you out, Vernon."

Vernon stiffly raised his hand to wave goodbye as he walked behind my mother, but not before turning his head and giving us a look that could slice through boulders.

I couldn't hear what was being said, but there was a brief conversation between them outside the front door. My mother returned to my bedroom holding a spoon and vigorously shaking a bottle of Pepto Bismol.

"Patsy, you're still here? I thought you were going home?"

Patsy sat on my bed, rocking back and forth, arms wrapped around her knees. "I'm feeling a little better now, Mrs. Cole."

"Oh? That's good!"

"Is it okay if I stay?"

"Of course, Patsy, and what about you, Sam? You feeling better too?"

"Uh, huh," I said.

"Hmmm... interesting, I suppose miracles DO happen. You sure I can't interest you kids in a swig of Pepto Bismol? It will knock out whatever is left that ails you."

Whatever *swig* meant, it couldn't be good if Pepto Bismol was involved.

We shook our heads.

"I get the impression you guys weren't really that sick."

Patsy spoke up before I could think up a good lie.

"No, Ma'am."

My mother sat next to Patsy. "All right, be honest, Patsy. Does Vernon make you uncomfortable?"

Patsy looked relieved. "Yes, Mrs. Cole."

"Can't say I blame you, he makes me feel a little uncomfortable, too."

"His eyes?" I blurted.

"No, that's not it, Samuel. He can't help being cock-eyed. And you already know we don't judge people on how they look, right, young man?"

"Yes."

Patsy glanced at me like—Can I please tell her? I shook my head. She wanted to sing like a robin, but I was still under the threat of the belt.

"Nate claims that bad eye of Vernon's didn't come from birth, it came from one of the many fights he got into," my mother added.

Patsy and I exchanged looks.

"Just so you know, Samuel, I wasn't going to let you go over there without Patsy, anyway—sick or not. Call it a woman's intuition, but there's something a little odd about him, even though he seems nice on the surface," my mother said while staring out my bedroom window. "Except, I can't put a finger on it."

I could—he's the bogeyman.

"As far as I'm concerned, you kids don't ever have to go over there if you don't want to. And that's another thing... a grown man reading and collecting hundreds of comic books... that seems a little weird to me."

I didn't see THAT as a problem. Daddy liked reading my comics with me, even on his own when my mother wasn't around. Still, this was the first time I found joy in my mother being overprotective.

Soon as my mother left my room, Patsy moaned, "Vernon's not going to quit. He wants to get us alone and then..."

"I know, Patsy, I know... I'll figure out something."

"When???"

"Soon."

"I hope so."

Me too.

Chapter 18

A couple of days later we had our first summer heat-wave with the temperature over 100 degrees in Los Angeles. There was no ocean breeze, and the Santa Ana winds made the heat worse. Everyone on Fisher Place had their windows open and fans blowing. We had fans in the living room crisscrossing across buckets of melting ice, to make it cooler.

Nighttime was a little better, but it was still about 80 degrees and tropically humid. Even with the clattering fan blowing harshly over my bed, my pajamas clung to my sweaty body. I couldn't stand it anymore and ended up peeling them off and lying on the bed in my underpants.

Time after time, I parted the curtains to see if Patsy was awake and gazing out the window, too. Like my bedroom, hers was located at the back of their house. Tonight, Patsy's window was open about a quarter of the way. Her curtains flapped against the window, meaning her fan was set on high, too.

Usually our parents made us go to bed around the same time: 9 or 9:30. Some nights, I'd catch Patsy's little Wonder Bread face smashed against her window. She'd break into a grin as soon as I opened my curtains. On those nights we'd play a game of opening and shutting our curtains and making funny faces until one of us grew tired and quit.

Disappointed she wasn't awake, I drew the curtains

closed and plopped down on my back on my bed. The spotlight hanging from the garage roof had burned out a bulb last night, so it would have been pitch-black outdoors except for the patches of light cast by the bright full moon. My father had attached the spotlight onto the garage due to all the problems we'd experienced with stuff being thrown in our backyard. Lately, nothing had occurred. I guess many of the "evil-doers" had moved.

I turned on my flashlight to amuse myself by creating animals and weird shadow shapes on the wall until they began creeping me out. I switched to reading comic books by flashlight for a long time until my eyes got strained. I flipped the flashlight off, let out a bored sigh, and lay on my back, playing with my fingers as I stared up at the ceiling.

The only noise in my room was the fan until I heard my parents in their bedroom giggling. Then I heard squeaky bedsprings and the bed rocking and banging against the wall. What kind of games were they playing in there? I thought, hey, maybe they'll let me play too since they're still awake. I sat up in bed and thought about going into their bedroom, but the noise stopped and it got real quiet. I waited a few minutes to see if they were still playing, but then I heard my father's heavy snores competing with the whirring of their bedroom fan.

All at once I heard rustling noises outside. It was probably an opossum. The first time I saw one was on a quiet night like this a couple of weeks ago. I was headed down the hallway in my pajamas, getting ready to go to bed. My father stood at the backdoor gazing out the window. He gestured for me to come to him.

"Daddy, what..."

He shushed me with a finger to his lips. He gently grabbed my arm, nudged the door open, and ushered me outside. We tiptoed over to what looked like a cat lying dead on its side.

Had he found Patsy's lost cat?

That's what I thought until I saw its giant rat tail and the long snout jutting out of a monstrous, pasty white face. My father poked this creature several times with a switch from the tree. It didn't flinch.

"What is it, Daddy?" I whispered, grabbing his hand.

"It's an opossum, first one I've seen since we've moved here."

"Is it dead?"

"Nah. It's pretending to be."

I had never seen any animal other than Lassie pretend to be dead. Even so, you could see Lassie breathing. This creature showed no signs of life.

"Are you sure it's alive?"

"I'm sure, Champ. Possums are tricky. Let's go inside, you'll see."

We went inside and peeped out my bedroom window. The opossum still lay unmoving on the ground.

"Daddy, I told you, it's dead."

"Shhhhh... don't talk. Just keep your eyes on it."

We waited another 10 minutes. Nothing. It was past my bedtime. I could barely keep my eyes open.

My father elbowed me. "Are you still looking?"

"Uh, huh."

The possum's ears twitched, and then it raised its head and looked around. It stood up and, incredibly, ambled onto the lawn.

"What I tell you? Next time you'll believe your old man, won't ya? Possums are experts at playing dead. That's how they protect themselves from predators wanting to eat them. They believe it's dead, get bored, and go away."

I switched to another window trying to find the opossum, but for such a slow-moving animal it had already disappeared into the darkness.

My father had told me opossums usually only come out at night. It sounded as though there might be another one outside my window. I grabbed the flashlight, ready to flip the switch on and shine it in its ugly face. The curtain was cracked a teensy bit as I peeked out. Guess I was wrong. I expected to see the possum clambering along the wall, but saw nothing. Daddy said I had to be patient, so I waited for Mr. Opossum to make his move.

My head jerked toward a noise on Patsy's side of the wall, underneath her window. What if the opossum decided to climb inside her window? My flashlight was ready to act like a spotlight when it popped up.

Except, what appeared was not a possum.

What I saw were hands wearing black gloves raising Patsy's window higher. The longer I studied the figure at her window, the better my vision got. It was a man with his back to me in dark clothing and wearing a black ski mask.

OH MY GOD!

A burglar was trying to get inside Patsy's house!! As I tried to get a closer view of him I accidentally tapped my flashlight against the bedpost. Instantly I drew back from the window as the silhouetted figure spun around. My heart pumped fiercely as I prayed he hadn't seen me.

After a few moments passed, I peeped through the slit of the curtain again. The silhouetted person hadn't moved a muscle. His head jerked stiffly from side to side like a hawk searching for his prey. His body looked familiar. It never dawned on me who the burglar was until he raised the window high enough for him to crawl inside as smoothly and as silently as a deadly snake.

VERNON.

Chapter 19

My face felt like it had burst into flames! I should have raced into my parents' bedroom and yelled for them to call the police. That's what I should have done... but I was struck with fear and an inability to move. Patsy and her mother were in danger and I was feeling like I was chained to my bed. Right before my eyes, Vernon slipped into the McGuire's house. Patsy was right. He planned to kidnap her and kill her.

And I'd be the next one on his agenda.

I had promised Patsy I would figure something out, but I failed her.

Before long, Vernon was back at the window. He carried something bundled in his arms. In the moonlight I saw a lock of red hair that spilled outside of the blanket.

Patsy!

Was she still alive? I clapped my trembling hands against my head and squeezed as hard as I could. I needed to DO SOMETHING! If Patsy was still alive she might stand a chance—if I did something!

Out of nowhere, Mattie's words swirled into my head like a cyclone: "God helps those that help themselves, Samuel. If you're waiting around thinking God's gonna do everything for you then you'll just be wasting your time. God helps those that help themselves—remember that and you'll be all right."

For so long I had waited for God to answer my prayers.

It had seemed like I wasn't in his favor and he'd never speak to me. Well, maybe He was talking in my head now!

I leaped off the bed screaming in agony, "Daddy, Daddy, help!"

The sheer volume of that scream was aided by me stubbing my toe against the metal bed support as I charged to their bedroom. I attempted to turn the doorknob but the door was locked. I banged with all my strength on the door.

"Daddy, Mommy, hurry up, open the door! Patsy's in trouble! She's been kidnapped!"

My mother was the first one to open the door, fumbling with her robe as she put it on. My father searched for his pants. He clicked on the bedside lamp.

"Child, what in heaven's name is wrong? You have a nightmare? Calm down. Everything is all right. Here, let me give you a hug."

"NO! It's not all right!" I shouted harshly to my shocked mother. "Call the police! We need to go outside and help Patsy—the bogeyman's gonna kill her!"

"Okay, young man, enough!" my father ordered, zipping up his pants. "There's no such thing as a bogeyman!"

"Yes there is!" I screamed at him while backing away. "I'm not making this up. Why won't you believe me?" I cried, hopping up and down.

Daddy eyed me the same way he had when I had that fit at Mattie's.

"I'm not putting up with no temper tantrums in the middle of a hot ass night; especially when I've gotta be at work in a few hours!"

Patsy didn't have much time. Vernon may have already taken off with her to some place we'd never find.

My eyes shot to my mother's. "Mommy, you've got to believe me! It's Vernon. He's got Patsy! I saw him steal her out of her bedroom!"

Something clicked in her when she gazed into my eyes.

"Grant, go out there! I'll call the police. Samuel is telling the truth!"

"Oh come on, Jolene! This boy had a nightmare, that's all! You don't REALLY believe..."

I didn't have time for them to debate this. I raced into the living room, unlocked the bolted door, and sprinted outside.

My mother screamed, "SAMUEL, COME BACK... GRANT, GO AFTER HIM!"

I flew out the door with no game plan. My only goal was to find Patsy before it was too late. I stood in the middle of our front lawn, quickly trying to adjust to the darkness. At least the streetlamps were on in front and with the moonlight, the streets were better lit than the backyard.

Plus, there was a ray of hope.

Vernon's car was parked in the McGuire's driveway!

Which meant they were still here.

I didn't see anything until I gaped at Patsy's side of the hedges. My insides exploded when I spied Vernon crouched and huddled against the hedges. He possessively clutched a bundled-up Patsy. Obviously, he'd been waiting for the exact right moment to escape to his car and drive away. From the streetlamp's reflection, his eyes glowered at me from the eye sockets of his ski mask.

I let out an earsplitting, "PATSY!!!"

Vernon ran from his hideout still holding onto Patsy. Once he spotted my shirtless father standing on the porch searching for me, he dropped Patsy and fled to his car. My father bolted off the porch, hurdled the hedges past me, and chased after him.

I ran to Patsy, who was lying on the grass.

"Patsy? Patsy? Are you okay? Please be alive," I cried.

I shook Patsy and wiggled her arms, but she didn't stir. She was still in her pajamas. I didn't spot any bruises on her. She was breathing, even snoring a little. I leaned my back up against the hedge and laid Patsy's head in my lap with her body stretched out on the grass. I stroked her head as I fearfully watched the battle between my father and Vernon.

Daddy tackled Vernon before he could reach the car door handle and ripped off his ski mask. He smashed his head into the grass and tried to pin Vernon's arms behind his back, but Vernon was strong, too. He pulled one arm away, jammed it into his pocket, and quickly pulled it out and jabbed his fingers into Daddy's eyes. Daddy fell back like he'd been shot, howling in pain as his hands covered his eyes. He vigorously rubbed them over and over. He scooted on the grass to the coiled water hose in the McGuire's front yard and turned it on full blast, trying to flush whatever was stinging his eyes. I was so busy watching Daddy, I lost track of Vernon.

Until I heard my mother shout from the porch, "Grant, look out!"

The car trunk was open, and Vernon rushed my father wielding a shovel like a baseball bat. Daddy recovered just in time to spray Vernon dead in the face with the water rushing furiously out of the hose. Luckily Vernon, swinging the shovel at my father, slipped on the wet grass. My father rolled out of the way and Vernon smacked only the muddy grass.

Vernon hurriedly wiped the water off his face with the sleeve of his black shirt. He gripped the handle of the shovel and tried to strike again, but the shovel was stuck in the ground. Those few seconds were just what Daddy needed. He bounced up, eyes blinking rapidly. I don't think he could see that good, but he could see well enough to lunge forward and fiercely sock Vernon on the side of his face. He continued to hammer Vernon with a bunch of punches. At one point he hit Vernon with a savage left cross that cracked Vernon's jaw so loud it echoed. Vernon's body awkwardly spun to the right, and blood drooled from his mouth. He clumsily stood on unsteady legs in a boxing pose.

Daddy circled him, fists balled, arm cocked, and ready to level Vernon with one final blow. During the ongoing fight, I realized that my mother stood back from the fighters holding the shovel she'd pulled from the ground like it was a magic broom. She waited to clobber Vernon if my father didn't finish him off.

Daddy didn't have to throw another punch. Vernon's legs withered and he dropped to his knees, both hands holding his clearly broken jaw. My father lifted him in a smothering bear hug and slammed him so hard against Vernon's prized automobile it created zigzagging cracks in the window. Moaning heavily, Vernon slid to the ground with his backside against his cherished vehicle. Daddy grabbed him by the collar and threw him face down onto the lawn. He straddled him and roughly pinned his arms behind his back.

By this time, a crowd had gathered on the sidewalk and the lawn around my father and Vernon, trying to figure out what was going on. They seeped out of their homes—men, women, and children looking like a Sears' sleepwear ad.

During the chaos I saw lights blink on in the McGuire household—room after room. Patsy's mother frantically screamed her name in each one. Finally the front door flew open and Mrs. McGuire ran out on the porch.

"Patsy! Patsy!" she yelled, stunned to see the crowd in her front yard. "What is going on out here?" she asked, her eyes desperately skirting the area. "Where's my daughter? Patsy!"

"Hazel, she's with Samuel—over there!" my mother replied, pointing at us with the shovel. She held it like she was on guard duty.

Mrs. McGuire barreled her way through to us as fast as possible while clutching her pregnant belly. She squatted down next to me and with some difficulty managed to sit on the grass. She pulled Patsy into her arms.

"Patsy? Honey? Wake up... Talk to me, darling. Are you okay? Looks like she's breathing fine. What happened, Samuel?"

"Vernon tried to kidnap her, Mrs. McGuire!"

I pointed at Vernon who struggled to get out from underneath my father. His face was swollen like a blimp and his lower lip bloody... like a vampire's.

"He did what? Tried to steal my daughter? Why? What was he planning to do? I don't understand... Oh Jesus, I can't take this... I wish her Daddy was here!"

"It's okay, Mrs. McGuire, I told my parents and my father ran out and beat him up before he could get away."

"Oh, Samuel, you are the best! I don't know what else to say. Thank you so much!" She kissed me on the check. "That bastard better not have harmed her... or I swear I'll..."

Patsy's eyes fluttered. "Mommy?"

"Thank goodness! It's so good to hear your voice. Do you feel okay?" She squeezed Patsy's cheeks and kissed her nonstop on the forehead.

"I think so," Patsy responded, groggily. "Why do you keep kissing me?"

"Because I love you and you are safe now."

"How come we're outside on the grass at night? What are all these people doing here? Samuel?"

"Hi Patsy."

She pushed herself up as she sleepily rubbed her eyes.

"Looks like our girl is back," my mother remarked as

she joined us, still armed with her trusty shovel.

"Hi Mrs. Cole. Why are you holding a shovel?"

My mother smiled. "It's a long story, Patsy."

"Why is Samuel in his underwear?"

I was so happy to see her alive, her stupid questions didn't annoy me.

Mrs. McGuire hugged her, tears rolling freely down her cheeks. "Heroes don't care about what they look like when they're saving people. Samuel saved your life, honey."

"He did?" Patsy gasped. "Then why are you crying, Mommy?"

"Because I don't know what I would have done if Samuel hadn't seen Vernon trying to take off with you."

Mrs. McGuire wiped the teardrops off Patsy's shoulder.

"He came after me? I told you Samuel!"

Patsy locked her arms around my neck in one of her strangle hugs. "Thank you for saving me, Samuel Scott Cole; you really are Superman!"

I tried to change the subject because my face was getting flushed. "My father is the one who beat him up... see?"

She was so out of it, it was the first time she noticed my father sitting on top of Vernon.

"Your father really *can* beat up monsters," she proclaimed admiringly.

"Told you," I replied proudly.

Mrs. McGuire said, "Oooh this is all too much; I need to go use the bathroom. Jolene, you'll watch my little girl?"

"Of course, Hazel, take your time."

Meanwhile, Daddy kept Vernon's arms bound while he waited for the police to arrive. His eyes were deeply reddened from whatever Vernon smeared in them. My father was truly a hero! Though, I'm not sure all the neighbors agreed with me. I heard grumblings.

"That ain't right... a colored man sitting on top of a White man."

"Uh, huh. We're taking their word for it... How do we know for sure it was Vernon that abducted that child? Anybody else see what happened?"

"Yeah. Vernon's been our neighbor since he was a little boy, those people have lived here barely three months. Should we be trusting them?"

"I know. Look at Vernon's face! That Negro beat him up pretty bad. Anyone call a doctor?"

"What were they fighting about anyway? Vernon never bothered anyone. Always nice and respectful. I knew his grandparents... good people."

"Yep. Never had ANY trouble on this block until THEY moved in."

"I say we ought to do something. Look at what that Negro did to him!"

"And why's his wife got that shovel? If you ask me, something ain't right."

"Police on their way yet? We need to know the truth."

"Back where I come from, there'd be no questions... there'd be a lynching."

My father looked around uncomfortably.

The Clark brothers ordinarily would have joined in with the talk, but they just stood on the sidewalk hands in their pockets and smirking at Vernon. They seemed real pleased to see Vernon get it.

At last, sirens blasting, police cars drove up from every direction. Shining, bright lights flashed from cars, a helicopter flew overhead, flashlights lit up the entire front yard, making it look like daylight. This was the scene I imagined would happen the day my father reported the damage to our car when we moved in. Policemen leaped out of their cars, guns drawn and prepared for action... except, the guns were pointed at my father instead of Vernon as they encircled them.

"Freeze! And don't move an inch till we tell you to. I mean it; raise your hands high up in the air! Now!"

"Ma'am, I need you to put that shovel down!" one of the cops ordered my mother, gun raised.

My mother moved very slowly, carefully laying the shovel on the grass. "Officer, I'm the one who placed the phone call."

"Didn't ask. Keep your mouth shut until we're ready to talk to you."

"Hey, man, you can't talk to my wife that way!" Daddy growled.

The cop put his gun back in his holster. He dragged my father off of Vernon and shoved him. "What are you gonna do about it, boy?"

Daddy didn't flinch or budge when the cop pulled out his baton and shoved it under his chin.

"Grant, stay cool... I'm fine. Let them work it out, hon. It's all right."

The cop slapped handcuffs on him. Then demanded he get down on his knees and keep his head bowed. Anger ripped through me. I wanted my father to haul off on him like he did to Vernon.

It hurt to see my father like this. I jumped up and cried, "That's my Daddy. Leave him alone! He's a hero!"

Patsy jumped up, too. "Yeah! Mr. Cole saved me! Get your hands off him!"

My mother wrapped her arms around us. "Both of you, keep quiet or you'll make it worse! You hear me?" she commanded, her body trembling mightily.

I started to object, but when I looked into her eyes it shut me down instantly. I'd never seen her look so afraid.

Vernon still lay on the ground. When a policeman reached down to help him up he began spitting and coughing more than he had been.

Speaking in a garbled voice he uttered, "Boy, am I glad you guys showed up! I'm lucky to be alive! I'm sure you can see what he did to me."

The crowd began grumbling again. Jerry Clark's father waddled over and patted Vernon on the back, glaring at my father. Vernon leaned against his battered car like it was a life support.

No one slapped any handcuffs on Vernon. Instead, one of the policemen kindly asked, "Are you all right, buddy?"

"About like my car, officer," Vernon muttered, "both of us are broken up." He chuckled, then winced in pain as he fingered his blown up jaw.

One of the women in the crowd handed him a towel.

"Thank you so much, Mrs. Bernard, I need this." He wiped his bloodied face, drawing more sympathy.

Just then, our favorite cops, Thomas and Mackey, jumped the curb with their car and rolled up onto the grass as people quickly moved out of the way. Lieutenant Thomas surprisingly carried a legal pad like he actually intended to file a full report.

"Okay, guys, we got this," Thomas stated. "I know both of the parties involved here, so let's see if we can make some sense of this. Looks like all hell broke out," he exclaimed. "Officers, bring Mr. Cole over here, please."

My mother shuddered as they forcefully grabbed my handcuffed father and jerked him up to his feet. My father looked sideways in our direction and then smiled. I don't know where it came from, maybe the Holy Ghost snuck inside him or he was just laughing about the craziness of it all as the policemen escorted him to Mackey and Thomas with their guns still drawn.

"No need for that. He's already in handcuffs," Thomas said.

"Yes, sir, Lieutenant," one of the policemen responded. He motioned for the other officers to holster their weapons.

Sergeant Mackey pulled out a cigar from his breast pocket as he inspected Vernon's face. "Damn, he got you pretty good!"

Chapter 20

"**Okay, give me the** straight scoop. Who phoned this in?" Thomas asked.

"I did," my mother answered. "I reported that Vernon kidnapped Patsy from her bedroom!"

"She's a liar," Vernon argued.

Even in handcuffs, it took several officers to restrain my father from going after him.

"So Vernon, why is your car parked in the McGuire's driveway at four in the morning?" Mackey asked, blowing clouds of smoke into the air.

"I was going to my graveyard shift at the airport when I saw this madman carrying that poor little girl bundled up in a blanket. He tried to duck down by the side of the house when he saw me. I pulled up into the driveway. When he saw me he dropped her on the ground and charged at me with blood in his eyes. He yanked me out the car and hit me with that dang shovel his wife is holding!"

Daddy snapped, "Stop lying. You grabbed that shovel from the trunk of your car and tried to knock my head off with it! The trunk of your car is still open."

Vernon shot my father a dirty look. "So what! That doesn't mean anything. It popped open when you attacked me!"

Mr. Clark suddenly yelled out, "You need to arrest that nig—uh, HIM before he hurts another decent citizen. Vernon is a wonderful neighbor. He maintains his property, is

217

always nice to people... He's never given anyone any reason to complain. But ever since these people have moved in, nothing but problems. That's why we put our property up for sale. Once their type moves in, property values drop. Look what he did to Vernon! His son's no different, just like him. He beat up my kid for no reason. My son was scared to hit him back and I'm glad he didn't. That kid probably carries a switchblade in his back pocket."

Once again it took some doing to restrain Daddy, handcuffs and all.

"See what I'm talking about—they're animals!"

One policeman that grabbed my father held him in a choke hold. My father's eyes bulged and started tearing.

"Stop it, you're hurting him, he can't breathe!" my mother screamed.

"Get your hands off my Daddy!"

"All right, ease up," Thomas instructed the officer, who took his time letting go. My father keeled over, coughing and hacking.

My mother couldn't hold back any longer. "Officers, I'm telling you—you've got the wrong man in handcuffs! Vernon's lying through his teeth. I swear on the Bible, he's the one who snuck into Patsy bedroom and kidnapped her!"

"Of course she'd stick up for her husband! I'd never do anything like that to that sweet little girl. Everyone on this block will vouch for me!"

A few people cheered. One hollered, "That's right. Vernon's a great guy, just like his grandparents!"

"See? People know me. But what do we know about him? Thank goodness I saw him with little Patsy in that blanket! God only knows what he planned to do with her. Just look at those bloodshot eyes! You can tell he's been drinking. Doesn't that say something to you?"

"Mr. Cole, your eyes *are* pretty red." Mackey shined a

flashlight in Daddy's eyes. "Did you have a little nip to cool off tonight?"

"I didn't have a thing to drink. I was in bed before Samuel woke me. My eyes are red because Vernon poked some substance in my eyes while we were fighting."

Patsy walked up to Officers Thomas and Mackey. "Why are you bothering Mr. Cole? He's not the bad guy." She pointed her finger accusingly at Vernon. "HE IS! He's the bogeyman! And HE kidnapped me!"

I heard a few chuckles.

"How would you know, darling?" Vernon said sweetly. "You were sleeping in your bed."

"How do you know if I was asleep in my bed, Mr. Doru?" Patsy asked, in an even sweeter voice than Vernon. Patsy put on her best act, too.

"Well, I mean, you had to be asleep. What kid isn't sleeping at this hour?"

I went and grabbed the ski mask still lying on the grass.

"Me."

Vernon tried to smile it off. "He doesn't know what he's talking about."

"Shut up, Vernon," Officer Thomas ordered. "What are you saying, Sam?"

"I couldn't sleep because it's so hot. So I looked out my window for Patsy to see if she was awake. That's when I saw Vernon push up her window and climb into her bedroom. He wore this black ski mask my father pulled off him."

"Oh that's so ridiculous! He's just trying to protect his Daddy! I didn't..."

"My partner told you to be quiet and let the kid speak. Don't say another goddamn word cuz I ain't as nice as him!"

Vernon got stone-faced; but I saw nervousness creep

into his eyes.

Officer Mackey nodded to me. "Go ahead, Sammy."

"I'm telling the truth, Officer Mackey, this is the mask Mr. Doru had on."

"Oh yeah? Let me see, kid."

I handed the ski mask to Officer Mackey. He examined it and turned it inside out as he pulled at the threads.

"Well, well... isn't this interesting?" Mackey reached over and held up some strands of straight brown hair against my father's head. "Doesn't look like these hairs belong to you, Mr. Cole."

He then dangled the hairs before Vernon's eyes. "Well looky here... I think we found a perfect match, partner."

"You don't say," Officer Thomas remarked.

Vernon grimaced as he rubbed his jaw.

Funny, Vernon didn't look so scary to me anymore. He wouldn't even look at me. I grabbed his hand and he jerked it away.

"Look! He's still wearing the gloves he had on when he grabbed Patsy! Isn't it too hot to wear gloves? Look at me. I don't have nuthin' on cuz it's so hot."

"*Anything* on... and it's *because* it's so hot," my mother corrected. "Speaking of, put this robe on before you catch a cold."

She'd snatched my robe before she ran outside, but with all the drama taking place she never put it on me.

Mackey bumped his belly against Vernon and blew smoke in his face.

"Kid's got a point, man. Why are you wearing gloves on a night like this?"

Vernon didn't answer. He just bowed his head.

Now Officer Thomas got in his face and put his hand underneath his chin to raise his head. "What's wrong Doru? You had all kinds of stuff to say earlier."

Jerry's father backed up and vanished into the crowd.

When Patsy's mother came back outside, she was shocked. "Hey! What are you idiots doing?" She marched up to Officers Thomas and Mackey.

Patsy's mother was normally very soft-spoken... but uh, uh... not on this night!

"Why in God's world is Grant Cole in handcuffs?"

Thomas adjusted his police cap. "Ma'am, we did what we felt we needed to do to sort everything out and get at the bottom of the truth."

"The TRUTH is, you and everyone else here oughta be ashamed for treating an innocent man and good Samaritan like a criminal!"

"Mrs. McGuire, we didn't know... From our viewpoint it looked like Mr. Cole was beating up a helpless man."

"The way it looked? The way it WAS is that Grant saved my precious little girl from that disgusting piece of filth standing next to you! Just keep me away from your guns because if I get a chance, he won't be standing any longer!"

She wrapped her arms protectively around Patsy. "If Samuel hadn't seen him climbing though our back window, my Lord... I can't even imagine..."

"Mommy don't cry... remember? We only want my little brother to hear good things before he's born," Patsy said, tenderly rubbing her mother's stomach.

"You're right, honey, you are SO right... I'm sorry."

That didn't stop Mrs. McGuire from ordering the police around: "What are you doing standing there? Get those handcuffs off Mr. Cole—this instant!"

Officer Mackey had already started to do that.

Still, Mrs. McGuire had more to say: "Grant deserves every ounce of gratitude this neighborhood and police force has to offer. Not insults. He did nothing wrong and everything right."

She placed a warm, comforting hand on my father's

big shoulders.

"People, listen to me, and listen good... Be thankful Grant Cole chose to live here, because for all we know, one day it may have been one of your kid's lives he rescued from whatever hell this horrible beast intended."

Officer Mackey patted my father on the shoulder.

"Really sorry about this mess up, Mr. Cole. But like I told you what my Grandfather Mackey used to say: 'When you make a mistake, all you can do is try and make a little sunshine out of the rain.' I'm giving you the Mackey promise—we'll make it right. This dirt bag will be in prison for a very long time."

Daddy rubbed his wrists. All of a sudden Daddy's face looked at peace. The anger faded right after he heard Officer Mackey call him "Mr. Cole."

My mother and father hugged for a long time and waved me in to join them. Mrs. McGuire and Patsy hugged my Dad, too.

I heard some gasps from the onlookers.

Mrs. McGuire didn't care.

"Thank you so much, Grant. I can't thank you enough for what you did."

"Oh that's not necessary..."

"Yes it is! And I'm sure once I tell my husband, John, he will be calling to express his thanks. He's always been so worried about us, and he'll feel a thousand times better knowing you and your family were our protectors."

"Well, I'm looking forward to speaking with him. Thank you, Hazel, for the nice things you said."

"You shouldn't be thanking me," she said loudly enough for the people avoiding eye contact with her. "All of us should be thanking you!! Well, I guess that's how it is when you're dealing with a world full of morons."

Officer Mackey dropped his cigar on the grass. He picked it up and poked it back in his mouth before slapping handcuffs on Vernon. I was surprised Vernon's hands weren't chopped off at the wrist the way Mackey clamped them on.

"Get in the car! What were you going to do with her? Huh? Tell me! Huh?" Mackey yelled at Vernon.

Vernon kept his head bowed.

Mackey snatched him by the collar of his shirt. Puffing on his cigar he snarled, "I wish I could line you up against the wall and shoot you a million times. But I probably still wouldn't be satisfied!"

Officer Thomas came up to my father, hand out, and said, "I am very sorry, Mr. Cole. I hope you'll find it within you to forgive us... *morons*." He glanced at Mrs. McGuire. She smiled and quietly applauded.

My father shook his hand. "He's going to jail... that's all that matters."

"Hopefully, he'll get there," Thomas said as he watched Mackey open the car door and shoved Vernon, making him bump his head on the side of the police car's roof. Mackey then pushed his head down and booted him into the car.

"I always thought Vernon seemed a little *different*, but, man, you just never know sometimes about people."

"No you don't," Daddy agreed.

Patsy tapped Thomas's arm. "Officer Thomas, can I talk to you?"

"Of course you can, young lady. What do you want to talk about?"

She looked at me. "Samuel, can I tell him?"

My parents looked at me curiously. I sighed, "Um... I guess so, yes."

"All right, will I have to arrest you guys?" Thomas joked.

"No, sir. Officer, do you remember Suzie?"

"Suzie?"

"She lived in Samuel's house before they moved in."

"Oh, wait... you're talking about the North family, their daughter, Susan?"

"Yes, sir."

"Go ahead. What about her?" he asked, cocking his head.

Patsy hesitated and looked at me again.

I nodded.

"Me and Samuel were in Vernon's house, and I saw Suzie's bracelet on Vernon's bookshelf in his bedroom and—"

Mrs. McGuire cupped Patsy's shoulders. "You were in Vernon's house? In his bedroom? Why?"

My parents were on me like bookends. "What were you doing at Vernon's? Who gave you permission to go over there?"

Patsy jumped in. "We thought he was a vampire, so we tried to find evidence inside his house so we could prove it."

"A vampire? Did Samuel put this notion in your head?" My father's red eyes fixed on me.

"Mr. Cole, I'm the one who kept pushing him to go with me since Vernon was going to show us his comic books. It was not his fault, I made him do it."

"No, sorry Patsy, it was his fault," my father argued.

Just in time, Officer Thomas interrupted. "Hold on folks, I'm hearing something more serious here. Patsy, what did you say about Suzie's bracelet?"

"I saw it on his bookshelf. I was scared to grab it, but I've got my missing cat Comet's collar... it was there on Vernon's bookshelf, too. I can go get it if you want me to."

"Sure, why don't you do that."

Patsy dashed into the house.

Officer Thomas no longer looked amused. He glanced at Mrs. McGuire.

She shrugged. "I had no idea."

"Did you kids find anything else, Samuel?"

"Uh, huh. Vernon's got a big pet snake, a boa constrictor named Freda."

My mother was stunned. "You were in that house with a boa constrictor?"

"Yes," I said proudly, knowing she was very frightened of snakes.

"He keeps one in the house?" Officer Thomas questioned.

"Uh, huh... she's over five feet and not even full grown yet."

"Mercy me," my mother gasped, wrapping my Daddy's arm around her.

Patsy ran back, out of breath. "Here's my cat's collar. I think he fed Comet to his snake."

Mrs. McGuire peeked over Officer Thomas' shoulder in disbelief.

"Oh, Jesus in heaven, it's Comet's, it definitely is," Mrs. McGuire said, her face drawn. "What in the world would he be doing with it?"

"Samuel said Vernon is the bogeyman, and I believe him. He told me how the bogeyman steals kids from their parents and does bad things to them."

Thomas rotated the collar in his hands. "Unfortunately, Patsy, Samuel might be right, Vernon just might be the bogeyman."

Thomas seemed uncertain of his next move as he stared in wonder at Vernon sitting in the patrol car.

"Patsy, are you sure that was Suzie's bracelet you saw?"

"Yes! She wore it all the time—she was my babysitter, right, Mommy?"

"That's right," Mrs. McGuire replied barely above a whisper.

"And that's not the only bracelet I saw, Officer Thomas. He had all kinds of bracelets and necklaces and rings on the shelf. Didn't he, Samuel?"

"Uh, huh, lots of them!"

Thomas lifted the brim of his hat and looked at Vernon again. "Was he aware you knew it was Suzie's bracelet?"

"He said he was giving it to a friend's daughter for her birthday. But he knew I didn't believe him and that's when he started acting all funny."

"If you search his house, you'll see Suzie's bracelet and a lot of other stuff," I said.

Thomas toyed with the brim of his hat. "You kids may have stumbled onto something big, and in our own back-yard... unbelievable."

He looked at Daddy. "Well, Mr. Cole, if you thought it was a long night before, it's about to get a whole lot lon-ger."

"It's okay, Officer, didn't plan on sleeping much after this anyway."

"Patsy, you won't mind if I hold on to your pet's collar as evidence will you? I need to take it down to the station to get it tested."

"Okay."

"I'm sorry about your cat," he offered warmly.

"Thank you. Do you think this will help you find Suz-ie?" Patsy's eyes glimmered with hope.

"I really don't know, Patsy. But, it may give us some better answers."

Patsy grabbed my hand and clutched her mother's waist.

Officer Thomas shook his head again as he stared at us in astonishment. "Man, you kids... this night... I don't know... this may be a game changer... thanks."

Thomas jogged over to the remaining policemen. They huddled around him. Soon they crossed the street purposefully to Vernon's house. Mackey bumped his own head scrambling to get out of the squad car, eager to join them.

Vernon no longer slumped in the backseat of the patrol car; instead he jolted upright like an inflated doll hit with a blast of air. His eyes ballooned. He mashed his face against the window as he watched the police filing into his home. He started rocking back and forth, twisting and turning in his seat, and bouncing up and down in the squad car. He let out a blood curdling scream before shouting, "You can't just go inside a man's house! That's private property! Get the hell out of my house! You better not touch Freda! If you hurt her, I swear I'll kill every single one of you. Do you hear me? Get out of my damn house!"

My mother clapped her hands over my ears but that didn't help.

Eventually Vernon wore himself out. He slumped back down.

"Daddy, am I going to get a whipping?"

He looked at my mother and she grinned. He put his arm around me.

"Champ, we decided to give you a pass on this one."

Patsy leaned into me. "See Samuel... I knew we shoulda told your Daddy a long time ago. Look what happened... the bogeyman is gonna get whipped instead of you!"

Some of the less moronic souls on our block came over and shook my father's hand, patted him on the back, and praised him for his courageous actions. I could tell Daddy deeply appreciated it; his face brightened with each thank you.

Chapter 21

Patsy and I were so crazy excited! We stayed awake until sunrise, camped out on the grass on a blanket with a sheet wrapped around us. I stayed awake longer than Patsy. She had been asleep when Vernon kidnapped her.

Our block was covered with more police than I'd ever seen in my life! There were news reporters everywhere and helicopters flying overhead. The police busily cordoned off Vernon's house and yard with yellow line tape!

Despite all the insanity, I barely kept my eyes open. Patsy had already fallen asleep. My final memory was seeing Daddy and Mr. Wolfberg sitting on Patsy's porch, talking very softly with serious expressions. I stayed awake long enough to overhear bits of their conversation.

"Grant, you're kidding me."

"I kid you not, Nate. The cops found a flashlight, rope, gloves, and plastic trash bags in the trunk of his car, including the shovel he took out when he went head hunting after me. Got a real sick feeling in my stomach seeing all that."

"Got that same feeling, Grant... and to think this kind of evil lived across the street is hard to fathom. I knew he was an odd duck, but I never thought..."

"Me either... To think how this night could have ended..."

"You don't have to, Grant. It ended with you stopping this sick man."

"I almost didn't, Nate. Sam was telling me the truth and I didn't believe him. It took him running out the door and forcing me to follow before I saw he wasn't making up stories. Nate, what kind of father am I, if I don't trust my own son? What if I hadn't been there? Vernon could have gone after Samuel too... I..."

"Shhhh, Grant, don't torture yourself over the what ifs... You WERE there! You saved a girl's life and maybe more lives than you'll ever know."

Daddy took out a handkerchief and wiped his eyes.

I meant to get up and go hug my father and tell him how much I loved him and how proud I was of him... but then I fell asleep. It's okay. He knew.

When we first moved to Fisher Place, I'd learned to hate the sound of the phone ringing. Rarely was it good news. More often it was someone cursing and saying ugly things about us or making death threats. A knock on the door made us jump and peep through the curtains. Instead of finding a good neighbor standing there, we'd find a package of dog poop on the porch and/or hate letters in our mail slot.

After Vernon Doru's arrest, all of that ended. Thereafter, news reporters called the most often and knocked on our door begging for interviews, stories, and information about "Vernon, the Bogeyman Killer." Yes, "the Bogeyman Killer." A reporter coined the term in an article after finding out that Patsy and I called Vernon the bogeyman.

Articles were published calling my father a hero and a credit to his race. He liked the hero part, but it may have bothered him a little to be called a credit to his race. I heard him say, "Saving someone's life has nothing to do with color." Still, he smiled and graciously said thank you to those who believed they were paying him the highest compliment by saying it.

He told us, "I guess you've got to start somewhere

when you're a pioneer."

Our neighbors on the block got interviewed, too, like Jerry Clark's father. During breakfast several days after the incident, my father was reading the *Los Angeles Examiner* and almost fell out of his chair.

"Jolene, you won't believe what Harold Clark said to this reporter."

"What did Mr. Wonderful have to say this time?"

"I never trusted Vernon. I knew he was up to no good, especially when he threatened my sons who are such good boys! I'm glad our neighbor, Grant Cole, got him though. Luckily, colored guys can fight!"

I didn't know why my parents got a kick out of it. I didn't find it funny at all.

Most of the information that came out about Vernon was carried in every local and national newspaper and magazine and appeared on television news programs. My parents did their best to shield the dark truth from me. Still, no matter how hard they tried, some things were difficult to hide, especially in Ike's Place.

As soon as we walked in the barbershop, Ike announced, "Hey everybody, strike up the band, 'Sugar Ray' Cole has just entered the room!" It led to lots of hand slaps and pats on the back for my Dad.

Once word spread that Grant Cole was hanging out at Ike's, soon the barbershop became standing room only. Everyone wanted to hear Daddy tell what *really* went down.

My father's status on our old block become as legendary as mine had in the schoolyard after my episodes with the mole men and Edgar. The difference was my father really didn't want to discuss it, particularly with me there.

"So Cole, that nut case actually came at you with a shovel?" Ike asked.

"Yeah, man, swinging it like he was Mickey Mantle!"

"But I hear you tagged him out before strike three!" Chester yelled, slamming his domino down for 20 points as BB frowned.

"I don't know, man... if it was me, I would have got my gun and shot his ass!" BB commented, sucking on his lip as he studied the dominoes on the card table. He held one domino to his chest to prevent Chester from sneaking a peek.

"And the PO-lice would have treated you like them Mexicans did to Davy Crockett at the Alamo—you'd look like Swiss cheese by the time they got through with you!" Mr. Sullivan proclaimed as he whipped through the *Jet* magazines. "My man Grant did what he had to do."

"And they still cuffed you up, Cole? Even after you rescued that little girl?"

"Fraid so, Ike."

"Didn't you explain to them what happened?"

"Tried to, but it ain't real easy with guns staring you in the face."

This caused a ton of grumbling and head shaking in the shop.

"Shoot first, ask questions later, huh?"

"That about sums it up, Ike."

"You made us proud, man, cuz I can't imagine what's it's like living over there in them vanilla suburbs. Can't be too easy on a brotha," a man remarked.

"Thank you, man. It's tough sometimes, but we deal with it the best we can." He looked at me. "That's what being a pioneer is all about."

A few "Amens" and "Right Ons" echoed in the shop.

"Grant, so that crazy fool killed that girl who lived in your house before you moved in and then buried her in the mountains?" Ike questioned before he started cutting the man's hair in his chair. "Now they saying there might be even more?"

Daddy nodded, then glanced at me.

Ike caught it and said, "Hey, the adults want to talk some more. Why don't you kids go into the backroom? Got a TV in there. You can watch cartoons."

Any time the adults tell you "the adults want to talk" when they have already been talking, means it's gotten real serious. Ike herded five of us kids into his backroom and turned on the TV. Perfect timing—*Abbott and Costello Meet Frankenstein* had just started. One kid burst into tears when it came time for him to get his haircut because he wouldn't be able to keep watching it with us.

***

That day in the barbershop was how I found out for sure Vernon murdered Suzie. I questioned my father about it as soon as we left the barbershop. He sighed, but didn't seem surprised I asked. He admitted that Vernon murdered her and may have done other bad things to her and other girls they found buried in the San Gabriel mountains.

He said Vernon used a dangerous liquid called chloroform on Patsy when he snuck into her bedroom. It makes you fall asleep. He also used it on other girls he kidnapped. It was the chloroform Vernon had on his fingertips when he jabbed them in my father's eyes, which was why his eyes burned so badly during their battle.

Daddy never talked much about religion or God, but he did say he thought Vernon had the Devil inside of him to cause him to commit such evil doings.

"Daddy, do you think Vernon planned to kill Patsy?"

Daddy stared out the windshield before answering.

"I don't know, son... I'm just glad, thanks to you, we never had to find out."

He shared more with me on the way home. He said for sure Vernon stole Patsy's cat Comet and fed him to Freda. He told me the police also discovered Vernon cruised neighborhood after neighborhood searching for rats, cats, and small dogs to feed alive to his boa constrictor. They didn't have to be lost. He'd steal them out of a yard or lure them into his car with food.

Daddy said, one day, when I'm much older, he'd tell me more about Vernon. It was more important for me to know that the danger was over. He'd be locked in prison forever for all the bad things he did to so many girls. Daddy said we'll never have to worry again and could sleep peacefully now that the bogeyman was gone.

This was a conversation I'd have to have with Mattie someday. I knew the Holy Ghost could get inside you and make you do good things... but the Devil could jump inside you, too, and make you do bad things?

After Vernon's arrest, Patsy and I never spoke his name to each other again.

***

A week after Vernon was thrown in jail, Patsy and I sat on a blanket in the front yard playing the card game, War. The Clark brothers strolled past us without saying a word, but not giving us dirty looks either. No one in the neighborhood caused us any further trouble. No more hate mail, dog mess, or trash was ever thrown in our yard. Except for the Wolfbergs and the McGuires, no one invited us over for dinner either, but there were more friendly waves after Vernon's imprisonment.

This didn't mean if we drove a couple blocks away some idiot didn't call us horrible racial slurs, but at least we didn't hear it on our block anymore.

The humane society came and picked up Freda. The whole block turned out to watch them cart the snake away. I felt kind of proud because we knew about Freda first. Patsy didn't watch. I understood why. It was because of Freda her pet cat, Comet, was no longer in her life.

While we played cards, the North's black station wagon rolled up. As usual Mrs. North was on the passenger's side. I'd always hoped that one day I'd be able to run up to the car and say, "Hi, Mrs. North! Your daughter's in the house waiting for you!"

Unfortunately, that would not be the case. However, it surprised me when she rolled down her window. She had never done that before.

"Hi Patsy! Hello Samuel!" Shockingly, a trace of a smile peeked out between the lines in her face.

I shyly waved. "Hi!"

I didn't even know she knew my name.

She folded her hands to her chest. "Thank God, my Suzie has come home and now she's finally at rest. Thank you so much, kids."

Her husband put his arm around her and waved.

This was the first time she didn't cry, but I sure wanted to.

"Please send my appreciation and love to your families."

"Okay, Mr. and Mrs. North," Patsy replied for both of us.

She took a long look at the house before they drove away.

I never saw them again after that.

***

Things got really good when I spied a big moving van in Jerry's driveway! The bogeyman was in prison and the Clark family left the neighborhood forever.

Funny enough, another pioneering Negro family later moved into their house, but it was too bad they had no kids to play with. The Jones' were an elderly couple whose two kids were already grown and had families of their own.

235

***

A couple of weeks later, instead of climbing over the wall, Patsy opened the front gate. She was almost unrecognizable. I was used to seeing her in pigtails and wearing a Los Angeles Dodgers' cap or the army cap her father sent her. She skipped into the backyard wearing a polka dot sundress. And her hair was not in pigtails. I never realized how long, full, and beautiful it was. The sun highlighted the gold streaks in her red hair that rippled down her back like shiny flames. Seeing her as a pretty girl unexpectedly made me nervous. I knew things were getting bad when I tried to figure out how many nickels I had in my piggy-bank.

"Hi, Sam!"

"Hi," I replied, suddenly trying too hard to act cool.

"Do you like my hair? My mother washed it with this new shampoo." She whirled around and around and ran her fingers through it.

"It looks… okay."

"Doesn't it smell nice and clean?"

She flipped her hair in my face. It did smell really good.

"It's so soft. Here feel it."

Before I could say no, she grabbed my hand and rubbed my palm against her very soft hair.

"Doesn't it feel good?"

"Yeah, I guess," I answered coolly while turning a trillion shades of purple.

I picked up the basketball and dribbled. She grabbed the ball from me and dribbled around me.

"Aren't you going to try to steal the ball away from me, silly boy?"

I wasn't used to her talking like that. She still couldn't dribble as she patted it awkwardly with her hands. I could have easily stolen it from her except at that moment I felt like Superman reaching for a Kryptonite basketball.

"What's wrong? C'mon, try and get it!"

She backed into me, whipping her hair into my face. I started feeling all tingly inside.

"What's wrong with you today?"

"I don't know... I guess I'm tired or something." I sat down against the wall.

"Me too. But I can't sit on the ground because my dress might get dirty and I don't want my mother to get mad."

So she sat down in my lap.

The sweet scent of her hair drove me crazy.

I yelled, "Your hair is in my face!"

Truth was, I didn't really want her to move.

"I'm sorry," she said, flipping it over her shoulder. She must have liked the smell of her own hair because she kept grabbing strands and sniffing them.

I loved the way she looked, but I also wished for the tomboy Patsy so I could be myself again.

"Why don't you just go home and change your clothes so you won't get dirty?" I didn't really want her to get up, but being cool was difficult.

"Am I too heavy? You want me to get up?"

"No, I don't care. Do what you want."

She leaned back into me again, but grabbed a lock of her hair and swept it across the top of my head. "You look funny with red hair," she laughed, dangling the strands over my forehead.

"Stop!" I giggled. It tickled.

She abruptly stopped playing and got real quiet. She bounced up. Her hair was all matted in the back from my sweat. She brushed her fingers through it to get rid of the tangles and readjusted her headband. Then she picked up the basketball and held it, staring at it like it was a crystal ball.

In a faraway voice she said, "I'm gonna see my Daddy."

"You are? That's good! You and your mom flying to

Germany?"

"No, we're driving to Dallas."

"Where is that?"

"In Texas, silly."

"Where's Texas?"

"I don't know, really far away."

"When are you going?"

"Today." She tossed the ball into the air.

"When are you coming back?"

The ball bounced off her chest and rolled onto the grass.

"We're moving, Samuel."

That caught me completely off-guard. I didn't know how to take it. My stomach twisted painfully.

"Because of me?"

"No, silly monster," she said softly. "My Daddy got stationed there."

"You *have* to go?"

"I don't want to. I asked Daddy why can't he get stationed here? He said he tried but the Army won't let him."

Anger flushed through me. I grabbed the ball and threw it over the fence.

"I'm sorry, Samuel... Daddy's making us go!"

"You can move in with us. My parents really like you."

She thought about it and then shook her head.

"No, it would hurt Daddy's feelings. I can't do that... he's my father."

"So you're leaving, like everybody else? Who am I supposed to play with? Who's gonna be my friend now? You hate me, too, that's why you're moving!"

Tears rolled down her cheeks. "Not me, Samuel... I love you."

She closed her eyes tight, grabbed my face, and pressed her lips hard against mine.

She kissed me on the lips just like they did in the movies!

It lasted about two seconds and then she took off running, hair flying behind her. Before she turned the corner and disappeared I heard, "Bye, Samuel!"

I waved my arms, and yelled, "Bye, Patsy!" as loud as I could.

Epilogue

Later that day, I saw a moving van parked in front of Patsy's house. From my bedroom I listened to furniture being moved into the truck. Feeling betrayed, I refused to step outside. Instead, I stayed inside my room reading my comic books, but not doing a very good job of it. My mind was elsewhere.

My mother walked in.

"Aren't you coming outside to say goodbye to Patsy and her mom?"

"No."

"That's not very neighborly."

I pretended to read.

"Come on. I know it's hard for you... but we ought to say goodbye."

"I already did!"

I didn't care if my mother got on me about yelling at her.

But she didn't.

She massaged my neck. "You're really going to miss Patsy, aren't you? I know you guys were very close."

Tears streamed down my face as I turned the page of the book I wasn't reading.

"We already said goodbye to each other, Mom."

"All right. I'll take your word for it. I will ask for their new address, though, so you guys can write each other. Just because someone moves away doesn't mean you can't stay in contact and remain friends."

I put the book down long enough to give my mother an appreciative smile.

She gently squeezed my shoulder and walked out.

***

The next morning, I stayed in my room listening to music on the radio instead of going outside and shooting the basketball like I usually did. I couldn't stand the thought of not seeing Patsy peeking through the curtains or making a funny face at her bedroom window. I already missed her wave and seeing her either climbing over the wall or running through my front gate ready to play. I wasn't ready to go outside to an empty court... not yet.

There was a soft knock on my door.

"Sam, can I come in?"

"Yes, Daddy."

My father walked into my bedroom with my basketball. "Hey, Champ, did you know you left your ball outside?"

"Oh, thanks," I muttered, not really excited about seeing it right now. I figured Patsy or her mother threw it back over the wall.

"I hate to tell you this, Champ, but it looks like it got all marked up."

I groaned. That's all I needed to hear. Patsy was gone and now somebody messed up my basketball.

"Daddy, can you just throw it away?"

"Son, I can't throw away a perfectly good ball. Besides, I think you might want to read the message on it first before we make that kind of decision."

He winked and handed the ball to me before walking out and softly closing the door behind him.

I was about to toss it into the closet, but curiosity got the better of me. I turned the ball over to the marked side.

On it was a carefully drawn, huge bright red heart. In the center of the heart were words in large bold letters:

Patsy
Loves
Samuel

I gazed at it for a very long time. No more playing with *this* basketball—I'd never want to get it dirty. Nope. I'd have to shoot hoops with my sockball.

But Daddy... somehow, he knew what to do... the next day he bought me a new basketball. I placed the one Patsy signed on the bookshelf in my room, like it was a trophy.

My father did one other thing.

Days later I was sitting in my room and I heard him pull into the driveway. Around 15 minutes later, my mother yelled, "Samuel, get in here—AND I MEAN NOW!"

On no, what did I do? Did I leave my comic books on the floor again? She said she'd throw them away the next time I did that. I slowly walked into the living room, expecting to get yelled at.

Both of them were seated on the couch, serious expressions on their faces. I waited for a scolding until I heard a sharp yelp near my right. There on the carpet, legs and fat paws splayed in a most awkward sit, was the most beautiful puppy I had ever seen in my life.

He cocked his head and returned my stare, tongue yo-yoing. The dog demandingly barked again, and I screamed with delight. I bundled him in my arms, and he wrapped his paws around my neck and swabbed my face with his tongue.

"The color of his fur... is so beautiful..."

"Yep. It's a silver Labrador... kinda rare, in the Lab world," my father remarked proudly. "My boss is a dog

breeder. Said he can't show the dog because he's not a tra-
ditional Lab color. He asked me if my son might want him.
I told him, I don't know, we'll have to ask him!"

"I saw the other ones, he was the best looking," my
mother added.

"You mean I can have him? He's mine?"

Both of them nodded, sporting huge grins.

"I love him! Thank you! Thank you! Thank you!!" I
muttered into his fur as I held his wiggling body. The smell
of a new car was nice, but the smell of a new puppy was
even better.

"You're welcome. We just thought you might need a
best friend right now," my father said, collecting my mother in his arms.

I did... and this time, I didn't have to worry about *my*
friend moving away.

Acknowledgments

I would like to express my sincere gratitude to Geoff Habiger of Artemesia Publishing for his wholehearted support, enthusiasm, and faith that Samuel Scott Cole's story is impactful and needs to be told. When I submitted the manuscript of *The New Frontier* to Geoff, he "got it" immediately. His open mind, insightful suggestions, expertise, and understanding of what I was trying to accomplish writing this young adult novel have powered it in the direction it needs to go. Moreover, I truly appreciate him asking for my input on designing the book cover. This doesn't always happen with publishers. It's been a pleasure and an honor partnering with Geoff to get Samuel's story out to the world.

My heartfelt thanks to the marvelously talented illustrator, Hillary Wilson, for her exceptional artwork. Hillary's magnificent book cover design captured the flavor and essence of the story.

Final thanks goes to copy editor, Lisa McCoy. She did an excellent job of conscientiously reading, editing, and offering suggestions that helped to solidly enhance the story.

About the Author

Wayne L. Wilson, has authored novels, screenplays, PSAs, memoirs, biographies, history books, college textbooks, and a wide-ranging array of books for children and young adults. Furthermore, he's served as a ghostwriter for various books and publications. Wilson received a MA in Education from UCLA and a BA in Sociology from UCSB. Prior to becoming an established writer he owned and operated a manufacturing company that published innovative multicultural greeting cards and related gift items. Wilson is a member of the Writer's Guild of America. When he's not writing Wayne is usually found playing with his German Shepherd, Koda.

About the Author